Momma's Boy

a novel by
Rodney Mallory

Publishing Associates, Inc.
Atlanta, Georgia

For book orders, author appearance inquires and interviews contact the
publishers in writing at: Publishing Associates, Inc. 5020 Montcalm Drive
Atlanta, GA 30331.
E-mail: Fcpublish@aol.com.
Book Design: Everett Chase
Layout: Eric Fitchpatric
Cover art and set director: Vivian Taylor
Cover photograph: Michael Taylor
   Maxx Photography Studio, Atlanta, GA

Dedication

To my *heart*,
Sharon Mallory, (Momma)

and to my *soul*,
Nadiya Mallory, (my little girl).

Acknowledgements

First, I would like to thank the Creator, whom without, absolutely nothing is possible. Nuff Said.

Now for the mere mortals! My sisters, Gwen, Chrystal, and Stacey, you have provided me with enough love, laughter and drama to last a lifetime. I really appreciate and love you very much. To my pops, Leon Mallory thanks for loving Sharon's kids as if they were your own. To my bestest friend Corey. You are my brother, thanks for having my back, and I forgive you for getting us kicked off the bus back in 82. To Mr. Gardener Clark, Dr. Nan McJamerson, and all of my other professors at Grambling State University for seeing something special in me.

To Phedra Owens, where ever you are... hello! The Elerbee family, thanks for the help. To my man, Shannon Flonnoury, thanks for putting your money where my pen is, I will not forget it. Darryl and Tiffany Felker, I want to be as happy as you are some day. Roger Jackson, Reggie White (my barber), and Aaron Pankratz, thanks for the conversations; you all helped me write this book in ways that you will never know. To the ladies of West Manor, for providing me with positive feedback about the book, Mrs. Cynthia May, Amelia Woodruff, Tracy Hope, Sonja Gamble, Sheila Brookins, Connie Olivieria, Sheriko Davis and Janice Hurly.

Thanks for the encouragement, Ms. Grace Hutchinson, and the good people at Spelman's Nursery School! Much love to Romona White, you forced me to take a long look in the mirror, and I am a better man for it. Thanks to Dione May, for adding the attitude and beauty to the cover. Thomas Lovelace, of T's Hair Designs, for helpin a brotha out! To my aunts Carol, Elmereta, and Denise, my Uncle Curtis, my Grandmother Carolyn, my cousins' CJ, Quint, Keith, Laron, Gene, Aisha, Cornine and Collin see you on the next holiday. Mr. Fred Cleveland, thanks for helping me with this. There is plenty more where this came from. Teresa Creecy thanks for the contacts and support. Fred and Brenda Robinson, you have always shown me unconditional love and support. Fred, I wrote the majority of this book on your laptop, I would probably still be on chapter one if it were not for you.

RIP aunts Debra, Sandra, Elmer Sallee, GeJuane Sallee, Roger Brown and my room mate Monty Dupree, nuff said!

To contact me for book signings, personal appearances, or to order books, I can be reached via e-mail at: Oneluv35@aol.com. I would love to hear from you.

My Mama

My Mama
Sweet as sweet could be
However could I measure her love for me

My Mama
In Church she sings, prays and shouts
but if you bother her kids, she'd cuss you out!

My Mama
Ain't she truly something?
Makes soul food meals with next to nothing.

My Mama
beautiful and bold
had it rough coming up, but her heart is pure gold.

Hey Mama,
What's in the kitchen?
"collard greens, macaroni, cornbread and chicken."

The Blues, O'Jays and Al Green
Reminiscing about the hard times that we've seen.
At night she'd tuck in my covers
And then I tell God how much I love her.

Momma's Boy

Man, I hate that sound. That ringing has been ending my dreams and fantasies since I can remember. It pierces the silence and brings me crashing back into the harsh realities of life. The realities that more times than not I wish were someone else's. But there not...they're mine. The sound is my alarm clock.

Have you ever noticed that when you need, want, or, long for sleep most, morning comes twice as fast? I aimlessly search for the snooze button; I find it, and stop that unbearably irritating sound. As I return to sleep I close my eyes tightly and search again for Nia Long; she seems to be hiding. I love it when she is playful like this. Oh, there she is, waiting for me on the beach. 'Ready or not, here I come.' I am close enough to smell her perfume (the oil that I bought for her when we first landed in Jamaica). She gets up to greet me with open arms and Damn! I don't believe this, I barely have a chance to blink and the alarm is going off again? Who invented that damn snooze button anyway?! Probably the same person who invented that cheap peanut butter. Sounded like a good idea, but in reality, it ain't worth the trouble. I get up and sit on the edge of my bed, trying to gather my senses. If only that dream were true, maybe if I close my eyes tight enough, Nia will come through that door in five, four, three, two, one... nothin'. I wish I could get a job that paid for having a vivid imagination. Oh, well.

Wow, what a night. This is the last day that I will be

here in this capacity. In momma's house as a resident, that is. How time flies. I finally get up. I smell breakfast. The aroma brings back memories. Memories of burnt hair, perfume and bacon. Smells like Sunday morning. It's almost as if it were yesterday.

"Ouch Mamma! you burned my neck," my sister yelled.

"Well, if you sit your little *fast tail* still, I wouldn't burn you. Ain't nobody tell you to go to that party last night, and sweat your hair out," my mother snapped back.

I don't know who started calling the hair on the back of your neck the kitchen, or how much sense it makes, but my sisters had more dishes in their kitchens than the Waffle House. I don't think anyone in our family slept in the big house during slavery. I probably came from a long line of field hands, that is, after being taken from our throne. My family and I are all the color of Mississippi mud, deep dark, with eyes that could pierce the soul, and hair nappy enough to clean a pan of three-day-old lasagna. Needless to say, when the Jerhi Curl came out my sister was the first one in line. Man, those were the days; no worries, no cares. Oh, where was I? That's right, the smell. I follow that smell and there I see her. She is wearing that powder blue robe that I bought her for her birthday.

"I made your breakfast" she whispered, trying to mask the tears in her voice.

"Thanks, but you know I can't drive on a full stomach, I'll get sleepy" I replied, as I tried to look her in the eye.

"Baby, you've got to eat something" she said while avoiding my eyes.

"Are you crying? Come on, I am only going to Atlanta, not to war" I said as I gave her a reassuring hug and a kiss on her cheek.

Now this may sound like an exchange from a man to his girl friend, but this is my mother. I am her youngest child and only son. Momma's Boy and proud of it. The unconditional love between a mother and son is so deep, so strong, so unyielding that unless you are in one, you would not understand. She nurtured me at my worst, and guided me to my best. It's as if we share a soul. I can't imagine life without her. I don't know how long I have left on this earth, but I hope I die before she does. Listen to Boyz II Men's "A Song for Momma" and that would give you some insight to possibly even scratch the surface but, like I said, you have to be in one to understand. I am sure that a father and his daughter have there own love Jones going on, but I only speak from what I know.

Believe me, I have been teased and taunted many times about our closeness, for our special relationship. The time when I got the wind knocked out of me when I played little league football, and she carried me..., yes, carried me off of the football field. The time when she got kicked out of a basketball game for cursing out the referee for not calling a foul on the opposing team. The time she was going to take on the neighborhood bully for picking on me. The time that she cried like a baby when she first dropped me off at college (Grambling State University). It took me two semesters to live that one down. My boys were cracking up a week into our first semester as they talked about how some new fish and his mom were crying like babies when she dropped him off.

I laughed along as much as I could, thinking that I had escaped ridicule, until my roommate Monty could not contain himself any longer, and told them that it was me. It took me a whole year to live that one down. Thanks Monty (RIP). I could go on, but I think you get the picture. I kissed her again on the cheek, grabbed a couple strips of turkey bacon, and headed to the shower.

Walking down the hall at mom's house is like taking a trip down memory lane. (Rest in peace Minnie Riperton). Wow, I was a funny looking kid; big head, little body, big teeth. Thank God for the weight room and the dentist. Nothing however beats my sisters. I swear that in this dimly lit hall, they both look like a ghetto version of Mickey Mouse with those Afro puffs in their

3

heads. I love showing pictures from back in the day to any male that comes to visit them. A picture is worth a thousand words and laughs.

Ahhhhh, nothing wakes me like a nice hot shower. If you want to experience true serenity, try a hot shower and a Miles Davis CD. This is so relaxing. I feel like that white lady in the old Calgon commercial (take me away!). Eyes shut, hot water engulfing me, massaging me. Its actually hypnotic, almost orgasmic. Almost. Damn! I can't believe this. Just as I was entering "my zone," my sister decides to wash clothes. So much for hot water. Siblings usually know exactly which buttons to push. She knows that I can't get going in the morning without my hot shower. I've had my share of cold showers in my day, but this wasn't the time or the place. Believe me, I know too well.

As I put my unmatched luggage in my truck, I could feel Mamma's tearful eyes watching me. My departure seems to be killing her softly. I guess this is the official cutting of the umbilical cord. She could tolerate me going to college, because she was still my primary care-giver, she knew I'd be back and my leave was temporary. This however was permanent. Her baby boy was taking the step into manhood. We had a serious co-dependent relationship going on. We both needed each other in the worst way, we leaned on each other like the sides of the letter "A", removed one side, and the balance was gone. It worked fine as a child, but I'm a man now. Right? What women would put up with me knowing I needed mom for breath. We share a heart. She is my mother, my father, my inspiration. I need to leave and see what I am made of, but I feel guilty. Can I make it without her? Can she make it without me? Why do I feel guilty, I am doing the right thing."

I headed outside; it seems awfully dry and hot today.

"Yo Eric, you really leavin' da hood, man?"

That was Lil' Mike from down the street. He has been my shadow for as long as I can remember. He was 17

4

years old and entering his senior year in high school. Talk about being a brat! His dad died in an accident at General Motors when he was nine. Needless to say, his moms got paid. She bought him everything that he needed, and even more that he didn't. He always had the latest pair of Jordan's. You would think that he had stock in Tommy Hillfiger, and he had a better car than my mom, and she has a job. You know the kind of car that you get after you graduate from college, and put in at least a good five years on the job. What does he have to look forward to? He was good kid, a smart kid, but used his good looks and charm to get his way. The girls loved him and he knew it. I was the only one who could keep his head from getting too big. His looks, charm and money did not impress me. He looked up to me; I was like a big brother to him. His mom often talked to me when she could not deal with him. She even wrote me letters about his progress or her problems with him while I was off at school. Mike needed to grow up with the quickness, and understand that the world does not center around him.

"Yeah man, gotta go spread my wings... see what I'm made of. You feel me?" I replied, while packing the truck.

"You gone keep in touch?"

"Come on, man. You know I got cha' back. I ain't gone leave ya hangin' like that."

"I never been to Atlanta before. I heard they got all kind of Honey's down there!"

"That's true, but you know what they say; too much honey is bad for you."

"Well, you know *me*."

Mike laughed and looked away. I knew he wanted to talk about something. I could tell. A person's word may say one thing, but their body language tells the real story.

"Mike, I can tell something is on ya mind. Talk to me, man. Holdin' stuff in ain't healthy. What's goin' on?"

"Naw, I'm cool. I gotta go, I didn't tell moms that I was leavin'."

Still not looking me, his body let me know that he was

lyin' his butt off.

"That never stopped you before. Talk to me, dog. What's really goin' on?"

"I don't know man, the hood is getting dangerous, man. I mean, who can I talk to when you leave? One of my moms punk boyfriends? They don't like me, and I sure don't like them!"

I looked at Mike's face. Beneath the tough exterior, was a child, a baby, longing for the attention of a man. This was the plight of many of our children in the hood. At least he could rationalize why his pops wasn't around. At least he had peace in knowing that Popa *was not* a rolling stone. I could not say that. My father is a musician. Haven't seen him since I was in high school, and that was because he had a concert here in the city. I've got no love for him. He knows where I am, how to get in touch with me, but does he? No. If he were on fire, I wouldn't piss on him. But any way, I was speaking about Mike. His mother tried to fill the void left by his father with material things. That's equivalent to building a house on quicksand. His mother loved him, but she created a monster. I am the type of Momma's boy who appreciates the beauty, strength and perseverance of the Black woman. I have vivid memories of my mother struggling to keep us safe, fed, and loved. Paying bills with rubber checks; "robbing Peter to pay Paul," as she would put it. I have seen Mamma making a way out of no way. Of Mamma stretching a pot of beans and some Jiffy corn bread out for an entire week. My sisters and I had gas out of this world for that week. I was the self-proclaimed King of self-made bubble bath. I may not have always had my share of applebutter sandwiches back in the day, but we were never hungry. Mike was the type of Mamma's boy who expects women to fill his every desire and need, while he sits back and does nothing. He was almost a minor league pimp. It sounds cold, but you should see how he waits for his mom on payday. Even in our poverty I was spoiled, but he was a brat. There is a

difference. We were both products of our environment.
Mike was getting ready for his last year of high school.
His talents knew no limits. He was college material, did-
n't study much, but maintained a "B" average. The kind
of student that I envied so much; never cracked a book,
but made excellent grades. A brother like me had to
think of games, gimmicks and music to remember facts.
I still owe Jermaine Jackson a thank you note for helping
me pass a spelling test back in the day. You remember
that song, *Serious?* In one verse he spells the word serious (which was also a spelling word), I can here him now.
S-E-R-I-O-U-S, baby lets get serious." I always did think
Jermaine was underrated. Because of him, I made a 70%
on my spelling test, and was able to go to recess for a serious game of "it." Anyway, back to Mike. He wanted to
go to Morehouse College. Not for the education per say,
but because of what he heard about the women at
Spelman, Clark, and Morris Brown. Atlanta has four
HBCU's (Historically Black College & Universities) in a
five mile radius, which made it an ideal location for the
party formally known as *Freaknik.* Atlanta is also known
for its upwardly mobile, independent, beautiful sistahs as
well as its strip clubs. Mention Magic City to most
brothahs who've been to Atlanta, and I guarantee you if
they have not been there, they've heard about it.

"Something else is bothering you man, speak up man, I
gotta hit the road pretty soon, so what up?"
"Aiight, you remember Tonya don't you, she lives on
46th and Arlington, you played ball with her older brother?"
"Yeah, I remember her, she's a cutie, I heard she was out there
though."
"Man, that trick claim she's pregnant. But I know two
other dudes that hit it around the same time I did, so I
know it ain't mine!"
"Hit it? We talkin' baseball or sex? You mean you ain't
protecting yourself? I even gave you some jimmies one
day! Haven't you learned from these other brothers out

7

here? Learn from it!"

"Man, if my pops was still here..."

"Oh, hell naw! You can't blame this one on pops not being here. I mean, you see this foolishness too much from your boys around the way to make the same mistake. I don't have to smoke crack to realize that it ain't good for you. I can just walk down 10th & Delaware. What if she's burnin', huh? Then what? You been checked out?"

"Calm down, E! Naw, I ain't burnin'. It's been almost two months."

"How long does it take for AIDS to show symptoms?"

"Later for that man, I ain't gay! I don't get down like that, I ain't got no AIDS!"

I took a deep breath. Ignorance is at an all time high, and common sense isn't all that common.

"You don't have to be gay to have AIDS. You got that nice computer, do some research instead of downloading nude pictures on kitty cat.com!"

He laughed, "Man, you trippin' now. I'm gone be aiight, believe that."

"You still need to take a test, especially if you know two other dudes that hit it. Do you know who those other dudes have been with, and who their partners have been with? This AIDS ain't no joke. Magic is living a normal life with it, but can you afford the same treatment that he can? Well, does your mom know, about the her possibly becoming a granny?"

"Hell no! She'd kill me."

"When will you know if the baby's yours?"

"It really don't matter at this point, she is going to Ohio to stay with her aunt for the summer, her mom is making her have an abortion."

"Well, how do you feel about that?"

"I don't know how to feel. I mean, I know it ain't right, but what can *I* do, you know? This ain't gone happen again, you can bet on that. I'm not giving up sex, but I won't ride bare back again. Believe that!"

"I here you, dog. I've had a scare before too. Luckily, final exams had her stressed and she missed her period.

Be careful though man, cause an extra 7 pounds can keep you out of college, and anything else you may have been thinking of. You feel me?"

"Indeed, well I'm a get on back to the crib. Be careful, man. And don't forget about me? I'll be movin' down there pretty soon for school, but I better talk to you way before then."

"Alright man, stay up."

We embraced the way brothers do. I headed back to the house to get the rest of my things and to say my final good-byes.

As I walked through the kitchen and turned the corner, I felt a familiar punch on my arm. That was my sister's way of giving me a hug. "You call that a hit, you need to take your skinny butt in the kitchen and eat a sandwich, you too light in the ass."

"Momma, Eric is in here cursing. Shut up, black..." she said.

Dang, she hasn't called me that in a long time. My sisters and cousins would call me black as a child because of my complexion. She wasn't fair herself, but I was by far the darkest (next to my grandmother). They did not mean any harm by it, but it hurt to be called 'Blackie.' If you recall, being black wasn't very "in" in the late seventies. I would never tell them that they hurt me with the name calling, because it would hurt them to know that they were hurting me on a totally different level. That's why I am such a Spike Lee fan. "School Daze" really helped me understand my color on a whole different level.

"So, did you enjoy your cold shower, or are you used to them by now?" she ribbed.

"Naw, it was actually cool, that's how I like my showers, short and sweet, just like your boyfriend."

"At least I *got* somebody."

"Nope, you got *someone*. That midget, dwarf doesn't

9

have a body. Move, girl. I gotta finish packing."

We shared a laugh, then she really gave me a hug, a real hug.

"You be careful down there. And don't drive like you crazy either, you know how those red-neck state troupers are in the South. I'd hate for you to become that strange fruit.

"Fruit? What are you talking about?"

"Brothers that hang from a tree. Getting stopped in the South can be dangerous," she said softly as her eyes got watery. She walked off.

This was turning into a bitter-sweet moment. I guess you never know how much you mean to people until you leave them. I went into my bedroom and sat on the edge of the bed for the last time. I just know this room will be a den by Christmas. It's funny how parents say they will miss you, but turn your room into a den before you even get a chance to get your mail forwarded. I lay back on my twin-sized bed as I looked at my posters of Walter Payton, Isaiah Thomas, Michael Jordan and Magic. I thought, when I was younger that I would play pro ball, but then again, what young Black kid doesn't? If these walls could talk, what would they say? "You know you can go blind if you do that too fast." Ha, I crack myself up sometimes. What am I doing? I am stalling for time. Do I really want to leave the nest? It's not too late to call Corey and tell him that I changed my mind. Yeah, that's it, I need to save up some more money, give me until the first of the year, I'll be there. Nah, I can't do that. As it is, people expect me to stay right here and live with my Momma until I turn forty-five, a modern day Lamont Sanford. They've been saying it as long as I can remember. "He ain't gone be no good, always up under his Momma." The Curse of the Momma's Boy.

"Eric, telephone... It's Corey," yelled my mother.

His ears must have been burning.

"Hello."

"Man, you still there?"

"How did you graduate from college asking dumb questions like that? I am where you called."

"You trippin', you should be half-way here by now, why are you still there, oh, don't tell me, ya moms started crying, you started feeling guilty, and you haven't left yet right?"

I hate it when he reads me like that.

"Naw man, I was out late last night doin' my thang, so I slept a little longer than I expected to."

" Well you up now, so come on"

"I can't come if I am talking to you, so get off the phone, I hollah."

"Aiight dog. Be careful, peace."

"Mom, Debbie, I gotta go, come give me some love" I yelled.

My mom put a bear hug on me that would put Yogi to shame, she would not let go. "You two are sick, when I left for the service, you had a smile on your face, and gave me a high five on my way out. The momma's boy leaves, and you act like he's going to war. Atlanta is only eight hours away!" kidded my sister.

"Shut up girl, you wouldn't understand until you had your own son. My baby is leaving me, and I will hold on to him as long as he allows me too,"said my mother.

"Don't be jealous, your older than I am, you should have been gone" I added.

"Will you two be nice for one second, get in here and give your brother a hug." We were all engulfed in a group hug. It feels good to be loved; you should never take that for granted. I tried to inhale, and with the breath, suck out every ounce of love that lingered in the air, for I new I would need it again in the near future, but be too far to access it. I wish they sold love by the case, I would invest.

I looked down at Mom and Debbie and they were both crying. "Listen, mom, Deb, I've gotta go, I want to beat rush hour," Shoot, they had me crying now. Women!

The Drive

- Eric -

Here we go. Let me take one last drive through the hood before I get on the highway. Mercy mercy me, things aren't what they used to be. Back in the day, we would be outside, running up and down the street, getting grass stains in our Toughskins, playing football on the way to school. Can you imaging trying to get one of these kids in a pair of Toughskins now? They don't even know what Toughskins are, if it ain't FUBU, Lugz, Polo, Tommy, Nike or any other name brand, they're not trying to be seen in it. We were always outside, getting some sort of exercise, even if it were hitting girls on their booties and running, hoping they would catch you. Well not me, it was more the lighter skinned boys with the "good hair." A nappy headed, Hershey colored brother like me would sit back and wish it were me getting chased. I would have given any thing to have a little Debarge in me back then, and every other dark skinned brother, who heard the phrase, "he's cute, to be so dark." If I had a nickel for every time, I heard that, I could afford a pair of Air-Jordan's. Two pair. Big ups to His Airness though, brothers like him, Wesley Snipes, Dominique Wilkins, and Mr. Smooth himself, Denzel Washington, made it cool to be dark. My dark complexion is "in" now. How in the hell can a color be in? I can't change, so if the Silvers have a reunion tour, I guess I am just S.O.L. I'm glad that darn Chico Debarge is a solo act. Where was I? Oh yeah, the neighborhood. Kids don't even play outside like they used to. The neighborhood just hadn't been the same since they closed down our schools and made us travel to the suburbs. I remember the first day of school in the suburbs; the Whites were picketing because they did not want us there. And this was in the 80's! I wasn't worried at all because when super sistah (my mom) heard about this, she got on the bus with me, and I know she was packing a 9mm. Of course she would not admit it, but I know sistah girl very well. She can be elegant one moment, and knock yo ass out the next. What a Lady. That's my momma. Wasn't that the name of a T.V. show back in the day? Well, anyway, let me get my butt on the highway.

Driving can be therapeutic if you have a lot on your mind. Lately, I have had the same thing on my mind though. Relationships. More specifically, why have I not found a meaningful one? I have been out of college for well over three years now, and I have only had one real relationship, one real girlfriend, and that was in college. Phelicia. That was the one time in my life that I was compelled to actively persuade someone, and I was determined I was going to get her by any means necessary. We would still be together if I had allowed her time to heal from the relationship that I rescued her from. That was over three years ago, and I have not had anyone significant since.

I often wonder what's wrong with me? Why is it so hard for me to find and maintain a relationship that I could possibly build upon? What am I looking for in a woman? And just like that, the radio Gods must have read my mind, because out of nowhere, my girl, The Songstress, came on. Anita Baker. That's what I want. The kind of love that Anita Baker sings about. I want that unconditional love. That Sweet love. I mean, if you actually listen to *Sweet Love*, there is nothing else to say. I would love to fall in love with someone who I could vibe with on that level. Say those words and mean them. I immediately stopped the car and dug through my meager collection of CD's and got out Anita and I let her take me down highway I-65, telling me how she loves me "Just Because," and as I headed through the mountains of Tennessee she tells me how I bring her joy. But my all time favorite was when she told me that she wanted me "from beginning to end, 365 days of the year, and she would bet everything on her wedding ring cause she's giving me the best that she's got. That's what I'm talking about. A sister like that will get that Nubian respect, the womanly worship, that praise and appreciation from me, every time. Every time. Thanks, Mrs. Baker for putting my ideal feelings into words.

Damn; I wish she were single. Yeah, I know she is older but she is fine, sincere, and she keeps her hair fresh, and what the hell, Stella got her groove back. If she were single, I could help Anita get hers. A brother can dream can't he? Well it probably wouldn't work out, besides; I would hate to break Nia Long's heart. Damn, the things that solitude and music conjures up. I wonder what it's going to be like in the ATL. Without mom. With my best friend. Can best friends live together and still remain best friends? I love Corey like a brother, but we are different in as many ways that we are alike. Corey is a ladies man, will talk to a woman in a heartbeat. To me that's brave. He's as brave as the first brother who refused to pick cotton. I'm not like that. I wish I were. I mostly sit back and fear rejection. Moreover, it's nothing for me to talk myself out of talking to someone. He normally has options on a Friday night; I have platinum BlockBuster card. I feel like that fat dude Norm, from "Cheers" when I go in there, they know me by name. It got so bad that I had my own section at the Mom -N-Pop video store. It was called "Eric's Pick of the week." That's bad...really bad. I sometimes wish I were like Corey. While he gets sick of his phone ringing, I sometimes wonder if my line has been disconnected without my knowledge. Corey is socially assertive; I tend to fade into the background, only wishing I could talk to the fine sister across the room. Don't get me wrong, eventually I do, but by the time I work up the nerve, she has been harassed by the knuckleheads so much, that she is already on the first syllable of the word "no" before I can ask her to dance. My timing sucks.

Atlanta, 97 miles. I know I was rollin', but six hours went by extremely quick. I'm not speeding either, I mean, these other cars are passing me like I am standing still.

What is that smell? Awwww man, I can't break down in this hick town. They think running water is something you chase. This is truly a patriotic town, filled with the RED (necks) WHITE (boys) (and black folks singing the) BLUE(s). This town is so small that the mayor is the fireman is the sheriff, is the judge, is the jury, is the owner of the largest strip club in town where his wife is the main stripper, is the nurse, is the teacher is the....

Getting Ready for a Party
- Corey -

Alright, where is my dog at, he should have had his butt here by now. I knew I should have flown up to help him drive. He probably punked out and changed his mind. His mother probably cried, he felt guilty, and decided not to move. Damn Momma's boy. Don't get me wrong, I've got nothing but love for my moms too, but damn, he was ridiculous. He needs to hurry up. I am so sick of this phone ringing. Thank God for caller I.D. Terri. Hell naw, I ain't pickin' it up.

"Corey, this is Terri. I know you there cause I saw your car when I drove by. Anyway, I heard you throwing a party tonight for your boy. Well, I'll be there, even though you didn't invite me, Bye."

That's all I need, I'm not trying to get sweated tonight, especially by her! She had her quality time. The thrill is gone. We did our thang, it didn't work out. She needs to move on. I ain't worried about it though, I'll get my boy Tony to run some interference for me. He's the type of brother that asks for permission to date someone after his boy has been out with her. I can't figure it out for the life of me; I don't want anything that my boys have had. He has had his eye on her every since she wore that shear dress and that thong at Roger's pajama party. I'll admit, she gave a few brothers whiplash that night. It felt good to know that she was going home with me. She even asked me what she should wear; I picked it out, but I had know idea she would actually put it on. Dang, is that the phone again? *'PAY PHONE.'* Let me get this, it might be Eric.

"Hello?"

"Corey, it's me I had to stop in Mayberry Tennessee, my car got hot,"

"You gone be alright, you need me to swoop you up? You can't be that far?"

"Naw, I'm cool. Some Gomer Pile type dude is changing my thermostat right now, he said I'd be ready in about 45 min."

"Aiight dawg, take my cell number down, I'm about to go get a haircut real quick, but hit me when you get close, I should not be that long though."

"Haircut? Man, you still trying to hold on to that last piece of hair? You need to get a bald head. In a minute you gone look like George Jefferson, let it go, brother. Jordan made it easy for brothers like you, let it go."

CLICK!

I hung up on his butt. Why I got to be the one to lose my hair, I ain't but 26, that ain't cool. Later for that, I'll cut it off when I have to, and now ain't the time. I'm keeping my fade. On the other hand, ladies do like tall bald brothers, right? I don't know if my head has the right shape for a bald head though, I might have some dents in their that I don't know about. Why me?

Vino's Barber shop. Ain't nothin' like the barbershop. The old-school barbershop is like a ghetto college. You want to get the 411 about anything in the hood, go to the barbershop. You will find more philosophers in there than at Harvard, droppin' knowledge. You always got the old-school player, and the new-school player. The militant brother who can't stand the man for keepin' us down, and the blind brother (barber) who is always sitting in his own chair, cause people scared he's gone take their hairline back too far. How is that brother paying his bills? I bet he lives with his momma. And everyone has a nickname. I have only been goin' there for three months now, so they haven't labeled me yet. I wonder what today's topic is? It's Saturday, around 1:00, so I missed the morning rush, I should be out in about an hour. "What's up, fellas?" I greeted them as I found my seat on a chair with springs poking you in the butt so stiff that it lets you know jail, or any other alternative life style does not suit you, if you know what I mean.

"Well, well, well, if it isn't MoJo," hollered the old dude with no customers. MoJo? How in the hell did I get that name? Oh well, I've heard worse.

"MoJo?" asked Reggie (the young player) "where did that come from?"

"He looks like this cat I knew back in Louisiana, tall, light pretty boy, screwed with this girl in Lake Charles, got her pregnant, didn't want to marry her. Man, her grandmomma put a MoJo on his ass. Made him some spaghetti and the fool ate it. He ain't left Louisiana in 30 years. I ain't never eatin' nothin' else with red sauce that a women cook for me, she ain't puttin' no MoJo on me."

"Man, you crazy as hell, that stuff ain't for real!"

"Tell that to my boy, he don't know if he comin' or goin'. I bet his draws are buried in the front yard, that's why he can't leave. You found you a women down here yet, MoJo?" he asked me.

"Naw, Pops. I'm just tryin' to see what Atlanta has to offer. They say it's at least five to one, so right now I'm just doin' some research." I replied.

"I hear ya, Mo. Don't let no female tie you down, get all you can, cause believe me, they all got a hidden agenda. Go for yours, Playa," said Reggie.

School was now in session.

"Check it out, Playa. You in the South now, so these

18

women got a whole different program. They lookin' for a husband, especially if they passed twenty-five. In the south, that's considered an old maid. So don't get caught up, as a matter of fact, don't even let them think that you might be that brother that is even capable of being caught up. Let 'em know you trying to be like Ali..., stickin' and movin'. If they can't be down with that, later for them. It's too many honies in Phatlanta to go out like that. You feel me?"

"Young boy, you don't know what the hell you talking about. Let 'em think you caught up, just spread 'em out a little bit. Atlanta is big enough. Get one in Stone Mountain, One in Decatur, one in College Park, and one in Mableton. And a big one for when it gets cold," sang the old player.

The Shop erupted in laughter, partly because it was funny, and partly because he sang when he talked. This laughter only made him cut up even more.

"You see MoJo, all true players are supposed to have a pair and a spare. You gotta make these women feel special, make 'em feel like they are the only thing on ya' mind. And that cell phone and that pager crap ya' young boys got, that ain't gone do nothin'' but get you found. Ain't no women gone have that kind of access to me! I see ya' when I wanna see ya'. Don't call me, I'll call you."

"I here ya', Ice. I'm just trying to get my feet wet, I've been here for about a year now, and Atlanta is definitely the place to be for a young Black Man. If you're lonely here, you've got no mackin' skills."

It was my turn in the chair.

"How you want, it my brother?" asked the Militant one, every one called him Rapp.

I let Rapp cut my hair all the time. He was too proud of himself and his brothers to let anyone leave his chair with a bad hair cut.

"I don't know, Rapp. It's getting kind of thin up there,

I almost got a sunroof goin' on up there. What do you think"?

"The hair cut don't make the man, the man makes the haircut. Besides, you got the right head for it, you're not one of them kidney bean head shaped brothers you should go ahead and let it go."

He took off his Kufi, "join the club, my brother. Always room for one more."

"Don't do it, dog. Don't let him talk you into it!" Said Reggie.

The whole shop laughed again. "You must want him to get some chemicals in his head like you. Nappy ain't good enough for you, prettyboy. You know good and well you ain't got no Indian in ya' family. Yo ass can't even go swimmin' without a plastic cap on ya' head." I don't know what possessed Reggie to get into a verbal confrontation with Rapp, that's how he got his name. He doesn't say much, but when he gets started I'd sure hate to be on the receiving end of one of Rapp's arguments.

"Do it, Rapp. Do it before I change my mind."

And like that, it was gone. I had a chrome dome, a baldly, smooth as a newborn babies butt. I was hairless. I don't want to see it, I bet I look like an ass with eyes. I bet if Michael Jordan wasn't rich, he'd be just another bald guy. Damn, why did I do this? I wonder how long it will take to grow back.?

"Here is the Mirror, my brother."

Oh well, here goes nothing...Damn...I look good, nice round head, gotie is on point, oh, I know its on now: "Ouch, what in the Hell is that?'

"My fault brother, its alcohol, get used to it, you don't want all of those razor bumps on your head do you?"

"Naw, you're right, but next time warn me, will you?"

"I did, you were just to busy admiring yourself in the mirror to hear me, my bad."

"It's cool, it's cool, take it easy Brotherman." As I gave

him 10 dollars, plus a 2-dollar tip, "Stay Black," he replied. Like I have a choice. "Aiight peeps, yaw stay cool, I'm out."

"Take it Slow, MoJo," said someone as I left the run down barbershop, Wow that Georgia sun feels good on my head. Let me open up the sunroof, and let the sun caress my head. Ahhhh!

2:15, alright, my boy should be here by now.

Welcome to Atlanta

- Eric -

Let me see, Exit 10 B. Cool, left at the light, two blocks... cool, there it is. Why do people turn the volume, down when they are looking for an address? It isn't like my ears can see. Oh well. Beep, beep.

"What's up, pahtna!!" I yelled as I hoped out of my ride.

"What's Up, Baby Boy. Damn, you been workin out? Trying to get a little buff on ya' boy or what?"

"You know man, gotta stay in shape, you never know who's watchin'."

"True, True."

Corey and me embraced the way brothers do; we've been inseparable since the fourth grade. Whenever you saw me, you saw him. He was the brother that I never had.

This is a nice spot. This is my new spot. Our new spot. As Corey and I looked at each other, I could tell that I made the right choice. He was just what I needed to get me out of my shell, and I was just what he needed to settle him down.

"I see you decided to go with the Lou Gosset, Jr. look?"

"Aww, later for you, man. Watch how the honies gone be sweatin ya' boy at the party tonight!"

"Party! What party?"

I hope he doesn't think I'm going to hang out tonight,

I just drove eight hours and I am tired as hell. Atlanta
ain't goin' nowhere, I can hang out anytime, but not
tonight.

"Your party. I'm throwin' you a *Surprise Welcome to
Atlanta Party,* bro. I invited every single sistah I know,
and I told them they could not get in without at least
two of their fine girlfriends. So, it's gonna be on, in about
five hours!"

"Come on, Black! I've been drivin for eight hours, I'm
tired, can't we do this some other time? Besides, couldn't
you have told me before throwing this party?"

"Why didn't I tell you? How in the hell is it a surprise
if I told you in advance? Stop bitchin. Take a nap, get
fresh, and let's see if you finally got some mackin' skills?"

The more things change the more they stay the same.
I can't be mad at him though, he has always looked out
for me, he was just trying to make sure I had a good time.
He probably thinks this will get my mind off of aban-
doning my mother. I wonder how she is doing, I hope
she stopped crying.

"What's on your mind E, you zoning on me?" Corey
snapped. " Look dog, ya' moms is going to be O.K., she
is the strongest woman that we both know. She's a sur-
vivor. Now bring your sensitive ass on, and help me get
this 'ole mismatch luggage up to the crib," he said as he
hit me in the head with a duffel bag.

"What the... Oh, it's on now, I said as I chased him up
the stairs to the second floor of the Spanish style apartment. Aww man..., this is nice. He really laid the place
out; he always did have good taste. Expensive, but good.
I see he put the money that I sent him to good use. I told
him to get whatever he thought we needed to get started
on the right foot, and he did just that. I really loved the
Black art. Well, it wasn't really Black art, it was just a
bunch of black and white posters of late great jazz artists
such as Miles, Ella, Monk, Parker, Dizzy and Coltrane,
matted beautifully in expensive frames. This made the

apartment look muscularly classy. I knew I would see black leather furniture, surrounded by all of the gadgets that the testosterone ladened male did not need, but could not live without. I saw remote controls everywhere. Everything had a place. I definitely had to pick up after myself for the first time in my life. I even sent him money to get me a nice king size bed. No furniture, cause I wanted to pick that out myself. I entered my room. "Good lookin' out Corey, I see I got the room with the private bathroom, I said as I entered the next frontier.

"I ain't stupid," he replied, "I know ya' mama's been pickin' up ya' dirty drawers since ya' got potty trained. I didn't want to take any chances on the company seein' how triflin you are. You my boy, and I love you like a play cousin, but yo ass is messy. We definitely have to set up some ground rules because I ain't about to be..."

SLAM!!!!!

I shut the door on him in mid sentence, I new he was right, but that was one thing I did not miss about home, getting fussed at. I never got spanked as a kid, because my mom knew raising her voice at me was even worse. The pain from catching a belt lasted for 10 to 15 minutes tops, but the image of the disappointment shown by my mom during a tongue-lashing is something that tore me up inside. Her words cut like a knife. If you truly love someone, words can hurt just as bad as sticks and stones. The thought of upsetting her, disappointing her, letting her down, is truly unbearable. Yeah, I new he was just joking, but he was serious at the same time. There is a little truth to every joke.

"Wake me up when it's time to get ready for the party, and bring the rest of my stuff in!"

I yelled out the door over Public Enemies classic *"Fight the Power."*

"What?" he yelled, who do you think I am, Benson?"

SLAM.

I went into the shower and let the water cascade over my tired body, I had the water as hot as I could stand it. The only thing missing was my Miles Davis C.D., and my sister flushing the toilet. I did not even use soap for the first five minutes; I just stood there, in complete solitude. Lights out, and in the shower. Complete serenity. I was in the light of my own darkness. The shelter of a clear mind is what keeps the sane sane.

While in the shower I thought about the party tonight. No one knows me down here, which gives me a perfect opportunity to change my image. What better time to convert from the boy next door, to the confident brother around the corner? That's what I'll do, present myself in such a way that all of the ladies will take notice. Women love the bad boys, right? Well, wait until they get a load of me. I've got to beware of the "friendship zone." I lived in the friendship zone. The kind of guy that the girls love when it's time to settle down. Anyway, I climbed out of the shower, dried off and put cocoa butter on all the right places. I learned that at an early age, ain't nothin' worse than an ashy dark brother. Back in the day I only put lotion on parts that would be exposed, and it worked until middle school. In middle school, we had to change into PE uniforms. So the first day of school came around, and I had no idea that we'd have to change that day, right? Wrong. My legs were so ashy, you would have thought I'd been rolling around in flour. I wasn't concerned about it cause my brand new heavily starched Levi's were hiding that scene of neglect. I had not been so embarrassed in my whole life, the older PE assistant called me the Ashman until he went off to high school. Children can be so cruel. He was the type of guy that would bully you and call you names to cover up the fact that he couldn't read. Luckily, Corey had some curl activator in his book bag. Yeah, I used curl activator for lotion before; I'd rather have shiny legs than ashy legs, any day. But even funnier than that, was a picture of

25

Corey with a Jeri Curl. The brother ruined more pillows and white white sheets than a Klansmen with a bladder problem.

Time to try out my new bed. Yeah, I could get used to this.It's king size; soft pillows and to topit off, its firm. I can't wait to break this bad boy in, put some miles on it, make the springs sing a sweet love song. Who am I kidding? With my recent track record, I would be surprised if any lady ever saw the inside of my room, let alone felt the firmness of my bed. I have a great opportunity to change that now though, I must project confidence, and I must project confidence (yawn) zzzzzzzzz.

"Hi, my name is Eric and I..."

"I know who you are, I'm Phelicia, we are in the same literature class."

"So Phelicia, how are you doing in that class? Dr. Reed can be tough."

"I'm doing O.K. not as well as you though, he seems to like to debate with you, I know you have an A. Can you help me study?"

Help her study, as fine as she is I will help her with more than studying. She has to be the most beautiful girl on campus, and she wants me to help her. If only she knew I only had a 2.4 G.P.A, she wouldn't be asking me! Wait a minute, we are still holding hands, I mean shaking hands, what's up with that?. She's still smiling at me; she wants more than just a study partner.

"Yeah, I can help you study, you let me know when and where. Better yet, I will give you my number, and you give me a call, alright?"

I reached in to my book bag to get a pen and a pad and she is shaking her head emphatically.

"Phelicia, you OK?"

"Yeah I'm fine, I gotta go, I'll talk with you later. Bye."

And just like that, she was gone. What happened? Is

my breath kicking? Do I have a booger in my nose? Is my high-up fade uneven? Wait a minute, who is that funny lookin' brother hittin' me with the ice grill? Do I know him? I know he ain't walking this way? Yep, he is.

"What up?" I said in my wanna be Barry White voice.

"Nothin' much, bro. I see you know my girl, huh?" he replied.

His girl? His girl? Awwww damn. How did someone so fine end up with someone who looks like booty? Life ain't fair, the dude look like a heavy weight fighter who has had a long rough career. You've seen em. It looks like their nose is kind of lopsided, their forehead looks like it's trying to hold their eyes hostage.

"Oh, you mean Phelicia, yeah we've got class together. Why, what's up? I replied, still trying to look tough. Anyone who looks like that can take a punch, and probably give out a few. Hell, I had some size on me, but honestly, I never had to fight, cause my mom and my sister could whip some ass.

"Ain't nothin' up dawg, just makin' my presence known. It's all good."

I normally don't pursue women, especially if they are in a relationship, but there are exceptions to every rule. Exception, thy name is Phelicia. We will meet again.

"I hear you dawg, I hollah." I walked to class to plan our next meeting.

27

Blue Lights and Music

- Corey -

"Yo E, wake up, dawg. It's almost eight o'clock," I hollered for the third time. He's always has been hard to wake up. Me, I sleep light. Always have. I guess it's because I am always doing something that I've got no business doing. Never knew when I'd have to make that quick get away. Besides, I've been caught with my pants down one time too many to sleep to soundly. Eric, on the other hand, sleeps like a fat baby because he's always doing the right thing. My man has a conscience as clear as a bell. His thing has always been about inner peace. I have never seen him do anything to spite anyone, to hurt any one, or to even get revenge, for that matter. Says his way of life is his religion, which is why he is at peace with himself by not having a church home. A brother like myself needs to stay in church, cause I can't resist temptation. Well, I can; I just don't. Hell, you only live once. I think he is a special type of brother. I don't see why he stays single so much. Well, let me take that back. He *is* the kind of brother that they want to marry after a brother like me dogs them out. I know that for a fact. These sistahs know I ain't no good, they know I am a playa. They know I stick and run with the effectiveness of a young Cassius Clay, yet they are always sweatin' me, no matter what. They like the challenge. They like my arrogance. Nothing more satisfying

28

than taming a wild dog. Whatever. And after I dog 'em out, they go cry on a brother like Eric's shoulder, he will restore their faith in men, then they come back to me. This cycle happens far too often.

I represent a challenge, spontaneity, I give them something to think about when their not with me. These sistahs come to me actin like they got gold between their legs, hell, I ain't mad at them, cause I know I got platinum between mine, and will let them know in second. Eric is the ideal man that they claim they want. They want him alright, on a layaway plan, put his nice ass on hold until they finish playin with the dogs. Once they've lived on the edge with me for a while, they look for the Eric's of the world. They say they want a good man. Whatever! They want a good man for the future and a freak like myself for the present. And what does Eric do while they are getting their freak on with me? Wishing he didn't have such a high sense of morals, so he can do what I am doing. He thinks about shit too much. Always empathizing with them, not wanting to hurt anyone, all the while, they ain't bit more thinkin about him. Women are all about getting what they can get from a brother. They put up that innocent, ain't no good men, male bashing front all the time, but I ain't buyin it. They say all we do is cheat. Who are we cheating with?? Damn sure not each other! I've never cheated on a sistah, with a brotha. I don't get down like that, and my boys don't get down like that. But after reading an E.Lynn Harris novel, I question everything. Twice with a microscope! Anyway, I don't do anything to a woman that she doesn't allow me to do. If they want to call us dogs, then they are dogs too, and you know the term for female dog don't you?? That's what I thought. Another reason that Eric is single all the time with no prospects is because of his moms. She did a hell of a job raising my man, and he worships the ground that she walks on, so much that any women that is going to get any QT (quality time) with him must have very similar characteristics. I mean his mom is strong, yet tender, beautiful, nurturing, sassy, smart and can cook her ass off. His mom is the sweetest thing he's ever known. If he could go back in time as someone else, he would marry her. No doubt. As long as he is looking for a version of his mother, he is going to come up short. They don't make that type of sistah anymore. Hell, especially in a big fast city like Atlanta. Too many big ballers, shot callers, and as long as these females know that there is a brother makin' mad lute... someone who can get there hair, nails, and feet done, good hard workin brothers like Eric don't stand a chance. These sistahs need a sponsor, not man. It's my job to school Eric. See if I can get him a players card, cause with out one he will get played. If he wants to meet a sistah who will appreciate him, he needs to go to some small town, and get a sistah who doesn't have cable T.V., and doesn't subscribe to all of these wishy washy female magazines. The only girl that he dated that even came close was a girl named Phelicia, and she was evil as a pregnant, out of work prostitute. She is the only girl that his mom and his sisters ever liked. She is the only girlfriend he ever had that couldn't stand me. I don't care though, the feelings were mutual. Eric is trying to find Ms. Right; I'm trying to find Ms. Right Now. He is looking for a number one female; I am looking for numbers 1 threw 5, not necessarily in that order though.

"What up, man," said Eric, as he rubbed his sleepy eyes. "What time is it jumpin off tonight?"

"Ten o'clock, but I've got to go to the club house and get everything squared away, my boy Roger will be there with the music in about twenty minutes, but he always runs late and that's another story." I replied, "just get ready, and I will come pick you up at 10:30, I've got a few honies for you to meet."

I left the apartment with a million and one things on

my mind; I've got to introduce the ATL to my boy in
true playa fashion. I hope everyone shows up tonight,
everyone but Terri. O.K., the balloons are on the club-
house mailbox, the place is well lit. Cool. We are in business. Hold up, I know that ain't Rogers car, he is here
early. Beep, beep. "What up, dawg. You here early,
either the world is gone end, or you got woman trouble."

"Man, these sistahs gone make a brother snap, man.
You can't be nice to these hoes, man," Roger said in a
tone that let me know that it ain't all good.

"Hoes? We said we would stop callin' the sistahs that.
Somebody must have pissed you smooth off!" I replied
while carrying his crate of records. No wonder cds are so
popular; records are too damn heavy.

"I know, dog. But I've got to call 'em like I see 'em," He
replied. "How about I told Dawn about this party two
weeks ago, and now she's upset that I refuse to go to
some lame ass sorority ball with her. Hell, she just found
out about it her self! She had the nerve to say next time
you want some, why don't you call Corey. That's cool
though, she don't know who she dealing with. She can't
use sex as a bargaining tool with me man, cause I've had
so much, that I can do without. See, when these females
know they can't use the ass as power, they have no more
power."

My man was in a zone. But what he said makes a lot of
sense. "Yo Rog, is she your woman or something? I mean,
you stressen the hell out of this situation."

"Naw, she ain't my woman, she was getting more QT
than any other woman. I was trying to settle... you know,
chill for a minute with her, head in the direction of making her the one. But she trippin,' dog. Had the nerve to
tell me some dumb shit like that, its too many women in
Atlanta for her to even fix her mouth to say call Corey
when you want some!"

"True, but she ain't wrong, ya' dig?" I said.

"What the hell you talking bout?" he wondered.

"I damn sure can't give you no ass, but I can take you to where plenty of it is, and I know plenty single females. This is Atlanta baby!!! These sistah can't control brothahs like us. We got what they want. We are single, no kids, educated, makin' legal money, benefits, fine as hell, and we keep it real. They got two choices, act right, or get left! A woman is only a woman. I don't care how fine, how built, or how smart, she is... she's still a woman. I don't care how she makes your toes curl at night, how well she cooks, how well she *backs that thang up*, she is still a woman. She bleeds like every woman, she puts her pants on one leg at a time like a woman, her breath stinks in the morning like every woman. She is a woman, and she can be replaced, because there are too many women. Look at Clark Atlanta's campus, all you see is women. Yeah its co-ed, but all you see are women. Same with Morris Brown, and don't mention Spelman..., its rediculous. Go downtown during lunch, and see how many corporate sistahs are down there, by they damn self. It's too many women in Atlanta for Dawn to talk trash like that. Don't let her see you sweat that foolishness man. Give her a couple days, don't even acknowledge her, if she don't come around, serve her some walkin papers. She's a nice girl and everything, but if she trippin' like that... I hollah. Anyway, the party is gone be crawlin with honey's tonight, and everybody loves the Dejay, so after tonight, you might not even want to hear Dawns name. You feel me?"

"That's why you my boy. Good looking out, man. I really needed to hear that, I get a little soft every now and then. Now lets get this stuff set up," Rog said.

We set the equipment up in no time flat. Roger hadn't Dejayed any parties since he was at Ball State in '94. He'd done it to make money, to pay for books, tuition and condoms. Not necessarily in that order though. I hope he still has skills, cause if he doesn't I've got mad jokes.

"Say Rog, you feelin' it man? I mean, you gone make it bounce, you gone keep it krunk, you gone bar-b-que or mildew?" That was my way of asking him was he going to keep the party hype.

"What's my name baby? Don't question me about that. Jordan came back and didn't miss a beat did he? I'm bringing it." he replied.

I hated to remind him that when Jordan first came back, the Bulls where put out of the playoffs by the Orlando Magic, he didn't return to his superman status until that second year back, but I did not want to burst his bubble.

People where finally starting to come in, and my man Roger was taking them on a hip-hop journey. No one was dancing yet, you know how we do. Wait on somebody else to get the part started, but their thirsty asses sure was drinkin like they thought I was going to say last call for alcohol.

Finally, the party is jumpin; Special Ed is telling us how he's got it made, while Rog is telling all the ladies to make some noise. Yeah, my man Rog is in a zone, he even referred himself by his DJ name, "Skillzz." I haven't heard that name in a minute. I make my way through the crowd and head toward the door, it's time to get my boy.

"Hey sexy, you gone save me a dance tonight?"

I knew that voice, and she had the nerve to grab my butt. Terri, damn! How did she find out about the party? Roger couldn't keep a secrete to save his life. I turned around, and Terri was looking good, she finally got that weave out of her head, toned down the make up, and she looked like she had been working out. Arms like Angela Basset while she was getting her groove back.

"Hey Terri," I said, sounding generally interested, as I gave her a hug, I noticed that the body was tight, "Where have you been hiding? I know it's been at least two months." I said.

"At least two months, I know you've been avoiding me, but that's ok, I'm through chasing. Oh, by the way, this is my cousin, Dionne. She just moved here a few months ago" she replied.

A few months ago, huh? About the same time that you stopped trying to blow my pager up.

"Nice to meet you, Dionne, I hope you enjoy the party. Listen, I would love to talk more, but I am going to pick up the guest of honor, and Terri, you look very nice, I look forward to dancing with you when I get back." I said, as I winked and walked out of the door, toward my car.

I can't believe how good she looked, and now she gonna try to play hard. I know I can ease back in though. She knows who put that arch in her back on a regular. She can't play hard with me, cause she showed her trump card. She showed up. There are well over seven different clubs in Atlanta that are off the chain on every Saturday night, and she shows up at my party. I know the game; I was born at night; not last night. I hope her cousin knows her way home, cause Terri is stayin' with me tonight.

The Guest of Honor

- Eric -

I don't know what to wear. Is it casual, or dressy? Is there a difference between the two? Moreover, if so, where is the fashion line drawn? What are they wearing in Atlanta any way? I mean, I know what's considered jiggy in the Midwest, but this here is the big leagues. I don't want to get arrested by the fashion police. Wait a minute, did I just say jiggy? Do they use that word here? What would Florida Evans say at a time like this? DAMN, DAMN, DAMN!!

I didn't even see what Corey had on. I got it, black. Can't go wrong with black. Besides, it's about the only thing that I have that is not wrinkled, so black it is. I hope I meet somebody tonight. Well, I am not currently trying to settle down. I wanna get acclimated to the ATL first, but having a sistah to keep you company is always a good thing.

"Yo' E, you ready to roll? The party is hyped, and the women are wondering where the guest of honor is. Lets bounce, baby boy!" yelled Corey.

I came out of my room, dressed in black from head to toe. Good thing I got my T.W.A. (teeny weenie afro) tighten up from my man Vino before if left. I sure hope Corey knows a good barber down here. But hell... he has a bald head, so what would he know?

"Damn, they gone be on you tonight, dog. You dark brothahs better take advantage of your looks now, cause us yellow brothers are coming back. Believe that!" spat Corey.

"Oh, its like that, huh? As long as you got me at least one sistah at the party, we gonna be just fine."

"One! Aw hell naw. I know you didn't say *one*. Don't get over here and let one girl lock you down. You need to work the room like you runnin' for office. Get the number, but don't write it down there. Slip into the bathroom and write it down before you forget it. Then come back out and do the same thing again. Don't let any female see you write down any numbers. You make 'em think you memorized it... make 'em feel special. And also, the other females won't see you writing down either. That way, they don't get a chance to start runnin' interference on the mackin' skills. That rule comes from Mackology 101. Hell, I need to write a book for mackin' rules, like those white girls did. But on the real, don't get hemmed up at the party, man. If I see you with any female for more than five minutes, just smooth your eyebrow out, and that will let me know to come rescue you."

I can't believe my man put this much energy in mackin'. I don't even have any mackin' skills. Never have. These high powered, independent sisters in Atlanta has probably heard every line in the book, what can I say that they haven't heard already. Damn, I think I may be in over my head.

"All right man, I'm ready. Shoot! Hold up a second dog, I didn't even call my mom to let her know that I made it in. She's gonna kill me." I remarked.

" What? All of these honeys waitin' to meet you, and all you can think about is your mom!? Damn! You a Momma's boy! Will you hurry yo' ass up? I'm ready to get my swerve on, and you holdin' up progress."

"Later for you, pretty boy. It won't take but a minute."

What was I thinking? I've been in Atlanta since 4:30, and haven't called her yet. I hope I didn't worry her too much.

"Hey, big head girl, where is ya' moms?"

"She's upstairs, and she gone curse you out. Why you just now calling her?" asked Debbie.

" I was tired. I mean, I meant to, but when I got here I couldn't keep my eyes open. Is she mad? Was she worried? I am so sorry." I pleaded.

"Boy, stop trippin'. Moms called you a long time ago. She knew how long it would take to get there, that hoe Corey answered the phone. He said you were asleep. He said you would call when you woke up. She has been crying all day. Sistah Brown from church thought you died. Mom told her that 'her baby was gone,' and she called the pastor. The whole church was over here in thirty minutes."

"What? You mean to tell me she couldn't get hold of herself long enough to say I was out of town?" I said in shock.

"Nope. All she said was 'Sistah Brown, my baby is gone. I hope he is going to a better place.' She cried and hung up the phone, and before I know it, the place was packed. They did bring food though, I ain't seen that much chicken since Froghorn Leghorn was pimpin' on the Loony Toones!" she said with a laugh. I can't believe that she thought that that was funny.

"Let me speak to momma! I don't believe this! I've been gone ten hours, and she's actin' like this? She's gonna have a nervous break down!

"Hey baby, I miss you already. Is everything O.K? Do you need any money?" my Mom asked.

"No mom, I'm fine. The apartments nice, the trip was OK, and I am well rested. I heard the church came by to pay their respects." I mused.

"Debra runs her mouth too damn much! It was all a

misunderstanding. Chile, you know how Sistah Brown is. Can't keep her mouth shut, always gossiping and jumping to conclusions. All I said was that you were gone, and I was too emotional to talk, and before I knew it, the pastor, the choir, and the deacon board was at my door with fried chicken and cole slaw. Well, at least I didn't have to cook. I'm not gone hold you, baby. Corey told me that you were going to a party. I just wanted to hear your voice. I love you, sweetie."

"Love you too, ma. Talk to you later."

"How much later?"

"How about we talk every Sunday, to save money."

"O.K., if you say so, but don't be mad if I can't wait that long. Have fun, and be careful."

"I will, ma. Love you." I hung up. This feels weird, I guess I'm grown now.

"Let's roll, man. I wanna see what Atlanta has to offer." I said

"Cool, its on. Lets bounce." Corey replied.

Corey ran his mouth the whole time about the women that were there when he left, but I tuned him out. He actually sounded like Charlie Brown's teacher. All I could think about was what would happen once we got there. I mean, he said that I was the guest of honor, but I hate the spotlight. I am a behind the scenes-type brother. It's bad enough that I don't know anyone in this city. Well, I did know Roger, but not that well.

"Come on, man. Snap out of it, we're here. I bet you haven't heard a word that I said, have you? Well, here we are. You ready?"

"What's my name, man. I was born ready. Let's do it." I said, knowing I was lying my butt off, I was as nervous as Al Sharpton in a blind man's barbershop.

Corey and I got out of the car. As I marveled at the cars, I tried to figure out whether or not I belonged here. I mean I saw nice cars. Benzes, Beamers, new Accords,

Acura's, and S.U.V.s where everywhere. We stepped into the party and it seemed like everyone was lookin' at us. Did I have a booger in my nose? Was my hair straight? I hope I have some breath mints. Do they still say jiggy?

"Come on, dog, lets head to the DJ both so we can get it started." Corey yelled over Eric B. and Rakim's classic, *"Move the Crowd."* On the way to the both, I shook about eight brother's hands, I didn't recognize any, but they all knew my name.

Roger was handling business on the turntables, but when he saw me, he stopped what he what he was doing and embraced me. The way brothers do.

"What's up kid, how you liven?" The native New Yorker said

"I'm chillin', how you feelin'?" I replied, trying to sound hip.

"I'm cool, you lookin' good kid. This party is off the chain, the sistahs are hyped, and they all trying to see if you bringin' it, you feel me?" He said. Just then Corey grabbed the mic and began to speak.

"Yo', let me hollah at yaw for a minute. This is my boy, Eric. He is brand new to the ATL, so lets show him some love. And ladies, the brotha is single, no kids, and he wears a size 14 shoe..."

I don't believe he went there. He is still talking but I don't know what he saying because now I feel like Kunta Kinte on the auction block, and I am being looked at by a bunch of beautiful black women masters, who need a love slave. Damn! Now they are all looking at my feet. Who in the hell started that rumor anyway, not that I am not blessed, but I don't go around saying, 'dude, you got big feet, how large are you'. I am my only point of reference. Talk about pressure. Penis size is important, but I saw this lady giving birth to a 10 pound baby on The Biology channel. I know my Johnson can not compare to a 10 pound baby, so I am very humble. I know my limitations. That's probably why white boys have been going down to "the Valley" for so long. They knew that they had short end of the stick.

I looked in the crowd and saw everyone giving me reassuring smiles and positive hand gestures when Corey handed the mic back to Rog, and said, "Let's do this, homeboy." He led me to the crowd, and I felt like a celebrity. The vibe was so positive, women giving me hugs, saying save me a dance, brothers dappin' me up. This is nice, I can get used to this.

"Hi Eric, my name is Terri, I was a friend of Corey's" said Terri.

"What do you mean was a friend, it's not like that is it?" butted in Corey.

"Don't play me, Corey. I tried like hell to keep in touch with you, but you had other things on your mind, and it wasn't me, so save it. Anyway Eric, I hope you enjoy Atlanta. Don't let your boy turn you into a dog... oh yeah, this is my cousin Dionne, she just moved here three months ago," replied Terri.

"Hello Dionne, nice to meet you," I said extending my hand to shake hers. "How about we go dance, it seems that these two have some catching up to do." I said, trying not to sound too corny. Dionne was very attractive, not pretty, but attractive. She was shorter than what I preferred, around 5'3, in 3 inch heels, but she had a shape that could rival a coke bottle. Wow, what a beautiful smile and she smells good. I wonder if she can cook? Cook what in the hell am I thinking, it's only a dance.

"Yeah, lets Dance" she replied. Her eyes traveled my body with the subtlety of Dennis Rodman in drag. Atlanta, here I am.

Playas' Paradise

- Corey -

Ican't believe she trying to act like she ain't feelin'
me. I knew I should have tapped it when I had the
chance, but then again, she wasn't bringin' it then
like she is now. She went from an under-rated free agent,
to a first round pick. She went from full-time geek, to
potential freak, in no time flat. Speaking of flat, ain't
nothin' flat on her. I can't help but to stare... me and
every other brothers in here. I can tell that her cuz from
the Chi. (Chicago), has been given her some beauty tips.

"Your boy seems cool, he has this real innocents about
him, I just hope Dionne doesn't hurt him out there."
Said Terri.
" Don't let the baby face fool you. My man can hold his
own." I responded.
"If you say so... Well, I'll talk to you later." Terri said as
she turned to walk away.
No she don't think she's just going to walk off like that!
"Hold on, Terri. What's your rush."
"Rush, I'm not in a rush. I'm just trying to go have fun,
get my dance on."
"Oh, we can't have fun together?"
"I've tried that already. You weren't feelin' me... or have
you forgotten? I don't believe in going backwards. I am
the same person that I was when you were dissin' me
back in May, so go do your thang, cause I'm sure gone do

mine." She snapped, as she walked off. And did she walk... had a stride that *oozed* confidence. That was attractive. I did not realize that she had that much swivel in her hips when she walked. If she can work her hips like that standing up, I can't wait to experience her again horozontally.

You know what though? I ain't sweatin' it. She can go on and do her thang. I had her once, and I can have her again. She showed up, she new I was going to be here. Hell it's my party. She still wants me. If she wants to play games, we can play games. She should know by now that you can't play games with a player. Besides, I play for keeps.

" Hey Corey, I like the new look, let me rub that head." That was Shelia.

"Which one" I replied. Sheila was a friend of one of my boys, his name is Tony. He used to sweat her all of the time, but she never liked him. He would invite her to all of our get togethers, fight parties, bar-b-ques, and card parties. I could tell she wanted to get with me though. She would always wink those beautiful dark eyes, and touch me whenever she laughed at my jokes. Usually a dead give away. I wouldn't mind given her a little Q.T. (quality time), if I were not so cool with Tony. Well actually, I am not that cool with Tony, he is Roger's boy, so we are cool by association. I told myself that I would not step to her unless Tony found another girl to sweat, or if a full year passed without me hearing her name out of his mouth. He tries to front like he doesn't like her, but I can tell.

"Are you flirting with me, Corey?" questioned Sheila.

"Naaah, I can't step to you like that, I don't want to step on any toes."

"You talkin' bout Tony? He and I are just friends, we work together, I don't sleep where I work."

"Is that right?"

Tony and Shelia worked from the same real estate

office. Selling homes is big business in Atlanta; new sub-
divisions go up quicker than Jacks beanstalk. I wouldn't
trust one of these new homes if they paid me. One good
Georgia storm, and you've got a water bed... whether you
wanted one or not.

"That's right, now back to my question," as she sub-
tracted some of the distance between the two of us,
"May I rub your head."

"Be my guest."

She grabbed my hand and took me to the floor. Even
though it was an up tempo song, we were dancing pelvis
to pelvis, while she repeatedly stroked my head and the
back of my neck. Naw girl, not the ear, that's my spot.
Oh, this is what they mean by "Your making it hard for
me." I know she feels the uprising that's taking place in
the south. Damn, now she's turning around. This hasn't
happened to me since college, I thought I had more control than this. I am so hard right now... a midget could
do chin-ups the third leg. At this point, I could pole
vault, joust, or put someone's eye out.

"I see your boy ain't the only one in here with a big
foot" she whispered in my ear.

"Yeah, and you know what they say about brothers
with big feet don't you?"

I leaned over and put my mouth real close to her ear
and said, "We have big shoes."

She looked at me and smiled and replied," Well, I
would love to try out those big shoes one day."

"Why put off tomorrow what you could do tonight?"

"What's up, dog." That was Tony.

Damn, I wonder if he saw how close we were dancing.

"What up, Tone." I replied, as I dapped him up, but he
wanted to embrace... like brothers do, not too close
though, I ain't trying to live an *Invisible Life*.

"How you feelin,' kid? Long time no see." Tone said.

"Yeah Tone, its been a while. Where you been hidin', bro?"

He gave me this sly grin, until he saw Shelia behind me.

There was a brief, awkward moment. The kind of moment when a kid realizes that the toy that he threw away was still in great playing condition but is too proud to ask for it back. Does that make sense? "Hey, what's goin' on, Sheila?" said Tony.

"Hey sweetie, how are you, give me some love" Sheila replied, cool as a fan. Nothing seems to phase her, let me make a mental note of that.

"I'm good, boo. Hey, this is my girl, Gail." Said Tony.

Tony had a new girl what a relief. If he has a girl, why was he lookin' like he lost his best friend a minute ago? He can't hide that shit, I know he's still feelin' Sheila, I can tell by his eyes. The eyes don't lie. We all exchanged pleasantries, and the half-happy couple walked off, hand in hand. Sheila and I continued our dance. Roger was now playing *"Back that Thang Up"*, and we could have been playing Simon Says, because Sheila did exactly what the song said. She didn't have much back up. She backed what she had with the skill and precision of Ben Carson. She hit the target with 95% accuracy. And again the south is rising. My cannon can't keep rising for these false alarms. Brothers know what I mean. Who ever called the condition *blue balls* was right. That is if by blue, they meant sad. Sad drooping and sore. Isn't it funny how you can tell when someone is watching you, I turned my head and there was Terri getting sweated by a brother who would have to jump to give Prince a high five, while watching me the whole time. Again she is showing her trump card, cause she is rolling her eyes at me. How you gone stare at someone, wait for him or her to look at you then roll your eyes. That is so sixth grade. Either you want me or you don't. Don't play games, especially with a player, cause you will get played.

"Listen Sheila, I am going to sit this next one out, I don't want to get too sweaty... at least not in here anyway."

"OK, that's cool, we will dance again" she said as she gave me a hug and a peck on the cheek. She made sure that her valley was pressed against my southern soldier, as she looked me square in the eye. She gave me a look that told me that we would have a civil war in the near future. I would be ready for the battle, equipped with my Trojans. Magnum that is.

I went over near where Terri was standing, and I totally ignored her. I began talking to some guy standing near the bar, he looked familiar, I think I played ball with him a few times at *Run-n-Shoot* last week.

"What's up dawg, you doin' ya' thing right?" I said

"Yeah you know, trying to see what's crak-u-laten." The guy said.

This brother has to be from Atlanta. What in the hell does crack-u-laten mean?

"True, where I know you from, dawg?"

"I work with Roger, I think we played ball at *Run-n-Shoot* last week."

Oh, now I remember. He was this was the fake ass Allen Iverson-type dude. I hated playing with this duck. The gym must have been named after him, cause all he wanted to do was run and shoot. You couldn't find his "D" if he had the alphabet tattooed on his chest.

"Don't act like you don't see me over here. You saw this midget, wave cap wearin'-brotha over here, and you didn't even come rescue me." It was Terri.

"Aren't you the one who did not want to be bothered about twenty minutes ago? I was givin' you your space."

"Corey, why are you trippin', one minute you don't want to be bothered, and now tonight you trying to show some interest?"

"Come on now, I ain't trippin', we've always been cool."

"Yeah, we've been cool, but tonight you act like you might wanna be starting something."

"Why you gotta analyze shit, lets just party. I came here to party with my boy, either you gone join us, or go back over there and talk to Stewart Little."

"You get on my nerves!"

"Yeah? I love you too. Now lets dance... if you can keep up."

"Whatever! Come on, boy."

The more we danced, the more I realize that she was going to make my starting five. I had a solid rotation of 5 women that I could call when I felt that Jones in my bones. Since I am a die hard hoop fan, I tried to put everything in hoop perspective. In the Chicago Bulls' glory days, they had two franchise players, Jordan and Pip, and three other role players around them that had a specific job to do. The question at hand is, can Terri break the starting five? And if so, is she a franchise player or a role player. She lives far enough not to just stop by, yet close enough for the all important booty call. The mentality, sex appeal, class, and "it" were all criteria to be a franchise player in the starting five. I have yet to define "it", but you can spot "it" when you see "it." A role player only needed the sex appeal. Low self-esteem didn't hurt either.

"What are you thinking about, Corey? A penny for your thoughts."

"Huh? I can't hear you... the music is too loud." I heard everything she said, I just needed an excuse to slip outside and talk to her. I didn't want all of my other "team members" to get jealous over playing time, especially Sheila, she had franchise potential.

"Lets step outside and get some fresh air, cause I can... like barely here you."

"Sure, lets go."

She grabbed my hand and headed toward the door. I felt every sistah in the place shooting visual daggers at me. A true player must think on his feet. Never be seen walking hand in hand with another female in the club... unless she is the youngest sister of the Jackson Family. I faked a sneeze, took the hand that she was holding to cover my nose, told her I had to go to the restroom for a booger check, and I would meet her outside. Mission accomplished.

I saw my boy Eric in the restroom writing down a phone number, I taught my boy well. "How they treating you, baby boy?"

"It's cool, these Atlanta women are a strange breed. Why do they all want to know what I do for a living? Hell I work!"

"It's like that, man. These sistahs want to know if you can match or exceed their salary. If not, they ain't tryin' to waste their time."

"I mean, I've met a couple of nice ones, but it feels more like a job interview than a conversation. You know?"

"I know, dawg. It's all a game, but don't let them set the rules. They've got an agenda, we've got an agenda. The question is, *who has the game to fulfill their agenda?*"

"Man, I'm not trying to play no games, I just want a good women to chill with, and..."

"Look dawg, this conversation is getting too deep for a restroom party. Lets finish this up later, I'm trying to scout out some new talent."

My boy looked like he was over his head. Women can sense that sensitive, vulnerable, Babyface; Brian McKnight shit a mile away. Nice lookin' brother, but too young to be that settled and sensitive. These sistahs won't appreciate him, unless they have been dogged out. On top of that, he doesn't look flashy enough to be a baller... not arrogant enough to be a challenge. He needs to start being a player, and learn the game. Or, hang out with the older crowd of divorced women at Harriston's Dinner Club, on Wednesday night with V-103's Frank Ski, because these women will eat him alive. "Come on, dawg. This is *your* party!" I dapped him up, and pulled him out of the john.

ॐ

Oh, What a Night

- Eric -

I'm starting to miss the comfort of good ole' Indiana. Surroundings were familiar, and my family was there. Yeah, it has it's share of rednecks and good ole boys, but it was home, and I new where I stood. Knew I was loved unconditionally. No matter how the women did or did not respond to me, I knew I had a safe haven, loving arms, and sound advice, biased, but sound nonetheless.

"Hey you?" said a sexy raspy voice from behind. I don't feel like being interviewed again. I don't have any current W-2 forms on me, and I don't have any business cards on fancy paper. My car is a '93 two door Honda Accord. It may not be a Navigator, but it sure as hell gets me from point a to point b. And I don't have to make a choice between paying a light bill or putting gas in my..., and I stress the word *my, cause its paid for,* car. I wish the party were over. If I had a key, I think I would slip on back to the apartment and call it a night, or better yet, if Dorothy had a pair of size 14 ruby sneakers, I'd click those bad boys three times, and get the hell out of Atlanta. It seems so cosmetic in here. I need substance. I finally turned around, and the lady that belonged to the voice was not bad on the retina, but then again, everyone in here seems pretty attractive.

"Hi, how are you?" I replied.

"I'm fine. You're Eric, right?"

"Yep, that's me. What's your name?"

"I'm Leslie. You don't seem like your enjoying yourself, you O.K.?'

"Yeah, I'm straight, just kind of tired. I drove from Indianapolis today, I've been up since 5:30 this morning."

"Really, so you're running on fumes, are you?"

Speaking of fumes, did she shower in her perfume or what?

"Yeah, you can say that, but the night is almost over, I need to get some zzzzzz's"

"Yeah I hear you, I had a long week at work. What kind of work do you do, Eric?"

"I am going to be running a community center in East Point."

"Really, how is the money in that... yadda yadda yadda."

I stopped listening when she mentioned money; I just nodded and smiled, thinking about my nice warm bed..."

What time is it... 9:45, seems like 6:45. I smell breakfast, I know Corey's ass ain't cooking, he cooks worse than I do. "What up, dawg? Oh, I'm sorry. I thought you were Corey," I said.

"I know I look rough in the morning, but I hope I don't look like a man, a bald man at that, I'm Sheila."

No, you don't look like a man, nice smooth long legs, smooth skin, no make up, no bra. Some guys have all the luck. I wake up with bad breath; Corey wakes up with a young Claire Huxtable.

"Mornin' Sheila. No, you look much better than Corey."

"Thanks, flattery will get you everywhere, and in case you are wondering, Corey went to the store to get some syrup for my famous apple pancakes. You want some?"

"Sure if its not too much trouble."

She keeps looking at me funny, not like she's trying to come on to me, but like she is reading me. I wonder what she's thinking?

"You're shy aren't you?"

"What makes you say that?"

"I don't know, you just seem like you are. Real innocent."

"Yeah, you're not the first one to say that, I'm pretty laid back, I can be quiet at times. I'm not as shy as people think I am though, I like to make sure that when I talk, I've actually got something meaningful to add to the discussion."

"Yeah, I can appreciate that, I hate when people talk loud, but say nothing. So, tell me, Eric, you leave any broken hearts in Indianapolis?"

"Yeah, just one. My moms."

She looked at me funny again, and now it looks like a light bulb went off over her head like in a cartoon.

"Are you a momma's boy, Eric?" she said this like she had something against mommas' boy's. Here we go again.

"You can say that, everyone else does."

"I feel sorry for any women that you date. I dated a mommas boy before, and before I realized what was going on, I felt like I was raising a child. A grown ass man-child. Had me callin' his momma for his favorite recipes, and that crap got old real quick. I didn't give a damn if his momma put sugar in her Jiffy Corn Bread, or if she put cheese in his grits. *Spoiled as hell.* Never again. No way in West Hell will I get myself into *that* again."

West Hell, dang, that was deep. Why do people like to label and judge everyone with similar circumstances in the same catorgory?

"Well, Shelia, I understand that you had a bad experience with that guy you dated in the past, but is it fair to assume that all of us are like that? I think you should appreciate a guy who loves his mother dearly. I would do anything for my mom, and any women that I get close to will get that same royal treatment."

"I hope you're different, you seem different, but I hope you don't compare every women that you date to your mother. That is the quickest way to run a women off."

"My mother taught me how to love and appreciate women. If that runs a women off, then she has done me a favor by running off."

Her words cut me like a rusty knife. I excused myself, and went to take a shower. Do I compare every woman I meet to my mother? How can I not? She is my point of reference? What is wrong with wanting a beautiful, intelligent, caring, strong sistah who can cook her face off? Nothing. Am I wrong for setting my standards high? No. Will I be single for the rest of my life."?

"Sheila, these pancakes are good, you make a brothah want to go back to sleep."

"Thank you, Eric. You know what? I have a girlfriend that I want you to meet."

Corey was trying to tell me not to take her up on it, using some sort of ghetto sign language, but how could I say 'no' to someone who cooks pancakes as well as my... Well, lets just say that she can cook very well.

"Yeah, we can do that, I start my new job on Monday, so I don't know what my schedule will be like, but we can set something up."

For the next hour or so the three of us made small talk about Atlanta, the social scene, and the traffic. They made traffic sound worse than getting your wisdom teeth pulled... with no novocaine. I could see those two play-ing footsey under the glass dinner table. She and I had great conversation, she barely even spoke to Corey. Not that I would go after my boy's girl (or flavor of the week) but she seemed to like my conversation, and if given the chance, we could talk on a deeper level. But she seemed drawn to Corey physically. They touched every chance they got. I began to feel like the chaperon that kids couldn't wait to leave so that they could get their freak on. Sometimes, I wish I had what Corey had, or should I say didn't have. A conscience. I sat there and fantasized about what it would be like to have casual (protected) sex with women. With Sheila. Shelia did not have a bra on, and it became obvious. After breakfast, the two of them tried to be smooth, and excused them selves to the bedroom. Within five minutes, I heard Will Downing, Gerald Albright, and the squeaking of the bed.

I rinsed off the dishes, and returned to my bedroom. There, I played Anita Baker's *Priceless* and reflected on the night before. I met quite of few women last night, and got three phone numbers. "Let me show you around Atlanta", they all said, but I did not feel a connection with any of them, especially once the small talk stopped and the interviewing began. Yeah, Dionne was nice, but she was a smoker. That really turned me off. Kimberly was cool, but everything on her was fake, the eyes, the hair, the nails, and the jewelry. The only girl I met who was halfway interesting is in the other room with my roommate, doing the do. Well, at least I wasn't a wallflower last night. I was somewhat assertive, which is rare. The reason that I said *somewhat* is because the finest girl at the party gave me that *come hither* stare and even shot me an angelic smile. I am a sucker for a pretty smile, and what did I do? Stood there, like a deer in someone's headlights. She finally got tired of me staring, and danced with someone else. I punked out. Not the first time, but I vow that it is my last. I think?

I dozed off when just as Anita Baker was trying to take my hand and lead me into love. Since I was a kid, the last thing that was on my mind, is normally what I dreamed of. This particular time, I dreamt about my first love, Phelicia.

We planned to meet in the lower level of the library. It took me a while to find her because up until that point, I thought the library was a social spot, much like the student union with out the juke box, chili cheese fries, and jungle juice.

"Hey Phelicia, what's goin' on?"

"Hey Eric, how are you?"

She stood up and gave me a hug. Not a hug where you lean toward someone and you barely touch chests, but the kind of hug you give someone that you are intimate with. A long hug. At that moment in time, I could not think of any place else in the whole wide world that I wanted to be. I didn't want it to end, then we looked each other in the eyes. I was lost in her eyes, and I did not want to be found. While in her eyes I saw our future. I knew I was too young to think about marriage, but I felt something strong. Something that both scared me, and made me happy at the same time. Something that made me want to tell her all of the embarrassing things about me that were reserved for the ones who witnessed them and were sworn to secrecy. There was enchantment between us; a magnetism. She smelled like Cocoa butter, and her bronze skin had soft red undertones. I never saw skin that smooth in my life. I wanted to rub her face to see if it were real. I wanted to kiss her in the worse way. She had the look of love in her eyes. I saw her soul. It was almost like a corny love story, but it was real. I swear I heard the music from the introductions of an old Disney Cartoon. You know the one when the goofy white dude is singing "when you wish upon a star." I felt innocent.

She finally released me, smoothed out her hair and sat down. She no longer looked me in the eye but acted as if she was uncomfortable.

"You O.K?" I asked.

"Yeah, I am fine. What page should we start on, do you have your notes, when is the mid-term?" she replied, she was talking a mile a minute. I could not let this moment pass and act as if *nothing happened. I felt something. I put my hand on hers. "Phelicia, look at me." She looked at me with those big, beautiful ebony eyes. She seemed scared. "I met your boyfriend today. I don't know him from a can a paint, but the way we hugged let me know that either he is not giving you what you need, or that I could give you something more. I felt something in that hug, and with your permission, I would like to hug you as often as possible. I like your smile; you have a beautiful smile. Give me a chance to make you happy, please... you won't regret it."*

Man, did I sound corny, but it came from within. Somewhere deep. I did not understand myself at the moment, but it felt good. I was expressing myself.

"Eric, I've known J.T. since high-school. He is a nice guy once you get to know him. He has been my boyfriend since eight grade"

"I don't want to know him, I want to know you. That hug we shared told me all that I need to know about you. Come with me." I grabbed her hand and led her to an empty stair well. There I took her in my arms, leaned against a wall, and held her for over two hours. We didn't kiss or fondle each other; we just held each other. In her arms, I felt safe. It was nothing sexual. We were connecting on a whole nother level. I haven't felt that safe since I hugged my mother. We spent many evenings "studying" in that stairwell. That became our spot. Same time every Monday, Tuesday and Thursday at 8:00. Thursday's were the best days, because the library was deserted. It was as if watching the Cosby Show and A Different World was mandatory for Black Colleges.

All in a Nights' Work

-Corey -

O.K. enough is enough. I know I hit it like a champ, and put her to sleep, but she's got to get up, its time for NFL Primetime. I know she's got somewhere to go, but if she doesn't, she's got to get the hell out of here. I didn't want her to stay the night; I hate that cuddling shit. On the other hand, ain't nothing like sex in the morning. Not a whole lot of fore play cause you got morning breath. And a brother like me wakes up with a rock in my jockeys on a regular. And the best thing about morning sex is that the *puddy tat* has had a chance to marinate all night. Well, she did cook breakfast for me and my boy, so I guess I can give her another 30 minutes, but that's it. The Titans and the Colts come on at 12:00. Shit, my arm is falling asleep.

All right, 30 minutes is up.

"Wake up, sleeping beauty." I whispered in her ear.

She smiled and looked me in the eye. No make up, hair all over her head, and she is cute.

"Oh, man, I was out like a baby, baby. Thanks for waking me up, I've got to show a house in Stone Mountain in an hour."

"You're kinda cute when you wake up."

"An orgasm gives you that glow, I feel so relaxed, I don't want to move."

I wish you didn't have to either I thought. Wait a second, I can't be getting soft, I mean she can definitely make my starting five, but that's it.

"I would ask you to take a shower with me, but you might wanna be startin' something" she said.

And then she stood up, butt naked. Butt-ass naked. I liked what I saw. I wanted her to stay. At that point, I didn't care about football, I didn't care what the analyst on ESPN thought about the daily matchup. I wanted to stay, cuddle, talk about the weather, politics, and why do fools fall in love.... the kind of shit you read about in Essence Magazine. I was loosing my edge. I smiled on the outside but on the inside I thought about relation-ships. I get like this when I am with quality women, kind of mushy and sensitive, but as soon as they are out of my sight, I looked for the next conquest. I was a true preda-tory player. She grabbed my robe and headed for the shower, I lay back on my bead and pondered me.

"How was your shower?" I asked. I kept my shirt off on purpose, and while she was gone I did at least twenty pushups. I saw her admiring her playground. She looked like she could use an extra hour of physical education.

"My shower was fine, it could have been better if you had washed my back for me."

Sheila did not realize it, but she just became a franchise player. I watched her get dressed in last nights clothing. She still looked as fresh as ever, she had that glow.

"So Corey, when will I hear from you again, or was this a one night stand?"

"You will hear from me again very soon, and this was definitely not a one night stand. And if I can remember correctly, we did very little standing last night."

"I know you got women coming out of the woodwork, so I won't hold my breath on that phone call, I know a player when I see one."

"Aww, come on, Sheila, you've got me all...."

"Corey, don't stress it. Don't try to explain, cause that

will piss me off. I am a big girl; I will just play this by ear, no definitions or expectations needed. I like you, but it is what it is, just do what you do, and we will take it day by day."

She kissed me on my lips, not a peck, and not a whole lot of passion, but a genuine kiss. I liked it. We looked at each other. I felt naked. Butt-ass naked. In that kiss, she stripped me. She hugged me again, tightly, and walked out. I heard her tell Eric bye on her way out, and I felt alone. I lay back in my bed, this time under the covers. I was in the wet spot, but I didn't care.

"Corey... telephone." Yelled Eric.

"I got it! Hello?"

"Hello, Corey, you alone?" it was Terri.

"Of course I am alone. What's goin' on?"

"When did she leave?"

"What are you talkin' bout? Ain't nobody been here but me and my boy."

"I saw the way you and what's her name where all over each other. You can't tell me that she didn't come back to your place."

"That's exactly what I am telling you. We danced, we talked, she left, I cleaned up the club house. Period."

"You must think I'm stuck on stupid."

"Look, Terri. First of all, I don't answer to anyone but my parents, and they are over eight hours away. Now I told you what happened. You got two choices; believe me, or not believe, cause I am watching the game in five minutes. How about that?"

"I see you ain't changed a bit. Always trying to play hard."

"Yeah, but I want to play with you, but you playin' hard to get."

"You had me, but you did not want me, or have you forgotten?"

"Can we discuss this later, how about over dinner?"

"Oh? So you takin' me out?"

"I ain't say all that... Why don't you cook a little sumthin sumthin; you said you had skills in the kitchen, hook a brother up."

"You getting on my nerves, what time you comin'?"

"Let me see, I guess the game will be over around 5:00. So, how does 6:00 sound?"

"OK, listen, bring Eric with you, I think my cousin was feelin' him."

"Alright, that's cool, check it out, don't make no pork, cause my boy don't eat that swine."

"His ass better eat what I cook, this ain't big momma's kitchen."

"You done got mean these days, I'll see you later, your five minutes are up."

"Bye, Corey. And don't come over here smellin' like no other bitch's perfume either." Click.

I see I still got it.

Assessing the Evening

-Eric -

I can hear Corey taking a shower. Undoubtedly washing off the passion of a woman that I could appreciate much more than he. I wonder how he feels about her, I mean, she seems like the total package and all. Humph, total package, I made that assumption based on one conversation. I can feel it though, if only I had met her first. She seems so right. Wait a minute, time out! That is my boys'... Umm, umm, damn! What is she? Is it my business what she is? I know what she is. OFF LIMITS. I know what I need, a guardian love angel. Yeah, that's it, a little black dwarf that sits on my shoulder, that only I can see, feel and hear. Someone who could actually whisper some sense in me as well as boost my ego. I have a tendency to fall for anyone who shows genuine interest in me, and that's not good. Because of that, in the rare occurrence that I do meet someone, I sometimes get too deep before I realize that that is not the person who is a good fit for me. I have this fear of being lonely. Not alone, because sometimes I like my space, but lonely. Growing up, I was never lonely. My sisters and my mom were always right behind the door, up the street or a holler away. My sisters were mean to me at times, but they where there. My mother was just the ultimate in security. Damn a blanket, no offense Linus, but mom wrapped me in so much love, and presence, even when she was not there, it is unexplainable. Now that I am a man, living alone, I'm feeling a void, and it has only been one day.

" ...Sup kid? How you feel?" Said an awfully refreshed Corey.

"I'm good, not as good as you though, you look like you in a zone."

"You know how I do. The game on yet?"

"They are still doin' the pre-game, you ain't missed nothin' yet. So what's up with you and Sheila? She seems like she's pretty straight."

"Oh, no doubt. Sheila is definitely on point, she has officially made my startin' five."

Startin' five. He's still using that basketball analogy to explain the ranking of his women, give me a break!

"Is that right? Well, how is the rest of the team looking?" I played along.

"Oh, I got a nice little squad. Terri is trying out for a spot. As a matter of fact, she and her girl is cooking for us later after the game. I think her cousin wants to holler at cha', dawg."

"Was that Terri who called you earlier?"

"Yeah, that was her. Tried to play hard, wanted to know who Sheila was, and if she stayed the night. She should know not to question me about something like that. It ain't like I'm gone say 'yeah, I hit it last night.'"

"Man, I don't know how you do it... got one fixin' you breakfast, and the other one fixin' you dinner."

"Like I told you last night E, you got to stick to your agenda. Last night I wanted sex... got it. Today, I want dinner... gone get it. And if I'm feeling her, I might need to give Terri a ride too. It's all about confidence."

Corey had a tendency of getting on his soapbox and preaching when he has had some success. Success in any field. This was his way of letting us mere mortals know that he is the man. I wasn't really trying to here what he was saying, but I had no way of getting out of hearing *His Highness.*

"Remember that Teddy Pendegrass song, when he is

yelling forcefully to turn off the lights? You see how women react to that song?... they love it. You know why? Teddy is displaying extreme confidence, and he is taking control. He has an agenda. Now don't get me wrong, I ain't for taking the drawers from no body, but I do project that certain game. The game that says, 'I am in the driver seat.' Not only am I *in* the driver seat, but it is your pleasure to ride with me. They try to play hard to get. Put up a little resistance, and I give them some ownership of the situation, but I got the keys."

"So, tell me, Macaroni Tony. What is your definition of game?"

As soon as I asked that question, I wish I hadn't. He reared back even further on the dark leather sofa and got into story-telling mode. It was as if he had been waiting for someone to ask him that forever. I felt like I was watching an old episode of the *Players Reading Rainbow*.

"Game? How can I explain it? Game, to me is a Mind Game. There is a certain reaction that I want to get from the ladies. And the only way I can get that reaction is by displaying certain *actions*. So what I do is display myself in such a way that can get that desired reaction. I know what ladies want, not what they say they but what they *really want*. I am looking for a team of females from the ages of 22-27. That is the age group that tends to live in the fast lane. They like an educated brother with a little thug in him. Someone with an edge. Someone unpredictable, with extreme confidence. Someone who is nice looking, but down plays his appearance. I know what they want... and I provide it. I am an actor, and I play my part well."

I knew Corey was a ladies man, and he acted as if he had ice in his veins, but I know him better than that. I grew up with him. Lived next door to him since the fifth grade. He and I were a lot alike. That is until he went to college. I don't know if it was pledging that changed him, or finding out that his hero was cheating on his mom. Corey had a half little sister that was a freshman in high school when he was a freshman in college, and his parents were never separated. I know I am not the best in math, but due to their ages, Pops had to have crept around on Corey's mom. And the kicker is, she didn't leave him. Corey's approach to females has been different since then. One thing I do know is that the man has a good heart. While in high school, he dated the same girl for two years, and was in love. My boy does have a heart, so I had to ask him about it. His heart.

"Does your heart ever get into it, I mean, do you ever feel somewhat attached to any of these women who you kick game to?"

And just like that his confidence seemed to be somewhat shaken, he was visibly shaken. He through his hands up to his temples, massaged them for a spell, then he rubbed his newly shaved head in a circular motion. His head reminded me of a crystal ball, and he was rubbing it in search for answers.

"Man, you know me better than anyone. At one time I was all about finding that special someone, and chillin'. Had no problem allowing my heart to get involved, I trusted women, and I wanted companionship. Until I got a double dose of reality. The last time that I allowed my heart to get into it was when I was dating this Delta at Ball State. I mean I turned my players' card in and everything. It was all about us. I knew she was the one, she was a couple of years older than me, and she had class, sass, and an onion for an ass."

Corey tilted his head all the way back, kind of reminded me of one of those Pez dispensers. He began to reflect, and it seemed as if, through his eyes, that he was actually there.

"I went to surprise her for Spring Break one semester. She lived in Evansville. I knew where she lived because I went out of my way to drop her off before. I got to her house and their she was, on her momma's porch, tonge wrestling with her high school sweetheart, and do you know what that bitch said?"

"Bitch, I thought you said you would never call a sistah a bitch?"

"I know, dawg. But this shit was foul, I got to call it like I see it man... This Bitch introduced me as her little boyfriend from school, and got mad because I was there. Had the audacity to say, 'this ain't school, you don't just pop up on me like this, I didn't invite you here.' And to make matters worse, she was on this dudes lap and never got up. As I walked away heart broken, all I could remember was this smug look on that niggas face, and her telling him that I must have bumped my head."

"Damn Corey, you never told me about that."

"I was too embarrassed to tell anyone, I got played like a game of Clue. And after that, that is just what I got, a Clue. I've been doin' my thing and getting what I can get since then. I mean, I got a heart, dog, I just ain't lettin' nobody get near it. When ever I do feel myself getting caught up, or warm and fuzzy, I think about that, and then I get even harder."

"So what you sayin' is that every other sistah in your path has to suffer for some chicken head from college?"

"Damn real, I ain't the one to get played, I've been burned once."

Corey's ears where turning red. One thing about light-skinned brothers is that when they're blood starts to boil, you can tell, just look at their ears. They turn plum red. I didn't know what to say next, so I said nothing. I pretended to be interested in the game. I was from Indianapolis, and would love to see the Colts win, but Tennessee has a black quarterback, from a Historically Black College, and I find it hard to root against him, so I could not get into the game like I wanted to, and eventually stopped paying attention. I eventually got real comfortable. It's something about me; Sunday morning and football, I eventually start to get lazy. I mean who can blame me; I did drive over eight hours yesterday, partied all night, and had some pancakes for breakfast. *Yawn.* I guess I can take a little catnap. The games don't get good until the second half, so what the hell. *Yawn.*

Again Phelicia and I are in the stairwell of the library. Our sanctuary. Our routine never changed, she would always arrive at 5:45, right when the cafeteria was at its peek. It was my stereotypical analogy that black-folks would not be interested in going to the library on a full stomach. I made sure I was there at 6:00, this would give her ten minutes to make small talk and not seem rushed. Time went by quickly while we were together, but it seems as if the world stood still. Nothing mattered but us. I was falling. Falling hard and quick. I had a hard time being with her in secrecy. I was so proud of this Nubian Goddess that I wanted everyone to know that she and I was she and I. I wanted to tell her I felt, but I promised her that I would be patient.

"How was your day? I asked

"It just got better?" She replied, and she looked up at me and I swear my heart skipped a beat. Yeah I know that it sounds corney, but it did.

"I love you, Phelicia."

And before I even gave it much thought, the words jumped out of my mouth. I tried to suck them back in, but was unsuccessful. She didn't answer. She parted her lips like she wanted to say something but she could not find the words. She hugged me tighter, and buried her head deeper in my chest.

"Did you hear me?"

She shook her head yes, and I began to feel something on my chest. I think she is crying.

"I gotta go." She said softly.

And as soon as she got that last word out of her mouth, the door from upstairs opened angrily. I knew who it was. And by the way she tensed up, she knew who it was. If there was another way out, she would have taken it, but it wasn't. The only way out was through the likes of her troll friend, J.T. I didn't like confrontation, but I wanted this confrontation. I knew after this confrontation, something would drastically change. I had a feeling that I was going to see if I could fight or not. I felt good about it though. What made me feel good is that I knew that after receiving or giving this ass kicking that I would know very soon where we stood. She looked at me with shear terror in her eyes. I tried to look confident, but deep down inside I was scared. I had to use my fear to my advantage. What would Shaft do in this situation? She let go of my embrace, and stood in front of me, almost as if she were going to protect me from him.

"What in the hell is wrong with you?" Damn, he sounded like Mr. T. I didn't know who he was talking to, but she answered.

He was on the last step, and coming fast. I put my hands around her waist, and switched positions with her, now I was standing in the path of this human bowling ball, hoping that he didn't roll a strike.

"J.T., lets go somewhere and talk!" she screamed

"Fuck that!" he spewed.

And just like that, he had a hand full of my shirt, and began to push me up against the wall. He was all in my face, stank breath and all, as he began to verbally assault me. I don't know what he was saying, but I'm sure he wasn't asking me who cut my hair. All I remember was that she was screaming at him, he was cursing her out, and calling me everything but a child of God. How was I looking in her eyes at this point? Like a straight punk, who was not able to protect her. The thought of that made me angry. I wanted to be everything to her; I could not let this happen like this. The thought of letting her down was driving me nuts. And at that point it occurred to me that his nuts where exposed, and my knee had a good ten inches to gain enough momentum to bring some pain. The say all is fair in love and war, and I was in a war. Sometimes when you are scared, the adrenaline builds up so much that you possess super human strength. I closed my eyes, and with all of my might, I lifted my right knee up so hard and quick that all I heard was him suck in a big breath, grab his nuts, and crumple to the floor in fetal position. Once he was there, I snapped, and began to kick him continually while reading him his rights. I think I told him that he didn't deserve a woman like that, and the he did not appreciate her, and that I did and every kick that he received was for every time he caused her pain. All the while she is telling me to stop because I was hurting him, and that I was scaring her. And that's when I stopped.

"Who's down there, what's goin on?" It was the schools rent-a-cop.

Closer Than a Brother

- Corey -

What the hell? I think my boy is having a nightmare or something. What is he saying?

"Eric, Eric, wake up man, you alight?" I said as I shook him, careful not to get kicked in the nuts. He woke up and immediately grabbed me by my throat.

"Chill out man, its me, Corey!" I yelled as his eyes got as big as saucers.

"Shit, my fault man, you O.K.," said an out of breath Eric. He sat down and held his chest, almost as if he were trying to keep it from escaping his person.

"Eric!" he wasn't listening, his mind was somewhere else, and I obviously was not invited, so I left him alone. He sat there. It wasn't hot but the beads of anxiety laced sweat on his forehead. I got a bottle of slightly chilled water from the fridge and sat it on the table in front of him. He reached for it, turned it up, and drained it. He then stood up and walked over to the patio, opened the door, walked out, sat on the lawn furniture. I followed.

"What's on ya' mind, dawg?"

"She got away man, she should be with me right now, yeah we had our differences, but should be here" he replied while staring toward the fourth rock from the sun.

"Who you talkin' bout?"

"I'm talkin' bout Phelicia, she got away! What happened to us?" he replied, talking to the air. While looking in my direction, but through me.

I wanted to say that she was crazy as hell, but I don't think that would have settled too well with him. Besides, from that throat grip that he gave me a minute ago I wasn't trying to catch a beat down. We yellow brothers bruise easily, you know.

"You tell me! I mean, whatever it was, had to be serious. That girl had you wide open."

"I know, its like, we weren't vibing our senior year, and then graduation came around and... man I don't know..."

"Yeah you do, stop bullshitin, if anybody knows its you, its been four years, and you still dreaming about her, you have had time to think about, analyze it, scrutinize it, verbaliziin' it, what happen man. Deal with it, I mean, what's really goin on?"

My man needs to deal with this now, he cant keep letting this shit fester like that. It's startin to stink! I know what happen; I've heard the story over and over again. His first mistake was that he fell to quick and to blindly. She wasn't over her first boyfriend yet when he swooped in and swept her off of her feet. You don't get serious with anyone on the rebound. If you know anything about basketball, you know about a rebound. You also know that rebounds can take funny bounces, and are unpredictable at times. Some bounce long, some bounce short, some are bricks, and some are airballs. You don't base your future on one shot; one rebound. As great a rebounder as Dennis Rodman was, there were always a few that he didn't get. You can be in what you think is the best possible position for a rebound, and the ball steel may not come to you. You might think you have it, it may even be headed in your direction, but it is still up for grabs. You must compete for every rebound. It never really belongs to you until you secure it and grab it tight, and even then if you bring it to a certain level people are trying to take it from you. Sometimes they are success-ful. At that point you must start throwing some elbows. I don't believe in fighting over a woman who is in limbo. My point is, you never should settle with anyone who is on the rebound.

"If things were going fine for us, she was going to move to Indianapolis after graduation. My mom even agreed to let her move in with her, while I got an apartment. She was about the only girl that my mother ever bonded with. I mean they got along well, my sisters even loved her. Everything was supposed to be smooth, but she never seemed to be all mine. She was with me, but she wasn't. When she felt herself getting close, she would push me away. Then we would not get along for a week, and she would come back apologize, and do the same thing again. Almost like she was scared to get close to me. When things were going great it was the best expe-rience that I ever had in my 26 years on this earth. She would not allow herself to love me completely. I could not see taking her to Indianapolis with me if things were not working out. If only I had another year of school to work things out with her."

"You blaming yourself for that man, if was meant to be, it would have been. You treated that girl like royalty, she couldn't ask for a better brother than you."

"What if it was meant to be, and I gave up to soon? What if I didn't try hard enough to make it work. I know I didn't give her time to heal, she needed more time and space, and all I gave her was an ultimatum. She is the one that got away. Where else will I find a woman as strong, smart, and beautiful. You should have seen the look on my mom's face when I told her that we were breaking up. She actually cried. It was graduation, but it seemed like a funeral."

"Oh, so that's it, you worried about finding someone that your mother approves of? Or better yet, someone that is like you mother?"

"Man, you are talking that crazy shit, I don't care if my mom approves, I am the one who has to live with her, not momma. She was nothing like my mother."

"Nigga please! You and I both know that if your mother ain't feeling her, she don't stand a chance past the first holiday. You even said how much Phelicia looked like she could be a part of your family, and you said that she had a lot in common with your mom. Hell, she can even cook as good as your mom. I bet you still got that picture of her and your mom in your wallet."

"Man, later for you."

"Prove me wrong then, pull out your wallet!"

"I ain't pullin' out shit."

"Cause you know I'm right. Boy, I know you. You want to marry someone like your mother. Pull out your wallet, and prove me wrong!"

He reached for his wallet and began to empty the contents out on the table. Business cards, old lottery tickets, tissues with phone numbers written on them as well as a couple pictures of Debbie and Sandy. There was also an old black and white picture with the words "From Amelia with love" written on it.

"Who is this?" I asked

"That's my mom, that picture is from her sophomore year in high school."

"Man, you are sick, that picture looks just like Phelicia and you know it."

"Man, fuck you."

"Naw dog, fuck ya' self, that looks just like your ex-girlfriend. That's some ole' Jerry Springer type shit there man."

"Whatever, man. You high yellow brothers think that all dark skinned sistahs look alike. Now do you see that picture that you were looking for... I didn't think so."

"Come on, man. Do you know who you are talking to? I know about the secret compartment. You know that rip on the inside of your wallet that you keep that emergency twenty-dollar bill in. I wanna see that.!"

He cracked a smile and reached for his wallet, but I was too quick, I grabbed it first, and ran into the apartment with Eric in hot pursuit. While in full stride I reached into the compartment, and there they were. *Smiling*. That picture has been in his possession since his senior year. It was taken at a surprise birthday party. His mom and sisters flew Phelicia up for the celebration. I was there. I took the picture. Phelicia didn't like me, because she knew I was a dog, and was afraid that dogs traveled in packs. I held the picture up like it was gold medal. He stopped.

"You got me, nothin' I can say."

He sat down, broad shoulders slumped, forehead in hand and laughed. Sometimes you laugh to keep from crying.

"I know you think that my relationships are dictated by my mother, but that's not true. I was in love with that girl, period. I love my mother, period. I love the qualities that my mother has, and I have no problem with saying she is a great woman. Finding a women like her is ideal, but the love for a companion, is totally different than the love for a parent."

My man had a Jones for that girl. I could see it in his face. The classic love story, boy meets girl, boy looses girl, and boy gets girl back.

"Where is she?"

"I don't know, man, somewhere in Louisiana... somewhere between Monroe and Shreveport probably."

"Go get her."

"What?"

"Go get her, find her, let her know that you still feeling her. Tell her you love her. Once you've been love, and you didn't cheat, and you did your best, a woman will always at least listen to what you have to say. You are that settle down type of brother, and you not gone rest easily until you find her. Besides, you not gone find a sister like her no time soon. If at all. Go find her... by any means necessary. You won't be happy until you do."

"It's to late, I had my chance, she wanted to make it work, I said no, she probably hates me. It's too late."

"It's never to late, do you think she loved you?"

"Yeah, no doubt about it."

" Its not too late then."

"I don't know dog, I mean what if she got somebody, I can't go out like that.!"

"When is Grambling's Homecoming?"

"I don't know, why you ask?"

"Road trip. We goin' down there."

"I don't know, man."

"I know you don't know, but I do. We goin'. I'll get on the net and find out when it is. Now get dressed cause Terri is cooking for us."

The thirty minute ride to College Park was a quiet one, we listened to the Hip-Hop of Hot 107.9 on the way over there, but eventually switched to 91.9 because jazz allows you to explore the depths of your mind. Hip-hop does the thinking for you, and leaves nothing to the imagination. The jazz seemed to be the soundtrack for the mood.

"What's up, dawg? You awfully quiet."

"I don't know, kid." said Eric, "You said that Dionne was feeling me, I don't know if I'm in the mood for conversation right now."

"Just be yourself, you gone be alright. We ain't got to stay long, just give me a sign and we can be out."

"You know good and well that if she is bringin' it when we get there, you'll be trying to get some."

"If I can get it now, I can get it later. If you wanna leave, let me know. Aiight?"

"Aiight, that's cool."

Comin' Out of a Shell

- Eric -

"Hey Corey" said Terri, as she gave him a full body hug, then gave me one too. Not like his though. My hug said 'hello friend.' His said, 'I'm cooking dinner, and I will be the dessert.' Terri was looking very nice, showing off her assets... so to speak. A small t-shirt that showed off her flat stomach and Capri pants that said she could be ready to try out for Corey's all-star team. According to Corey, Terri was a cute girl with an average shape. This is not the girl..., excuse me, woman that stood before me today. She has obviously been working out, and was wearing her hair in a short natural. This short cut made her look confident. I can appreciate a sister who is not afraid to go against the grain. I saw a picture of her with her perm on the wall and she didn't look bad, so I know it took a lot of confidence to get it all cut off.

"I hope you all are hungry," said Terri.

"It depends on what you got to eat" replied Corey with a grin on his face that said that he wasn't talking about the baked chicken that I smelled.

"You are bad, I hope you don't corrupt Eric," said a blushing Terri.

In comes Dionne. She was wearing a pair of walking shorts with a cut-off shirt. She had her navel pierced. Ouch.

"Hey fellas, what's goin on?"

"Sup Dionne" said Corey

"Hey Dionne, what's goin on?" That was me.

"Not much, just watching my Bears catch a beat down by the Atlanta Falcons of all people."

"Don't sleep on the Dirty Birds now, we didn't go to the Super Bowl a couple of years ago for nothing" joked Corey.

"Actually, they did go for nothing, came back with nothing, and they have nothing to show for it," replied Dionne.

The girl knew her sports, that was refreshing. She cursed like a sailor though. I know I may say a four-letter word occasionally, but after hearing the words coming from her mouth, she lost all sex appeal. Not that she wanted to, but I could not imagine kissing her with the trash that came from her mouth. She reminded me of one of the fellas. I would love to go to the E.S.P.N Zone with her, but not anywhere romantic. And that's pretty much how the day went, Dionne and I talked sports, while Corey and Terri flirted. They disappeared to her room later, but I don't think he got any cause the door was left cracked, and he did not make a b-line for the bathroom when he came out. I had a pretty good time. Dionne turned out to be someone I could really talk to. She didn't bite her tongue at all, and was painfully honest. She seemed like she could be corporate if she had to, or ghetto in a heartbeat. An educated, round the way girl, who grew up in a house full of men.

I had a good day at work today. I didn't even get lost. I think I am going to enjoy it, I know I like the hours. From 1:00 to 6:00. I go in early on days that I need to meet with corporate sponsors and I my hours change when the summer months roll around. My official title is program coordinator. I work with the pre-teens to around 15 years of age. My hours are set up like that because my kids don't really get their until around three o'clock. I am in charge of day to day operations as well as special events. My goal is to expose the children to everything and let help them understand that they have options. Today was an orientation.

On the way back to the house I decided to stop in the store to get something for dinner. All we had was mayonnaise, spoiled milk and Frosted Flakes that were chewy enough to rival Hubba Bubba. True bachelor fridge. I didn't quite know what I wanted, but it sure wasn't that. I stopped at the Publix up the street, I didn't have a list, but I knew what I wanted. Catfish. I was really impressed with how friendly southerners are. In Indy, speaking is not something that we did if we didn't know you. Down here, even the thug looking brothers gave you that familiar what's up nod if nothing else. While in the spice section I saw a woman that looked extremely familiar. She had eyes that I knew; I just didn't know where I met them. I wanted to get reacquainted with them I wanted to project my game. I picked up my Cajun spices and my lemon pepper seasoning and decided that I would make it a point to walk past her. I mean, what did I have to loose right? It was actually a great time to do it, my hair cut was still fresh, and I had on a tie. Me in a tie is about as rare as O.J. with a Black Woman, you would like to see it as often as possible, but you don't. I hate having anything around my neck. Blackmen in America has a hurtful history with things being around our neck. I liked the way it looked, but hated the way it felt. Anyway, it was time to do my famous Laurence Fishburn in the movie Deep Cover stride right up to her and try not to say anything stupid walk. As I got within two feet of her she abroptly turned toward me as if she could feel me coming. And being the smooth, suave brother that I am, I dropped everything that I was holding on the floor. If I weren't so dark, I would have turned red, but in this case I had to settle for burgundy. She bent down to help me retrieve my spices, fish an V-8 splash. I thanked her, and assured her that I wasn't really as clumsy as I looked, while all the while wishing I could hide behind the hot sauce bottle on the second shelf. No luck.

"I guess wearing a size 14 shoe does have some disadvantages to it" said the doe eyed stranger. How does she know what size shoe I wear? I immediately recognized her from the party. She is the one that held my eyes hostage with hers for what seemed like an eternity before getting frustrated with my inability to approach her.

"I thought you looked familiar, did you enjoy yourself at my party" I replied, while trying to act like I didn't actually do anything stupid.

"Yeah, it was O.K. considering that I got asked to dance by everyone but the one that I wanted to dance with."

Did she just flirt with me?

Silence.

"You do know I was talking about you, don't you?" She added.

"I was hoping that you were, but I was trying to figure out a way to tell you that ketchup is all over your suede shoes with out getting hit with bushel of bananas."

She looked down.

"You do realize that you owe me for these brand new Versachi pumps don't you?"

"Ouch, those look expensive, I am so sorry, you name the price, it might take me a minute but I will pay you back." I said sounding as humble as humanly possible.

"I'm joking, I can have these cleaned, but since you seem so sincere, how about bringing that fish to my house, and cooking me dinner. That way I can call it even."

"Sure, I can do that, where do you stay?"

"Here, let me give you my number, call me in an hour and I will give you directions."

She wrote the number down, and then she wrote her name.

"Nia, your name is Nia."

"That's what my license says, it means *purpose*. Why, you don't like my name or something?"

"No, it's a great name. Short, sweet and easy to spell." Didn't I sound special? I couldn't dare tell her that I was thinking about Nia Long.

"Eric, I will make the salad, the bread, and the baked potato, you just come and fry the fish. How about that?"

"Sounds like a plan," I said as I walked toward the express lane. It said ten items or less, and I know for a fact that this woman in front of me has over ten cans of soup alone. That's not very considerate, if its one thing that bothers me is inconsiderate people. My mom always taught me to consider the feelings of others, that way you don't burn any bridges. Although I was not happy about the woman with twenty items, I didn't mind waiting; it gave me time to reflect on my first date in Atlanta. It's a good thing that she didn't let my first, and second impression throw her off.

She said call in her in an hour, but I didn't want to seem desperate so I waited an hour and fifteen minutes. She gave me directions and luckily she didn't live very far, so there was very little chance of me getting lost. On the way out, I passed Corey on the steps.

"What's up, kid? Where you headin, you taking some food back to the store?"

"Long story, dawg. But in a nut shell, I am going to Nia's to fry some fish."

"Nia? When did you meet her?"

"We made eye contact at the party, and I saw her again at the grocery store, and the rest is history... or shall I say, my story."

"I hope you don't say no corny shit like that at her house, or you will be here for breakfast!"

"Oh, I see you got jokes huh, I'm out. By the way, you

got a messages from Terri, Yolanda, and Kay, I didn't erase them though."

"Yeah, that's what I'm talkin 'bout, three of my startin' five, checkin in to see when they are going to get some playin' time. Aiight man, I holla."

Telephone Connections

Corey

Let me go up in here and check my messages. "Hey Corey, this is Kay, I heard you had a party, my invitation must have gotten lost in the mail. Anyway, don't bother callin me, I'll be busy for a long time." Beep.

Typical Kay, always pouting. All she needs is some validation. I have not given her any attention lately. I'll give her a call, take her to dinner, and then let her fix me breakfast in bed.

"Corey, what's up, this is Terri. When are we gonna hook up again? Alone. Call me."

The new and improved Terri. Gotta appreciate a woman who improves herself.

"Hey sweetie, this is Yolanda. I had a long day in class, and I really need to see you... badly. Call me or page me, you got the number. Take care. Here from you later. Bye."

Who am I feeling today? Yolanda is always fun to be around, college student, energetic, not a nag cause she's got to study to maintain an excellent g.p.a. Only bad thing about her is that I have to pick her up, and take her back. She is a senior who stays on campus with no car. Don't worry, she is of legal age, 22. Terri? Not today, that would make it three days in a row, she would get used to that and expect that type of playing time on the regular.

Been their, fuck that. Kay, I don't feel like begging tonight, and with her, I would have to listen to her complain, and then think of a lie as to why I did not invite her. She would definitely have a wall that I would have to break down, but once that's broken... its all good. And I stress the word good. Kay is too high maintenance though. Everytime I see her, we..., make that, I, spend money. She has rich daddy that spoiled her to death, so she expects every man to do the same. She needs to marry a brother whose initials are A.T.M. On the other hand, she really knows how to make a man feel special. If she appreciates you, she really shows it. I can't afford her tonight, I'll wait until payday to call her, and until then I will send her a small bouquet of roses to her job. I can afford that. I wonder what Shelia is doing right now. She has been dominating my thoughts for a couple of days now. Let me give her a call to see what she is up to.

"Hi, this is Shelia Talley, I am currently unavailable, leave a message and I will call ya' when I call ya'. Onelove." Beep.

"Hey Shelia, this is Corey, call me when you get this message, the number is ... Click.

I wonder what she is up to? The phone is ringing already. I bet it's Shelia.

"Hello?"

"Hello, Corey. Where is my baby?"

"How's it going, Mrs. Dukes? Eric is out on his first date."

"Already? That must have been some party you threw him, don't you corrupt my son, Corey."

"Aw, come on, ma. You know me."

"Exactly, so like I said, don't corrupt my son, how is he doin'?"

"He's doin' well..." I didn't sound very convincing and I don't think she bought it either. I wanted to ask about Phelicia, I was determined to get him in touch her. His dream was so intense that I knew he still had issues with the Louisiana native. His mother could always read right through me.

"Talk to me, sweetie. What's really goin on?"

I hate it when she calls me that, she could get what ever she wanted out of me and she knew it. No wonder he worships this woman, she has that sixth sense when it comes to dealing with people. Not that Bruce Willis - "I see dead people" type thing, but she was just in tune constantly.

"Mrs. Dukes, don't do this to me."

"Corey?" This time she sang my name.

"Did he keep in touch with Phelicia after graduation, cause she is still on his mind constantly, to the point where it is effecting his sleep?"

"Is that so? Hmmm. He tries to hide the fact that he has feelings for her, but I caught him staring at her picture on several occasions. As a matter of fact, when I cleaned up his room yesterday, he had written quite a few letters to her, but he never mailed them, they where in a shoe box under his bed. Not that I was being nosey or anything."

"I'm not goin' to even touch that, Moms."

"You better not" she said with a sweet laugh. Eric is in trouble. He is never going to find a woman like the one on this phone. She has that type of personality that brings a smile to your face. I am smiling right now just talking to her. There must be something special about Phelicia, something I just don't see.

"Mrs. Dukes, I want to get those two together. I will be honest with you, he is still in love with her, and the big reason for that is that he sees you in her. He still has a picture of her in his wallet. He had a nightmare about loosing her. We have got to get them two together."

"I don't know about that, Corey. I am trying to let my baby be a man. I can't get myself wrapped up in that part of his life. I am trying to support him by letting him grow up to be his own man."

"He has been here for less than three days, and I can tell that the women down here are not going to appreciate what he is bringing to the table, he is so sensitive. I have seen people like him come down here before, and before you know it... they change. I don't want to see Eric like that. Like me."

Silence.

"Like you! What do you mean *like you?*"

"I understand the game that the women play down here, and you either become a player or you get played."

Silence. Dead silence. Ms. Dukes treated me like her favorite nephew, and she was quietly internalizing everything I said. I wish I knew what she was thinking right now.

"A player? Is that what you are Corey? A player? A player of women? A woman like your mother is a women, like I am a woman, that's what you are? She was saying this the same way a kid would say, "you mean Barney is not real? She heard me, but didn't want to except it. My dad is a player, and he hurt my mom, Eric's dad is a player, and he hurt Ms. Dukes.

"Ms. Duke, you don't understand."

"Well, why don't you help me understand."

Silence. Awkward silence.

"I am playing the game, mom Dukes, that's all. I am not hurting anyone, it's a game that we all play down here. All of the single, so called professionals play. Not ready to settle down, having fun, getting what makes you happy until you are ready to settle down. I am sewing my wild oat is all I am doing."

"This game that you have mastered, where are you meeting these umm... contestants, for lack of a better word?"

"Everywhere, I mean, the mall, the clubs, just hanging out.."

"I didn't hear you say the church, the library, plays, art

galleries, museums. The places that you go to now are the places where every one who is *playing the game* go. So, go somewhere else. You sound like you like being a player, in the game that you play?"

"Do I? Maybe I do, I am young, single, and not bad to look at, I enjoy the game because I got the mentality. Eric doesn't. His heart is not as hard as mine is." Remember that cartoon when they showed how big the Grinch that stole Christmas heart was. That's me. That's my heart. I got burned once. Been there fuck that.

"You are probably right, Mom Dukes. I am having fun, and following my dream of owning my own restaurant. The places that I go, and the people that I meet are all part of me living out my dream. I go to these places to both have fun, and learn about the environment that I want to be my livelihood. I also love women, and I am not trying to settle down. Eric has that settle down personality, and if he hangs with me with that mentality, then he is going to get taken advantage of."

"My baby, I mean my son, can handle himself. Some young lady will realize that he is a helluva man, and act right."

"I agree, but how many times will he get played before it gets to that? Furthermore, he found someone who will treat him like that. Phelicia. If the timing were better, they would be together right now, working on your grandkids."

I knew that would get her. She wants a grandson soooo bad. She wanted to relive the time spent with Eric as a baby.

"Phelicia, huh? You think they got something left in their tank?"

"Do I? I know they do."

"Let me set the record straight. I am not a fan of Phelicia. She hurt him worse than anyone. Her heart was unstable. One minute as warm as the sand on South Beach in June, the next minute cold as a polar bears' ass in January. He needs to think about why they broke up, not why they got together. But I think in order for him to move on, he must bring closure to that part of his life."

So I was all for him getting back with her so he can get away from wanting to be with her. I would not tell him that, but that's my agenda.

"Let's do it then." I said to the surprisingly energetic Mom Dukes. She agreed. I could hear the hope in her voice.

Fish to Fry: Who's Catching Who

-Eric -

This is a nice house. I like that, an independent sis-tah with her own place. A lot of brothers are intimidat-ed by a woman who makes her own money. They figure, if she's making money like that, what does she need me for? Later for that, I would love to be involved with an independent, money making sistah, that way we can share the bills. I don't like the damsel in distress types, cause you got to take care of them all of the time. Don't get me wrong, I am all for taking care of a womans' emotional, physical, and when possible, spiritual needs but financially, we can share that load. I am not cheap by any stretch of the imagination, but I do believe, if we both are getting paid, then we can take care of each other financially. I didn't ring the doorbell, because I have issues with them. Far too many times have I sat outside a door pushing a button that was not even hooked up. It's a thin line between ringing a bell, and pushing a button looking like a fool. I knocked on the door.

"It's open, come on in, Eric. Why didn't you ring the bell?" she said over her Emil Lareux CD.

"No reason, hey do you always leave your door open, Nia?" Damn, I love that name.

"No, but I saw when you pulled up, besides, my two

boyfriends are in my bedroom."

"Excuse me?"

"You heard me, my two boyfriends, Smith & Wesson" she chuckled as she came toward me with a cold bottle of water.

"Oh, you packin like that, huh?"

"Sistahs gotta do, what a sistah's gotta do; it's some crazy folks out there. My daddy taught me how to use a gun before I left for college." She handed me the water.

"Oh, what school did you go to?"

"I went to Florida A&M, and you?"

"I went to Grambling State University"

"How does it feel to have the second best band in the land?"

"Yeah, you're right. Grambling does have the second best band in the land, second to none."

"Whatever, man. Did you like Grambling?"

"Loved it, I think I learned just as much out of class than I did in class."

"That can be taken a couple of ways."

"Which way do you want to take it?"

"Which way do you want me to take it?" I know I'm not a rocket scientist, but I think she is flirting with me.

Awkward silence. Avoiding eyes. Awkward silence. Sexy grin. "Eric?" For some reason, she sounded even sexier now than ever. I looked at her.

"I'm sure you had the ladies all over you at Grambling, huh?

"Nah, I kept a low profile... I like it like that."

"Tall, dark, handsome, at a Black College, no such thing as a low profile. If you went to class and were a full-time student, the sistahs will find you."

"Nah, they weren't checking for me, I was just a face in the crowd."

"Yeah, right. And Terri McMillan is just another writer."

"What about you? How many hearts did you break in

school?"

"None, but mine was broken before. I dated this guy for two years who played football for FAMU and he had women all over Florida."

"How long did it take you to find out?"

"He had been screwing around on me since day one. I had some girlfriends who would tell me things, but I was blinded by what I thought was love. On top of that, I just thought they were jealous, I saw them checking my man out."

"Didn't you see any of the writing on the wall?"

"I saw the writing, but I didn't want to read it. And the bottom line is that this was the first man who I had ever been with, and he gave me multiple orgasms. I was so blind by love and lust that I would have believed him if he said water was dry."

Note to self, she is multiple-orgasmic. I sat and imagined that vision of lust for a moment when she abroptly said, "Eric, what are you thinking about?"

"Nothing, I was just, um... listening to you?"

"Yeah right, your mind is probably stuck on the multiple orgasms aren't you?"

"Naaaah I wasn't thinkin' about that, I was just... um."

"Get your mind out of the gutter and lets fry this fish."

"Gutter? Is that the way you view sex, as the gutter?"

"I never thought about it like that... well, ain't nothin' I got anywhere near the gutter."

As she said that, her voice got soft, and then her eyes held me hostage again. I was her prey, she was pursuing me. Trying to look through me. Trying to read me. I am sure she thought that she could have me if she wanted me, and I was pretty sure she was right. I played it cool , and changed the subject while avoiding her hypnotic, beautiful, dark brown eyes.

"How do you like your fish, Nia? Did I mention that I like the name?"

"Done."

"Are you doubting my cooking skills?"

"Just show me what you've got."

O.K. granted, I am naive about some things, but when she said, "Show me what you've got," I felt she was talking about something other than fish, and I wasn't mad at her one bit. I was enjoying our cunning conversation of double-meaning words.

We exchanged friendly flirtatious conversation while I fried the fish. I was attracted to her, and she was with me. I could read something in her eyes. She looked at me like she wanted me to stay as long as possible. We ate, smiled, talked, flirted and exchanged stories about college. We talked about relationships, and she shared with me the things that went wrong in hers. According to her, the men that she dated, started out as great guys, but once they had her, they did not do the same things that they once did to get her. She also seemed like she was hard on brothers who could not match her intellect. She was an accountant, and she was very well read. She was not tolerant of brothers who did not read, or were not up on current events.

"So Nia, how long have you been in Atlanta?"

"Three years in January."

"Have you met any brothers to keep your attention yet?"

"Not really, I have met some nice guys, but I have realized that I am kind of high maintenance, and that doesn't sit very well with most guys."

"High maintenance?"

"Yeah, I mean, I have been on my own for a few years and I have spoiled myself. I think I am worth it, so I do it. When guys ask me out, and ask for suggestions on what we should do on dates or outings, as I like to call them, I don't say 'lets go to McDonalds.'"

"Nia, are you a gold digger?"

"No, I'm not a gold digger, I am a gold owner, but if you

want to date me, I expect certain things. The guys who can do the nice things are normally shallow, and can only talk about themselves. And the ones who don't have a pot to piss in, are the ones who are actually quite interesting."

"Do they know that you think they are interesting?"

"They don't stick around long enough to find out, and the thing about it is, after about four dates or so, I don't mind footing the bill every now and then."

"Is anyone in the picture now?"

Just then, the phone rang. She casually got up to answer it, and after saying hello, I immediately heard panic in her voice. She said a few more things in what I like to call an urgent whisper, then she came to the sofa where I was. Her eyes that were once beautiful now looked like a deer that was caught in headlights. She didn't even try to mask the fear in her voice.

"Eric, I'm sorry, but you should probably go."

I stood up and while looking at her, I glimpsed over her shoulder, and I saw a black Expedition next time my meager Honda Accord.

"Is everything O.K.?"

"We will talk about it later, I'll call you later."

She said all of this while taking my hand and leading me to a door. The phone rang again, and I saw the siloulette in the huge truck and a guy with a phone to his ear.

Drama. I hate it. Try to avoid it. Can't stand it.

I gave her a look that said that I was neither feeling her, nor the potentially violent situation that I could be facing. I stepped out the door, while the phone continued to ring, swallowed hard and began to walk. This time I choose my *Shaft, 'bout to go kick somebody's ass* walk. Intimidation was half the battle. I learned that from the Detroit Piston Bad boys of the eighties. The door opened, and out stepped a guy who actually could have caused an eclipse if the sun were directly behind him. I looked at his plates, and that's when I realized that I was going to be confronted by an Atlanta Falcons Defensive Lineman. This brother gets paid to hit people every Sunday. Shit. Is he walking toward me, or toward the door? He stood in front of the path that I had to walk. Damn. The stare down was on.

"What's up, dog?" said the oversized Mandingo Warrior.

"Nothin' much, man. How you feelin'?" I said trying to sound cool and calm.

"I'm cool, what's up with you and Nia?"

"Just friends, dog, ain't nothin'."

"Aiight then, I holler."

He said this with a smirk on his face, that bully-type smirk that dares you to say the wrong thing, so he can see how much pain you can take.

He walked past, and walked right in like he owned the place. With the salary that he was making, he just might. She said that she was high maintenance, well who better to take care of a high maintenance woman than a big ballin, shot callin, football player. What does he have that I don't, other than an expensive ride, a seven-figure salary, and of course, Nia? Do I even want Nia? I thought I did, I thought I saw some chemistry. I thought I saw something in her eyes. Probably saw the same thing that every other brother sees. If she were beautiful to me, why wouldn't she be beautiful to any other brother with 20/20 vision?

As the door slammed, I immediately heard him talking in a very loud, angry tone. I don't know why I cared, considering that I just got played, but I did. No, I didn't want my butt kicked, but I would rather he kick mine than hers.

Look at me! She just played me, and I am worried if she is going to catch a beat down or not. I stood next to my car, while I listen to them argue over how insignificant to them that I am. I wanted to leave, but I was caught in a moral dilemma. If I leave, and she gets a

Nike up the butt, am I to blame, if I leave? She told me to leave. Did she tell me to leave because she feared for my safety? Is he a crazy ex-boyfriend, or a crazy current boyfriend? You know what the common thread is in both cases? The word *crazy*. If he were the team punter, or field goal kicker, I would not worry, I would probably open a can of whip-ass on him, because they are normally the smallest, and weakest on the team. But this brother was at least 6'5, 275. A grown ass man. I leaned on my car, and thought about what I would do if he actually hit me. And all I came up with was "fall." I could get paid though. I know a great civil lawyer. He would probably knock her head off. Just then, the door flew open, and he came toward me, looking at me like I was the opposing teams quarterback, with Nia hot on his heals. She was trying not to make a scene, she did live an a nice neighborhood.

"Tank, will you stop and talk to me, he has nothing to do with this" she said in a low yet stern tone.

"Nigga, what you still doin' here?" said Tank. I have never heard a more appropriate name in my life except for the stripper that goes by the name of Fantasy, but that's a whole nother topic.

"My car won't start," I said in a surpassingly sarcastic tone. Suprising to even me. Why was I waiving a red flag in front of this bull?

"Eric, I'm fine. You can leave, I will talk to you later" said Nia, looking at me with a desperate, 'please leave and save yourself before Godzilla steps on you' look.

"You better get on up away from here before I put something on yo' punk ass. You can't protect nobody but your damn self."

"Look here Tank, I understand you a big boy and all, but if you want to hit me and share that big-time salary that you're clockin, let me know. I got a friend who's a helluva lawyer." I replied.

It's a good thing that my jeans are baggy, cause if they

weren't he would have seen my knees knocking. He looked at me like he was letting my words marinate, and then called me a punk mutherfucker, and went back into the house mumbling under his breath.

"Eric, please go, I know you were here to help but I am fine, I promise. I will call you when he leaves. I'll call you."

I laughed, opened the door, turned and faced her and said, "Don't bother, when I want drama, I will go to Blockbusters" and I drove off.

I got in my car and searched for my Anita Baker CD. She sang *Fairy Tails*, while I headed toward I-285. As I let her words engulf me; I contemplated what she said. The song, in case you don't know talks about a little girl who dreamed of a Prince sweeping her off of her feet, and living happily ever after. She then says that the story ends, like stories do, and reality steps into view, no more living a lie in fairytales. I want a fairy tale. I am sick of the dating merry-go-round. I yearn for the stability of knowing whom I am going to be with, knowing that someone wants me to hurry home so we could embrace. And with that embrace, squeeze out the pressure and stress of the daily grind. I want the fairytale. I know what a good woman is like. I was raised by one. I know the potential that a woman's spirit has, her ability to help lift your soul. The power of her embrace. My mother has those powers. I feel terrible that she didn't have a man to share her life with. I know how good she is. She is the one that helped me understand the power of a woman. Uh oh, I just thought about what Corey said about finding a woman like my mother... was he right?

Corey

It's already 8:30, how long have I been sleeping? I normally can't sleep like this during the day, guess I'm scared I might miss something. Phone is ringing.

"Hello?"

"High, is um... Eric there?"

"No he's not, may I take a message?" The voice on the other end sounds emotional, and the number came up "unavailable" on the caller I.D.

"Girl who in the hell you talkin to, you need to show some respect!!" yelled a gruff voice who abroptly picked up the phone.

"I pay my own damn bills, so hang up my damn phone!"

"I know this ain't that punk ass nigga, Eric on the phone! replied the wannabe Mr. T type dude.

Dial tone.

What the hell is goin on? My boy's first date and he's already caught up in some drama. I can't believe this shit! His mother would kill Mayor Campbell and me if something happened to that boy. Let me star six nine that heffa. Shit unavailable.

The phone is ringing again.

"Look trick, I don't know what kind of Jerry Springer type shit you got goin on over there, but don't get my boy caught up in it."

"Uh... Corey, this is Sheila, are you O.K.?"

Oops.

"Hey Sheila, my bad, I would explain, but it's a long story. I'm getting ready to head out to find my boy."

"Oh, well I am 3 minutes from your spot, I can swing through and go with you, see you in a minute."

And just like that, she hung up after inviting herself over without my approval, and I don't mind one bit. How about that. I actually want her to come over. I think I am feeling Sheila in a way that I haven't felt any-one in a minute. I just heard a door slam, let me go meet her in the parking lot before she even gets out of the car so we can roll. I open the door and guess who I see lean-ing on his car.

Glad you Got my Back

-Corey -

"Yo, man..., you aiight?" I asked.

"Yeah, I'm cool. Just listening to Anita Baker, thinkin' 'bout some things... You feel me?" He was talking in voice that was so calm, it was eerie.

"I just got a weird phone call from some broad, and then her man picked up the phone and asked about some punk ass nigga named Eric."

"Is that right?" Still as calm as a nursery school during naptime.

"Yeah, that's right, so what's really goin on?"

"Sshhhh, I am listening to Anita" as he put his pointer over his mouth in schoolteacher mode.

"Anita, my ass! Something ain't right. You gotta tell me *something*, dawg!"

I was getting frustrated; I wanted to see if we needed to go regulate, like back in the day. I was ready to go to battle for, and with Eric. Just then, Sheila pulled up quickly, looking concerned. That's right girl, support your man. Not that I am her man, but I... um, ...let me be quiet while I am ahead.

She got out of the car and walked straight to Eric, touched his shoulder with one hand, and lifted his chin with the other, and said in a soft, concerned sweet voice.

"Are you O.K.?"

"Yeah, I'm cool; just vibin to Anita that's all" and he

looked at her with a gentle smile. Even though he was 8 inches taller and one hundred pounds heavier, he looked like a child talking to his mother after his first day of pre-school. His eyes looked sad.

"I know Corey is your boy, but if you ever want another perspective, call me anytime. I mean it."

"I will. Thanks, Sheila" he said as she gave him a hug. She looked like she tried to take his pain away with that hug, because she squeezed real tight, and almost rocked the gentle giant for about five seconds. She then let go of him and finally acknowledged my presence. I wasn't jealous though, I actually became more taken by her now than ever before. She walked toward me and gave me a hug and a kiss full on the lips. No tongue, but a sincere kiss on the lips, she then whispered.

"I hope these women realize what they are doing. I don't know what happened, but I wish I could talk to the women who put that pain in his eyes. I will be upstairs, talk to your boy, and then come on up. Take your time though, I ain't goin' nowhere."

I ain't goin' nowhere, huh? I kind of like the sound of that. Did I just think that?

I sauntered over to where my brother was, and leaned against the car.

"That's a good woman, Corey."

"I know."

"So what are you going to do?"

"I don't know, kid."

"Just don't hurt her, it's enough of that goin' on."

I think he was letting me in on what may have gone down. I didn't want to be nosey... Yes I did.

"What happened, man. I was getting ready to come lookin for you after I got that crazy phone call."

"Yeah? I appreciate it. I got caught up in some drama. Things were going well, dinner was cool, conversation was on point, and I was really feeling her, you know?"

"Yeah?"

"Then, the phone rang and it was her football playin' boyfriend. He showed up, we exchanged words, ... yadda yadda yadda, I left.... I am here."

"Yadda yadda hell! Did she tell you that she had a boyfriend?"

"Nope."

"Playin' games, just like I thought."

"Don't sweat it dog, you live and learn."

"Who was the ball player?"

"I didn't recognize him, she called him Tank, and he fit that name."

"Tank? Tank Sallee?"

"Hell, I don't know! But I didn't want no parts of that dude, man. I held my own."

"Held your own! Man, you don't hold your own against ProBowl Football linemen. You walk away, hell... run, if you need to!"

"Look man, I just told him that if he wanted to hit me, that I would see his big, rich ass in court. I could take a punch for a few hundred thousand dollars; I could use a new car, and my momma could too. I think she wants a P.T. Cruiser," he said with a laugh. Following that wise but funny remark he then stuck out his hand. I grabbed it and said, "Good lookin' out, man." We then embraced... like brothers do.

I will never admit to my eyes getting watery, but we looked at each other for at least one solid minute before he broke the silence.

"Corey, you got me down here, and Sheila up in the house, what's wrong with this picture?"

"Point well taken, Bro, I'm out."

I trotted upstairs to hear the sounds of a vacuum cleaner, and a Tribe Called Quest.

When I walked in, the apartment smelled of Pine sol, and potpourri. She had cleaned the living room, and the kitchen. Well, they weren't really dirty, but they could use some attention. I unplugged the vacuum cleaner.

"Shelia, what are you doing?"

"I always clean when I'm frustrated."

"Why are you frustrated?"

"I like Eric, he deserves better than that. I could tell he was hurt. I just don't want him to turn cold. Lord knows, a good man is hard to find."

I moved closer, and put my arms around her waist, pulling her closer to me.

"Have you met any lately?"

"Yeah, I have, he just doesn't know it."

I kissed her. She willingly kissed me back.

"Is that right?"

"Yeah, but I'm working on him. He has a soft heart, but there is a wall that I need to break down first."

I kissed her again. Longer, softer, fuller.

"Get a room, you to are making my stomach turn!!" It was Corey.

Sheila jumped out of my arms, almost as if she had been caught making out by her father.

"Hey Eric, you done listening to Anita?" quizzed Sheila.

"Yeah, for now, anyway. Music is my therapy."

"You need Jesus" I mused.

"Boy, you silly.... When is the last time you seen the inside of a church?" asked Sheila.

"Yesterday, I had Church's chicken for lunch." I shot back.

"Yo ass is goin' to hell for that one. Get your suit ready, both of you, if you can throw parties until the a.m., then you can go to church with me on Sunday. Service is at 11:00, and I will pick you up at 10:30."

"Is the cover charge still 10%, cause I haven't gotten my first check yet?" Joked Eric.

After he said that he and I burst out laughing, I laughed until my side hurt. I then looked at Sheila who did not share our humor. I reached out to give her a hug, but she shot me a look that put a tingle in my spine.

Eric saw the awkward moment that Sheila and I

shared, put that "oops" look his face and said, "Sheila, I'll be ready at 10:15." She smiled, at him, and turned her nose up at me.

"Yeah baby, I'll be ready at 10:14. As a matter of fact, you can pick out my suit..." trying to get one up on my boy.

"You better" said Shelia, then gave me a kiss, picked up her purse, and headed for the door.

"Sheila, where are you going?"

"Home, I got to drive all the way to Stone Mountain, I got an early meeting tomorrow."

I don't understand what's going on here; I don't want her to leave.

"You can't stay a little while longer? I mean, you just got here."

"What, you trying to get me to stay the night or something?"

"Yeah, that would be cool," as I pulled her closer yet again.

"Corey, my visitor is here."

"Visitor? Oh, you got another brother waitin at the house for you? It's like that, huh?"

"No, silly. My period is on."

"And?"

"Oh, you think that is the only reason that I want you to stay, for sex?"

She pulled me close to her this time; I could smell the peppermint on her breath.

She whispered in my ear. "You mean you don't want to make love to me tonight, Corey?"

I closed my eyes an absorbed everything that makes her, her. Her warmth, her smell, her skin, her sincerity, her intelligence, her smile... her. Those words broke me down. She was in my system like a love cancer, spreading throughout my body. Spreading fast. Every organ that the love spread to made my body and soul long to be taken by her in any way that she would have me. And like a normal reaction to a cancer, I realized that I didn't want it. I could not become victim to the love cancer that was Sheila. I had to do what I had to do to get rid of her; because if I didn't, I had a feeling that it would mean death... do us part. I didn't want to fall in love.

She pulled back and tried to look me in the eye, but I avoided hers.

"What's on your mind, Corey?"

I scrambled for a defense. Whenever you have to scramble for a defense, you are in trouble. Especially when the person on offense has many offensive weapons. That is why Michael Jordan was so effective on offense, he had more weapons than anyone else did. Sheila had many weapons on her side as well, and I was scrambling. "I was just thinking about what you said, I mean, Stone Mountain is a long drive, and it's already 9:45, we will get together some other time." I said this so nonchalantly that I surprised myself. I was as cool as a summer breeze, but I don't think she bought it. She was using one of her weapons to break me down. She knew me. I think she knew I was guarding my heart, because she'd just made reference to it a minute ago.

"That's interesting," she said as she took my hand while heading for the door, and she was as cool as an arctic breeze.

"What's interesting?"

"The sound of ice-melting, then refreezing again."

"What is that supposed to mean?"

"That ice-wall around your heart briefly started to melt, and when you realized it, it started to freeze again. Don't fight it Corey, listen to BoyzIIMen #7."

"Huh?"

And with that, she was gone. She got into her silver colored Accura, and disappeared into the night. BoyzIIMen number 7, what in the world does that mean? I'll ask Eric, I like the silky smooth quartet, but I don't have their latest CD. I went back into the apartment pondering what she said about the ice melting around my heart. She was almost right, but what she doesn't realize is that the ice not only began to melt, but when she whispered those sweet words into my ear, the ice melted, boiled, and began to evaporate. The question is: *Will I allow my heart to beat freely to the beat of love that was being played by Sheila, or follow my playeristic instinct, and allow her to be the franchise player, and nothing more?* The word 'more' is very significant, because I feel myself wanting just that... more. I want more from Sheila.

I think.

I can fall for her...

I think.

I want to be a one-woman man...

I think.

"Eric, where you at?" I yelled looking for my roommate.

"This apartment is only so big, where do you think I am?" said the smart-ass from his bedroom.

I opened the door and saw Eric lying across his bed, watching the ceiling fan go round.

"You got that BoyzIIMen CD?"

"Yeah, which one?"

"I guess the new one, I need to hear track number seven."

"Let me look. Why do you want to hear number seven?"

"Just heard some good things about it, that's all. Do you have it?"

"Hold on, you know I ain't organized my junk yet."

"Junk. Excellent term to use."

"Keep that up, and you won't be hearing *junk*."

And with that, I closed my mouth and waited patiently, kept my mouth shut, well... not all the way shut. I could not resist the temptation to hum the chorus to *Sanford and Son*. The junk in his room made me do it. He shot me a look that let me know under know certain terms was my sarcasm was neither needed or wanted right now. I stopped. My boy and I had a lot on our minds. I wanted to tell him about my conversation with his mother, but I knew he was not up for it at the moment. Our lives seemed to be ideal for a soap opera at the moment. He tossed me the CD, I thanked him and I headed toward the door.

"Yo Eric, your mother called.... She said give her a call when you get a chance."

"Is everything O.K.?"

"Everything is everything."

I closed the door, and proceeded to my much neater room.

Making a Better Impression

- Eric -

I decided to return momma's call. "Hey mom, what's up?"
"Hey baby, how you doing?" She replied.
"Oh, I can't complain. Well, I could, but it wouldn't help none."
"I heard you had a date today, how was it?"
"It was good, we just had dinner, listened to a little jazz."
"She sounds like a nice young lady, you think you'll see her again?"
"I don't think her boyfriend would like that."
"Boyfriend? What do you mean boyfriend. She didn't tell you she had one?"
"Nope, but everything is cool. No harm, no foul."
"Be careful, baby. I would hate to come down there and hurt one of those tramps for acting foolish."
"No, we wouldn't want that."
I know all to well that mom would go to any length that she could to assure my personal safety and happiness. It is up to me to set limitations on what role I would allow mom play in my life. It's like, I don't want to give her to much information, because she would give me advice that I don't want to hear, because if I listen to her, my final decisions are going to be laced with her opinions, and that is not the goal. The goal is independent thought and actions. Silence. I knew mom as well as she

knew me, and for her to be silent while talking to me long distance meant that something was on her mind.

"Hello? You there?"

"Yeah, I'm here. Just thinking, that's all.."

I can feel her setting me up; she wants me to say about what?

"About what?"

"You ever wonder what Phelicia may be doing? It's been three years since graduation. Have you spoken to her?"

"So mom, have you heard from Sandy?"

"Are you avoiding my question?"

"I sure am, cause I know where you are going with this."

"And where might I be going?"

"You want me to call her, and see if we have something special don't you?"

"Eric, that is your business, I was just looking through some old photo albums. You two look so happy together."

"Yeah, but all that glitters ain't gold."

"You trying to tell me you don't miss her at all, Eric?"

"Naw, I didn't say that, but its time to move on."

"Do you have her number?"

"Nope."

"Well, I do. Do you want it?"

"How did you get it?"

"She sent me a birthday card, and left her number, she said that she would love to hear from me."

"So why didn't you tell me back then."

"Because I knew you were trying to move on with your life."

"So what's changed since then, its only been three months, I'm still trying to move on."

Silence. I smell a set up here.

"Momma, have you been talking to Corey?"

"What?"

I know she heard me, she is trying to stall for time and think of a lie.

"What did Corey say to you?"

"What makes you think Corey said anything to me?"

Classic. Answering a question with a question.

"Come on, ma, what's really goin' on?"

"Eric, either you want the number or you don't. It would be a shame if you two had something special, but didn't act on it cause you being so hard headed. You are acting just like your father."

Ouch, low blow. I'd rather be compared to Adolph Hitler than him; I refuse to deal with that with her now, so I will let the comparison to the sperm donor slide. For now.

"I'll take the number, mom. But answer me this question."

"I'm listening..."

"Did Corey put you up to this?"

"That's not important, we are dealing with fate here"

"I knew it, why does everyone feel like they have to look out for me all the time, I mean just a little while ago Corey was ready to come and fight someone for me, then when I got home, his girl was hugging me and feeling sorry for me. I can take care of myself, believe it or not, I *am* grown."

"I know you're grown baby but... "

"See... see what I mean? "You said 'I know you're grown, baby.' You called me baby and grown in the same sentence."

"Let me tell you something, I don't care how grown you think you are, you will always be my baby..., you've just got to deal with it!"

"So you don't see me as a man, is that what you are telling me?"

"I never said that. You are a man; you are 25 years old. When you turn 50 you will be my baby, when you have children of your own, you will still be my baby."

"I get the point, mom, I understand what you are saying, but will you please do me a favor, and look at this from my point of view?"

"Which is?"

"I want to make decisions for myself without interference. There will be times when I will need your advice, and I won't hesitate to ask, but until then, let me make mistakes. Let me fall, and let me get hurt. I guarantee it will make me that much stronger."

She was quiet. I hope I didn't hurt her feelings. She needed to know that she did an excellent job raising me, and it is now time to put all of those lessons into action.

"Mom, you there?"

"I'm here, Eric."

"Are you O.K."

"Yeah, I knew this day was coming. As a parent, I tried to hold on to you as long as you would allow me to. Every night when I say my prayers, I ask God to watch over you and protect you. He hasn't failed me yet, and I've got faith that he won't."

"You make it seem like I am going to war, I'm just trying to live my life is all."

"I know baby, your right. From this point on, I will try to do better."

"Thanks mom."

"I am proud of the man that you have become, I really am."

"That makes me feel better, making you proud has always been very important to me."

"I want to ask you a question, but I don't want to overstep my boundaries?"

"Ask me."

"Do you want Phelicia's phone number?"

The more things change, the more they stay the same.

"Sure ma, I don't know when or if I will even call her, but I will take the number down."

"Good enough."

She gave me the number; told me she loved me, begged me to go to church this Sunday, and hung up. The number. What to do, what to do. I wonder if Corey told mom about my nightmare? Should I call Phelicia? I'm curious to see if anything is there or not. She meant the world to me. On one hand, I want to see if she and I have something special, but on the other hand I don't know if I want to put up with disappointment. What if I see her, and I am still feeling her like I was in college, and she is completely over me. Can I handle that? I don't know. I don't think I can. I think I need to move on with my life. I can find someone else, this is Phatlanta. All I need to do is be patient.

"Yo Eric, get the phone!" yelled Corey.

"Hello."

"Hey Eric, this is Nia, I need to talk to you."

"Nia, you don't owe me any explanations."

"No, I do, what happened today wasn't cool, I broke up with Tank over a month ago.."

"I don't think he received that memo."

"I'm being serious Eric."

"I am too, it's not that major, I had a good time, good food, now I am going to bed, take care."

I didn't even want to say her name. How could a person named Nia put me in danger?

"I want to see you again, Eric."

"I ain't got time to be playing no games. You obviously have some baggage that you haven't fully dealt with yet, and you put me in danger. Not cool."

"So what am I supposed to do, stop dating cause Tank can't deal with it? I cant do that, we have been apart for over a month, and I am ready to move on. I want to go out with you cause we had a good time."

"I don't know, Nia. I had a good time as well, but I don't wanna be watching my back because I pissed off some football player. He could do me in and hire Johnny

Cochran and be free as a bird. You probably wouldn't even come to my funeral, and if you did you would probably bring a date."

"Boy, you are silly, I wouldn't dare bring a date to your funeral. The wake maybe, but not the funeral."

"Ok, Ok, I guess I will let you off the hook."

"Really, you forgive me?"

"Yeah, everyone deserves a second chance."

"Great, now, I know it's late, but I need to come by and give you your good-bye hug, I didn't like the way we said good-bye earlier."

"You mean you want to come over right now?"

"Yeah, I won't stay long; I just don't like what happened today. The drama. I am so not like that, I can't stand drama. So may I come over?"

"Sure, I stay in apartment 35."

"Give me 5 minutes."

Fifteen minutes later...

"Hey, I see you made it," I said as I opened the door. She had on a red Nike sweat suite. She looked good in red. She looked good period. Her hair was pulled back into a ponytail, with no make-up on, I was impressed.

"Who's at the door, dog?" yelled Corey over my BoysIIMen CD. He poked his nosey head out of the door.

"This is Nia, Nia this is Corey."

"Corey, sorry about the phone call earlier, it was a big misunderstanding." pleaded Nia as she stepped to him with her hand extended as a show of peace.

"Oh, that was you? Aiight, it's cool, as long as that shit is squashed. You're beautiful and all, but you ain't worth dying for." Said a sarcastic Corey.

"O.K. I guess I deserved that one. Yeah, its over. The case of a ex-boyfriend who does not understand what the 'X' stands for."

"I know you, don't I? You look real familiar."

"I was at your party. My girlfriend Shelia invited me."

"Sheila?" we both said in unison.

"Yeah Sheila, we went to FAMU together."

"Small world, small ass world" said Corey as he shook his head, and returned to his room, where BoysIIMen massaged the air.

We were alone. We looked at each other. I felt awkward because I didn't know what she had in mind. I didn't want to play myself and assume that something was going to happen. Let me step back and assess the situation. She has on sweats, which means easy access. She has her hair pulled back, so there is not a worry about messing it up. She wants to get back onto my good side, always a good thing. She was here after 10:00 p.m. on a work night.... Booty Call. I think?

"You know what, Eric. You look real sneaky, what's on your mind?"

"I am going to plead the fifth on that one."

"Really, how often do you work out?" she asked as she slowly sauntered in my direction.

I think she is making reference to how my tank top fits. I worked out enough to look fit, not like a live in a gym. My arms had good definition, my shoulders are broad, and my stomach is O.K. I hate doing sit-ups, yet love to eat. That combination does not equal abs of steel.

"I work out when I get a chance, I wish I could do it more often."

"I think you look great. What kind of cologne are you wearing?"

"Wings, you like it?"

"I love it," she said as she put her arms across the tops of my shoulders. She was tall, and I love tall women. I didn't realize how tall she was until we embraced. She was 5'10," and had on tennis shoes, which gave her another one and a half inches, and I was 6'2", but I happened to be in my socks. As we embraced we rocked from side to side and eventually found the rhythm to whichever BoysIIMen ballad was playing at the time. As we swayed, her body pressed against mine like I had a Velcro waistline, but I am not complaining. She rested her head right next to my neck, and I could feel her warm sweet breath. Her mouth seemed extremely close to my neck, so close that I could feel moister of her breath. She better chill out, cause that's my spot. I then felt her lips and tongue on my neck. She definitely had my full attention at this point. When she felt the depth of my attention, she raised her head and looked at me with a sly smirk on her face. I looked at her and raised both eyebrows as if to say "now what?" She kissed me, I kissed her, we kissed each other. The kiss seemed to last forever. I had her, I honesty think that I could have taken her to the bedroom, and enjoyed what she had to offer right now. But did I want the responsibility that went along with it? I mean, if I sleep with her tonight, what would that mean in the morning? As good as she feels, I need to stop this now. Well, maybe not right now, but soon. At least in another hour.

We somehow made our way to the couch, and she was on top of me. Judging by her pelvic thrust, she wanted to do a bedroom dance with me, and I was more than up for the lesson. Yet I knew it was wrong. It felt right and wrong at the same time. While she was lifting my shirt, going for yet another one of my "spots" we heard Corey coming out of his room to go to the rest room. We both jumped up immediately like teenagers who were often caught by their parents making out on the sofa. We tried to look innocent.

"Go to your room, that is not the last thing that I want to see before I go to bed" said Corey.

"Don't hate" I replied.

"Whatever" he said as he made his way to the restroom. This fool is pissing with door wide open. We don't want to hear that! He is killing my flow.

"Close the door, man!" I yelled.

"Oh, my bad" he said, as he laughed to himself.

That was a stroke of reality. Now we both had a chance to evaluate the situation. To cool off, so to speak. We sat there on the couch, looking at each other. Trying to read each other's minds. What was she thinking? What am I thinking? Go for it. Well that's what the southern head is thinking, as the northern head is thinking about the morning after. The big picture. This is one time when I know I was being hard headed, pun intended. From my experiences, women have a harder time separating the physical with the emotional. Men can sleep around without getting attached, women can't. They say they can but if your doing them right, they will get attached, eventually. If you can make a woman smile, feel comfortable, and have an orgasm on the regular, she will get attached. I can make Nia smile, I can stimulate her mind, and judging by the fore play, I can stimulate her body, so I think she will be attached. Do I want her to be attached? I don't know. The situation of earlier with Tank still has me skeptical. What to do? What to do? We sat there looking at each other until Corey returned to his room. She broke the silence.

"Wow!"

"Wow? Is that a good thing?"

"I would say yes. I"m glad your boy came out when he did," she said.

"And why would that be?"

"Things were getting pretty steamy on this couch. How many hands do you have, they were everywhere."

"Are you complaining?"

"Do I look like I'm complaining?"

"Nah, you actually look pretty content."

"That"s one way of putting it."

We sat there in silence again. Small talk was over. The question of the night was what happens next? Normally the woman dictates what will happen next. Right now she knows whether or not she is going to give me some, or not. I can speculate but that means nothing. She knows. I am going to take control right now, and walk her to the door. This thing has to stop right now before the moment gets going again. We can not go into the bedroom. I refuse to sleep with any woman that I am not sure in which direction we are going in.

"Let's go into your room, Eric."

"Sure!"

I am so weak.

A Dinner Date with Sheila

-Corey-

"What up, man. How was work?" I asked Eric as he walked through the door. He had a real weary look on his face. You know the look were the creases in the forehead are real pronounced, your eyes are kind of glossy and you are looking deep in to nowhere? That's how he looked.

"Let me ask you a question. How in the hell can a person bring a precious life into the world, just to beat it to death? If you feel that strongly against having a child, keep your legs closed and you penis in ya' pants, better yet, where a condom. They don't cost that much. You know what? The same type of test that you gotta take to get license, should be the same type of test for you to have a child."

"Rough day, huh dog?"

"Rough does not even begin to describe it, I mean, I understand that life can be stressful, and I also know that children have a tendency to push all the wrong buttons at all the wrong times. But there has to be a limit as to how to physically discipline a child. What would possess a parent to beat a child until they bleed?"

"I hear you dog, but don't judge until you know the whole story."

"Judge hell! You should have seen this child's legs man,

he looks like he was beaten by a slave master."

"I hear you, dog. But if you don't know the whole story...."

"Man, fuck that! It's a thin line between spanking a child and assault! You know what? I need some air, I'm out!"

And just as soon as he was here, he was gone. He always did wear his feeling on his sleeve. Don't get me wrong, I am not for abuse, but back in the day, my pops wore my ass out, and I am a better man for it. As light as I am, the belt may have left a mark or two, but I don't consider that abuse. What I mean is that I would rather my pops whip me, than a cellmate. "Slam." That was the door. Where is he going? It aint like he know how to get anywhere. My pager is blowing up, let me see who this is. Sheila. I guess I'll call her back on her cell. This ain't cool; I know her cell number by heart.

"Hey Sheila, what's up, this is Corey?"

"I know your voice, what are you doing?"

"Just chillen, I've only been here for about ten minutes"

"Have you eaten yet?"

"Nope, I just got here."

"Let me take you to dinner."

Dinner now it seems to me that Sheila is not only try-ing to be my number one, but my only one. I want to go, but I aint trying to be nobody's man. You know what? I'll go, but I need to put my feelings in check, because I can't go out like that.

"Corey, you there?"

"Yeah, I am here, sure I will go."

"Good, I will pick you up in about 15 minutes, I am leaving my girl Nia's house, bye."

Nia? Naahh, it can't be the girl who was here last night...or could it?

25 minutes later...

So much for 15 minutes, women are never on time. Not

only that, when you check them on it, they get an attitude as if they are doing men a favor by gracing us with there tardy ass presence. I knew she was too good to be true. I am going to give her another 10 minutes, then I am out, ain't no woman gone keep me waiting, my time is just as valuable as hers is. I think I heard a door slamming, it had better be her. Oh, it's Corey.

"You aaight kid?"

"I'm cool doc, I just needed a drink."

"A drink, yo ass don't drink!"

"I know, I got an Oreo Blizzard from Dairy Queen" he chuckled.

"That's even worse, you know dairy products will have you fartin all over the place!"

"Later for you, you better hope I don't cut one right now!"

"Naw dawg, don't do that, Sheila is on her way over, she might think it was me."

"That's even better." he said as he let out a fart that had the base of Too Live Crew song.

"All hell, man. That's foul, go light a candle and check ya' draws, cause yo ass is rotten. Better yet, you need to burn ya' draws."

Perfect timing, Sheila would come now, and my place smells like rotten eggs. Let me grab my wallet and meet her in the parking lot. I can't let her in here with the house smelling like this.

"I'm out, stank man!" I said to the laughing gas man.

"Yo momma."

"My momma, huh, I would get on yo momma, but the line is too long, and I don't have change for a dime."

Slam!

"Hey Sheila, what's goin' on?"

"Hey sexy" she said as she gave me a kiss.

I didn't even care if the neighbors saw us kiss or not. Well I hope Tasha from across the lot didn't see, I think she wanna give me some.

"You want me to drive Sheila?" I asked, hoping she'd say no.

"Have you been to Show Case Eatery off of Old National Highway?"

"Show Case Who?" I said faking ignorance, of course I know where it is, as a matter of fact, I took Kay there last week. I even met the owner. Nice brother and he can cook his butt off.

"I'll drive man, get in."

Worked like a charm.

Phelicia on My Mind

- Eric -

Times like these. Days like these, I kinda wish I had someone I could talk to about my day. Someone who would just listen and not pass judgement. Just allow me to vent. Listening is a lost art. Instead of listening, most people are trying to figure out what they are going to say next after they hear the first thing that you say to them. That's not listening, that's preparing. It's O.K. to listen and not say anything. It really is. My mom is very good listener, she would understand. You know who else is a good listener? Phelicia. Well she was, but that was almost four years ago, people change. I wonder how much she has changed since then. I wonder if I should call her, just to say hi. Yeah that's it, call to say hi. Nothing else but a simple harmless hello. What if she doesn't want to hear from me? Yawn. What if she has a man? I think I will lay down and sleep on it. Yeah, that's what I will do, sleep on it. Yawn... When I wake up I will give her a call...zzzzzzzzzzzz

"Phelicia, what are you doing here?"
"I wanted to see you. See what happened at the disciplinary board."
"I am on probation for one year. Dean Whitting said if I as much as J-walk, I would be kicked out of school. He even made me call my mother, can you believe that? I felt like a kid in the

principal's office."

"It could have been worse ,you know," she replied.

The closer I looked at her, the more I realized that something was wrong. Her eyes were somewhat swollen, glossed over. She had been crying.

"What's the matter?" I said as I moved closer and reached for her delicate hand. She pulled it away.

"Nothing. J.T. and I are through."

"And you are crying? Shoot, that's reason to celebrate! That means we can finally be together."

"Eric, it's not that easy, we have a lot of history together."

"Hell, Blacks and Slave master's had a history together, but when they were set free, they moved on. Quickly."

"Are you trying to say that I was a slave in that relationship, cause I don't appreciate that shit one bit!" she snapped as she tried to walk away. I never heard her curse before. I didn't like it coming from her mouth. It didn't fit her. Some women seem natural saying words like that, but not her. I grabbed her. Not violently, but gently.

"No, no, no, I wasn't calling you a slave, that came out wrong" I said desperately while pulling her close to me. Tears streaked down her soft, cocoa brown skin.

"What I meant was, you just left a terrible situation, and you have an opportunity to move to a far better one. We can be together. We can be together right now."

She looked up at me with glossy eyes and said," I need time to heal, I need some space."

"But I need you. I thought this is what we both wanted. I thought you and I wanted it to be 'you and I.'"

"I do Eric, but..."

"No. No buts. Let's make it happen. I can help you heal."

"No you can't, I need to do this on my own. I also need space."

"Space? And what am I to do while you are having your space. You except me to wait around, as hard as I worked for us to be together? I'm just to wait an twiddle my thumbs until you are ready? You know how I feel about you, it is torture to be apart from you."

"Eric, you know how I feel about you too! Don't do this."

"Yeah, I thought I knew how you felt. If you felt as strongly as I do, there would be no question. We would be together. No matter what."

"Are you giving me an ultimatum, is that what this is?"

"I don't know what you want to call it, but I can bottom line it for you. I have fallen in love with you, and I thought the feelings were mutual. I want to be with you. I want to be your man. Either you want to be my woman right now, or you don't. I know what I want, and I am laying my cards on the table. Now it's you're turn."

She inhaled deeply. She exhaled deeply. She initially spoke to me with her eyes. She was almost pleading with me to understand, but as usual, I was being stubborn. I am extremely kind, and equally as stubborn. Especially if I think I have the right answer.

"Eric, I have dreams about us. I want you like you want me. And even though I am not ready, I will be your girl, your woman. But you've got to promise me that you will be patient with me. My relationship with J.T. represents the last six years of my life."

We embraced, and I felt her tears through my shirt. I also felt her body trembling with sobs of her emotions. Were they tears of joy, or pain?

"We are going to be O.K. baby, I promise, we are going to be fine" I promised.

Ring.Ring.. Ring

"Hello"

"Hey you. Were you asleep?"

"I was, but I'm up now"

"Were you dreaming about me?"

"Uh huh, sure was," I said while wiping the eye snot out of my eyes. Who ever this is messed up my dream.

"Do you know who you are talking to?"

Let's see, if I can lie my way out of this one.

I said, "How can I forget a voice like this one, of course

I know who this is?"

"Well in the words of Destiny's Child, *Say my name, say my name.*"

Oops. Whoever it is sings like she is in pain. This can't be hard, I don't know many females in Atlanta, and the ones that I know in Indianapolis don't have my number yet. The process of elimination works again.

"Nia" I said.

Silence on her part.

"Yeah it's me, so how was your day Mr. Eric?"

Here is my chance to check her listening skills.

"Well, if you really want to know, today was my first real test in a crisis situation"

"Good for you, hope you passed. Anyway, what are you doing this evening?"

Damn, can I finish? Oh, I see she is not a very good listener. Just because a person asks you how you are, doesn't mean that they really want to know, and she obviously didn't. I don't think I want to be bothered with her. She just rubbed me the wrong way. My evening will not include her.

"I have a lot of paperwork to do that's going to take me into the evening."

"That's too bad, I wanted to see you tonight, I enjoyed being held last night."

"Oh really?" We didn't do anything but lay in the spoon position. You know her backside to my front side. We were a perfect fit. All night she kept nudging her butt up to my groin, trying to play sleep, but I was wide awake, and standing at attention, I know she felt it. It was cool, but the blue balls that followed weren't.

"It was cool to be in your bed and not be attacked. I could lay next to you and not have sex anytime."

WHAT????? Lie next to me and not have sex! That can't be good. I don't want to be bothered with her tonight, but I don't want to get stuck in the friendship zone.

"Is that good or bad?"

"That's a turn on, you not attacking me, makes me want you even more."

"Yeah right, so much so that you fell asleep on me."

"Eric, do I need to come over there now and show you how much I want you?"

She wants me like that? I definitely did not see that coming. Now what? She wants me, but I am not feeling her because she is not a good listener. But on the other hand, I am sure I can think of another way of venting my frustration from a long draining day. I haven't had any in a while either. Nope can't do it, she seems like she might want to stay around, be a franchise type player. Franchise type player, I hope Corey isn't rubbing off on me, that's not my style.

"Listen Phelicia, let me finish this paper work and give you a call when I am finished, it may not take as long as I think it will."

Silence.

"What did you just call me Eric"

"I called you Nia." I think.

"No you didn't, you called me Phelicia" she said coldly.

"If I did, I am sorry. Phelicia is this little girl at the center who was all over me today, she's a sweet girl, but I've been calling her name all day, I didn't mean anything by it though." I hate lying like that, but I didn't feel that I had a choice. Oh well, no harm no foul.

"If you say so. Give me a call when you finish, I'll be here watching *Love & Basketball*."

She said this with an edge on her voice, I hope she didn't see through the little lie.

"Nia, you O.K.?"

"Yeah, I'm cool."

"You sure?'

"I said I am fine. I wouldn't lie about that." She put a little extra sauce on the word *lie*. I think she caught me.

"O.K., well, I will talk to you later, boo. Bye."

"Bye, Eric."

O.K., this is a bit much. I can't believe that I just called Nia, Phelicia. Is it something still there. I've got to call her. I keep having dreams about her, I almost physically assaulted my boy because of her, and I called another women Phelicia. It's only 8:35, she should still be up, I'm going to call her. I have to. I am going to do it right now before I talk myself out of it.

It's ringing. Damn, the answering machine.

"Hi, this is Phelicia, I can't make it to the phone at the moment, but leave a message and I will definitely call you back. Talk to ya' soon." Beep.

Why am I nervous? It has been forever since I've heard that voice, and it still captivates me. I feel like I did the first time we spoke. Do I hang up, leave a message? Leave a message.

"Hey Phelicia, this is Eric Dukes. Ummm, I was just calling to say hello and to see how you are doing; I would love to hear from you. Give me a call at 770-555-4545."

O.K. I did it. I feel better, I did it. It is time to either bring closure to this, or go to the next level.

The phone is ringing, what does Nia want now?

"Hello?"

"Eric?"

"Phelicia."

"Yes, this is Phelicia.Umm... hi."

"Hello, how are you doing?" I hesitantly asked.

"Aside from being shocked, I am doing well, how about you?"

"I am fine too, how is your family doing?" I said, still not quite knowing where to take the conversation.

"My family is good, everyone is healthy, so I can't complain, how is yours?"

"My family is great, mom is healthy, Debbie, and Sandy are doing well."

Silence. Loud deliberate silence.

"Eric."

"Yes."

"Can I ask you a question?"

"Sure."

"Why did you call me? I haven't spoken to you in over three years, what's really going on?"

"It's a long story."

"I like stories."

"I have been thinking about you, about us, an awful lot lately. Wondering how you were doing, wondering what types of twists and turns that your life has taken. Playing the what if game in my head."

"The what if game?"

"Yeah, you know, what if we had stayed together."

"The *what if* game? You have to mean what if you hadn't dumped me before graduation. What if we had stayed together like you promised me we would? What if I didn't get my hopes up high for us to be shot down. You mean *that* what if game? If it's a game to you, it's life for me, and I still don't see the humor!"

BOOOOM! She just dropped a bomb on me

"Phelicia, I didn't mean it as a game with your life. I mean we meant a lot to each other, and it would be a shame to not have any contact whatsoever."

"Look, it took me a long time to get over you, and I refuse to turn down that road again, so let me tell you about the twists and turns of my life, so we can bring some closure to your little what if game. I am a registered nurse, I am single, no kids, not dating. You wanna know why I am not dating Eric? 'Cause I don't trust men anymore. I don't have time for the pain. I pour myself into my work, and I am a big sister to a child who needs me. You know why I chose a child to love instead of a man? I'll tell you, children have unconditional love for you and they are honest. What do you know about honesty Eric? Not a damn thing! Were you honest when you said we would move to Indianapolis together? Were you being honest when you said that I was the woman that you wanted to spend the rest of your life with? Answer me, Eric!" As she spoke she got more and more angry, more and more intense. It's as if she had been holding this in for a long time, and was relieved that she let it out. I could hear the tears in her voice. I didn't know what to say. So I said.

"I'm sorry."

"Sorry, that's all you can say is sorry? Yeah, you are right. You are sorry..., a sorry excuse for a man. I am so sick and tired of you sorry ass men that I don't know what to do. I would never be a lesbian, but believe me, I understand. Well, look here, I got a life to live, so I am going to hang up now. Bye!"

"Wait! Don't hang up, please talk to me!"

"Talk? What do you want to talk to me about?"

What I say next will determine what happens to us next.

"I know where I went wrong with us, and I take full responsibility. I forced you into a relationship before you had time to heal. When I said I wanted to spend my life with you, I was being honest; I just couldn't see moving you all the way up north with the problems that we were having. I was scared. We were only twenty-one. I can tell you this though, when I said I was in love with you, I meant it. It was pure. I haven't felt that way since. Not a day goes by that you don't cross my mind."

I heard her crying softly.

"Eric, what do you want from me huh, what do you want from me?"

"I don't know, I just had to talk to you."

"Well, you've done that, now what."

"Phelicia."

"What?"

"Do you ever think about us?"

"Don't do this to me, Eric."

"Do you?"

"Eric, stop."

She began crying again, this times not as softly.

"Please answer my question."

"Answer your question, why would I answer that? I can't afford this type of emotional stress. Let me ask you a question. What if I say yes? Then what? What is you're plan?"

"My plan is to get to know you again, because...." I don't know how to finish the sentence. I know what I want to say, but am I really ready for the consequences of what I will say? I need to figure out what I want, because I'm not sure.

"Because what?"

"I want to see if anything was left."

"And what if it is, then what? Are you going to propose to me, and then spend the rest of your life with me, 'cause I have heard that before."

"Yes."

Silence. Dead silence, loud silence.

"Eric, do not break my heart again, I can not take it." She said this slow and deliberately. She sounded like a whispering robot, I guess she wanted to make sure that I heard every single emotion, of every single, syllable of every single word.

"I won't."

"Promise me, Eric."

"I promise."

"So, now what? What happens next?" Still in a whisper. Like she is real weak, on life support, uttering her last word.

"I want to talk to you as often as possible, I want to take a road trip to Monroe to see you, I want to take it day by day, because if it is something still between us, we will know..., it wont take long."

"Eric, I want to be as open as possible with you, because we are both grown. Although I am not dating anyone, I will have an occasional dinner and a movie with a man, how do you feel about that?"

"I will be honest with you, I don't want to think about you with another guy, but at this point, I am in no position to say no, but when I come to town, I want your undivided attention. Is that a deal?"

"Yes baby, that's a deal?"

Baby? Did she just call me baby? This big 'ole grin just crossed my face.

"I just moved to Atlanta a few days ago, and occasionally I will go on a date also, but as for now my focus is on you."

"I am looking at my caller I.D. right now, are you staying with Corey?"

"Yes."

"Is he still a hoe?"

"Ouch, that's kind of harsh, don't you think?"

"No! I know he is ya' boy and all, but we both know he is a player. I don't know where you and I are going with us, but if you for once think about hoeing around with Corey, you can just forget about us."

"If I didn't cheat on you in college, you know I won't do it now. College is the ideal place to sleep around... at least that's what I heard."

"First of all, we are going slow, so what ever you do will not be considered cheating on me right now, but when and if the time for us comes, we will discuss it."

"I feel you."

"I bet you'd like to" she laughed that sweet laugh that is forever recorded in my heart.

"Phelicia."

"Yes?"

"I am glad that we are again communicating, my mom would be so happy."

"Eric, please don't tell her just yet, she and I cried on the phone many a night talking about what could have been, I don't want to disappoint her again."

"When did you and my mom discuss us on the phone? She never told me that."

"Believe it or not, your mother has conversations separate from you. She even has a life outside of you."

"Ha, Ha, Ha" I said sarcastically.

"Listen Sweetie, I hate to cut you off, cause I am really enjoying you, but I have a Funk Aerobics class to go to, and I don't want to be late."

"O.K., you be careful out there."

"I will, love you, bye..." Click.

What did she just say? I think she said she loved me. I know she didn't mean to say that, cause you can't still be in love with someone that broke your heart and hasn't talked to you in over three years. I think. Does she love me? Do I love her?

Ring... Ring... Ring...

"Hello?"

"Hi, it's me again, I am sorry, I didn't mean to say that to you, it just felt like old times, and ... I am so sorry."

"It's O.K., it sounded natural. I guess on some level, we never stopped loving each other, so the feeling is mutual. We are still going to take it step by step, but, I love you too."

"Thanks, talk to you soon." Click.

I just said 'I love you' to her.

Shelia's Working On My Heart

- Corey -

I am really enjoying this dinner with Sheila, her confidence is refreshing. The dinner is excellent, and the
ambiance is on point, I just wish that damn waitress were
not so fine. She keeps looking at me like she wants to say
something, but she just grins when we make eye contact,
and goes on about her business. She is leaning down
extremely far when she puts food items on the table,
showing off her ample cleavage, and butterfly tattoo. I
bet the artist who had the pleasure of putting her tattoo
there, took his sweet time, and I ain't mad at him one bit.
"Corey, have you heard anything that I said?"
Damn, I didn't even know she was talking.
"Yes, I heard every word."
"O.K. then, tell me what I said then."
I have absolutely no idea what she said, but I can't let
her know that.
"Oh, you callin me a liar, you don't believe me?"
"No, I don't, you were so busy flirting with that perky
Black Barbie doll, that you hadn't heard anything I said
in the last five minutes!"

"Flirting, me, naw, I mean I will admit I did look, but that's it."

"Look, I know you are a man who has 20/20 vision, but don't disrespect me."

"I wasn't trying to disrespect you, I am sorry if that is what it seemed."

"I accept your apology, but she will not get a tip, believe that."

"Are you ready for a check sir, or would you like something else," said the amply shaped waitress. I felt that by her body language that she would offer me anything that I desired. The problem is, is that I know Sheila saw it as well.

"Excuse me, miss. May I have a word with you for a moment" said a stern Sheila. She then stood up and walked off to the side. Both the waitress and my eyes were as big as headlights s as we looked at each other. The P.Y.T. (pretty young thing) nervously followed Sheila over to the corridor, and disappeared. I hope Sheila is keeping her cool. Hell I hope she isn't leaving me. A few moments later, Sheila came back with that confident look on her face, said let's go, and we went. The unpaid check still on the table.

"Sheila, I didn't pay the check yet, we can't just leave like that."

"It's on Black Barbie."

And just like that we were out in the parking lot, getting in to her smoke gray Acura. It smelled like vanilla, and it was as clean as the board of health. I was quiet, but curious. What did she say, was I allowed to talk without getting cursed out? I wasn't really in the mood for any drama, cause I know I am not backing back down, and neither would she.

"Where to, sweetie?" she asked.

"Where to? Just like that huh, like nothing ever happened?"

"It's water under the bridge, I handled my business,

now lets move on."

This arrogant confidence is starting to get on my nerves, last time I checked, I did have on the pants in this relationship, the way she's flexing, I may as well have on a thong or something. I sure can't go out like that. Wait a minute, this ain't no relationship, what am I thinking. I don't know if I even want, better yet, I know I don't want a relationship.

"Actually, you can take me back to the house."

"What's wrong with you, Corey?"

"Ain't nothing wrong, I'm just not feeling this anymore."

"Feeling what, was I supposed to let her flaunt her big ole tiddies in ya face, and flirt with you like I wasn't there?"

" Later for her, was I flirting back? I mean you ruined the whole vibe that I was dealing with, you didn't have to take her to the side, and make a scene."

"A scene? Were we in the same restaurant? You didn't hear anything that I said over there. You have not seen a scene, I could read Barbie up one side and down the other, and would have been justified but I didn't. I have too much class for that. Too much control."

Control, she hit the nail right on the head. Always got to be in control. If she is in that much control, what use do I have?

"Control, that's all you think about is control."

Silence. I don't like this silence though; she is smiling and chuckling under her breath.

"Sheila, did I miss a joke, I could use a laugh right about now."

"I see you are use to the weak, pretty sistahs that sit back and let you maintain total control. Well, let me tell you something. I ain't her."

We pulled up into my apartment complex. Eric's light is off. Do I sit there and continue to talk, or do head on upstairs. I don't feel like talking to this control freak at the moment, but something wont let me leave.

She spoke, "Well, thanks for dinner. For the most part I had a great time, talk to you later."

"What, you kicking me out of your car now."

"No, but I know you probably need to go call one of your weak friends, to make sure you still go it."

"Got it? First of all, I never lost *it*." And if I need *it*, I don't need to call anyone to get *it*. What in the hell is *it*?"

She laughed. A sexy laugh, tilting her head back and letting it out.

"It, you know that sexy moncho thing that you do. That thing that makes the below average sistah, who knows that she is one out of eight per man in Atlanta. That "I'm in control of the situation thing that you do."

"I am in control of me, that's all that matters, I don't have time to try to control anyone else, I got better things to do."

"So, are you telling me that you are not upset?"

"Upset, nope not one bit, I just think it's time to bring this evening to a close."

"Like I said, I had a nice evening, and I will talk to you later, I tried to bring it to an end until you asked were you being kicked out. It's like you want to leave, but then again... something is holding you back."

She is so casually cool that she is pissen me off. Is something holding me back? Damn real something is holding me back. It's her. I like her, but I can't stand her right now.

"Nothing is holding me back, like I said I am in control of me, I'm out."

"Have a good one, Ice Man."

"What is that supposed to mean?"

"Nothing, boo. Give me a good night kiss before you go in."

I leaned over for a short, aunt-style kiss, but she grabbed the back of my head, and I didn't resist. She parted her lips ever so slightly, and we had a long deep kiss. I don't know how long we were engulfed in each other, but the windows were so fogged I couldn't see my apartment, and I had little beads of sweat on my bald-headed. She finally pulled back for air, and that's when I noticed that the radio was on. The song that blared from V 103's quiet storm was Janet Jackson's *Any Time Any Place*. Normally when I hear this song, I imagine Janet and me doin' our thing, but this time I imagined it was Shelia and I instead. This is major. Nobody has ever made me stop thinking about Janet. She smiled at me.

"It's melting again."

"Huh?"

"Nothing, Corey what are you thinking about?"

"That song. You and I were making a video that goes with this song."

"Really? Tell me about it."

"How about I show you." I said as I put my hand on her thigh.

"You are 6'3 and I am 5'8, I can deal with that anytime, but this car is not the place, lets go in."

"Let's go."

I got out of the car, and she went to the trunk. She is getting a night bag and outfit for work tomorrow. I just shook my head and smiled at her. She is a trip. I think I like her though.

"A girl's got to be prepared."

A girls got to be in control. We went up stairs, and there was Eric. Sitting in a pair of oversized Nike shorts and a tank top. Normally he would get up and speak, but I don't think he noticed us come in, probably because he was watching the *"The Best Man"* and Nia Long was in her negligee. I can't blame him one bit though.

"Hey Eric, how you doin?" said Sheila as she gave him a sisterly hug.

"I'm good, how about you?"

"I'm blessed."

"Sup, Black." I said.

"Ain't nothin', man. Just chillen."

"Corey, I am going to take a shower, I'll see you in a minute." said Sheila as she winked and walked that sexy walk that told me that I better not be to long.

"What you been up to, dog?"

He shook his head, still watching Ms. Long cuss out Taye Diggs.

"I called her."

"You called who?"

"I called Phelicia."

"For real?"

"For real."

"And?"

"It's still there, man. I can feel it, I mean the conversation was rough for the first few minutes, but after that it was like butter. Just like old times, it was all good."

Damn, that is not what I wanted to happen. She was evil then, and now she is going to be bitter and evil. I wanted her to act evil on the phone, and let him move on with his life. She probably played the sweet role, made him feel guilty, and had him eating shit within a ten-minute conversation.

"Aren't you happy for me, I thought you wanted this for me."

"I am happy, but take your time, man. A lot could happen in four years. I mean, what if she is fat or something?"

"Man get out of here, you remember how fine she was, don't you?"

"Exactly, how fine she was. She's from the south, and she never met a pork chop that she didn't like. It is easy to maintain a figure like that when your metabolism is high, but she is twenty-six now. You know what kind of junk she got in her trunk. You know better than I do that the girl can cook."

"Man, later for you, I don't care how she looks, we were

above that. We were in love, and once you are in love, looks are secondary."

"What planet do you live on? You know good and damn well that if that girl walks in here right now tippen the scale at 200 pounds, yo ass is leavin' quicker than a cat at the dog pound. Yeah, you may have loved her for her heart, but if there is no physical attraction "come on, dog" I mean, you in love with Nia Long, but you have no idea what her personality is like. Do you? You know that big girl that works at the Publix up the street? The manager? She has a beautiful personality, but I don't see you trying to hollar at her? Yeah personality is important, but any man that tells you that looks don't matter is lying his ass off."

"Whatever, man. She ain't fat. And I appreciate your support."

"Naw man, it ain't like that, I am just trying to keep it real. I don't want to see you get your hopes up high for a big fall. I want one of two things to happen. Number one, I want you and her to go your separate ways, or two I want you to live happily ever after. That's it, cause you gone be my boy no matter what, but something has to happen."

"Yeah, something is going to happen, but until it does, if you can't say anything positive, leave that subject alone, aiight?"

He looked me square in the eye and I could see the hope, the desire, the optimism in his eye. He resembled that child who looked out the window on the morning of December 25th; hoping with all his heart that what he wanted was under that tree. The tree was his life, and his gift is Phelicia. If he wants it that badly, then I want it for him. Who am I to get in the way of his dream? She and I did not see eye to eye, but it's not my eyes that she is interested in. If I dissed her now, I could do some serious damage to my relationship with Eric. To be perfectly honest, I wish I had that potential someone waiting for me. The potential of finding that person that compliments me, someone who could be for me what Ruby Dee is to Ossy Davis.

"You all O.K.?" said a freshly showered, beautifully scented Sheila. She wore a very nice pair of silk pair shorts and matching v-neck shirt. She didn't show very much skin, and she looked wholesome. Nice legs, very nice.

"Yeah, were O.K. Just having a man to man..." I said, "you *do know* brothers exhale too."

"Yeah, you all need to exhale, we all do, as long as your are growing in the process" she replied.

"Come on now, don't start getting all Essence Magazine on a brotha." I returned.

"You need to read it, instead of looking at the swim suites. Eric, I'm getting ready to get in your business, so if you want me out, just say so. Whatever happened to that girl that was trippen a few days ago?"

"Nothing much, we smoothed it out. She had an x-boyfriend that didn't want to be an x, and he popped up unexpectantly."

I forgot that Sheila told me that she had a friend named Nia, I wonder if this was the same one that Eric kicked it with? What a small world.

"Sheila, don't you have a friend named Nia that went to FAMU with you, and lives in this area?"

"Yeah."

"Eric, isn't that girl that caused the drama named Nia also?"

"What?" Replied Sheila.

"I think the drama queen, and your girl are the same one?"

"You know my girl Nia, Eric?"

"I think so, does she have an ex named Tank?"

"Tank? She broke up with that fool over three months ago. He popped up? When did you meet her?"

"O.K., which question should I answer first? Yes he did pop up out of no where, and I saw her at the party, and I saw her again at the store, struck up a conversation, and the rest is history.

"Really? That's cool, she's cool, maybe we can double one day?"

"Not so fast, Sheila. My man is taking a trip down memory lane, she doesn't stand a chance. I replied.

"Slow down boss, we are taking it one day at a time. I am going to keep in touch with her. Nia, we had a pretty good vibe."

"Yeah, and I bet you said her name about a million times."

"Corey, what are you talking about?"

"Hey ain't talking about nothing."

Sheila then turned to me and mouthed the words '*I want you, right now.*'

"We'll talk later, Eric. I'm turning in. I'm tired." She said that and disappeared down the hall.

"Bro, I wanna be like you when I grow up. I don't know what your plans are, but you have a good woman back there, man."

"I know man, I know, I just ain't ready for her. If I bring it to her on that level, I can't be half steppen."

"Why would you not want to bring it to her on that level? What more could you want from a woman?"

I sat and thought about what he said, and I didn't have an answer. She was everything that I wanted, and needed for a woman to be, so what is my problem. Well, for starters, I am only 26, and..." That's my only reason is that I am 26? Nope, that's not the only reason. My other reasons are: Kay, Tracey, Erica, Trenna, Retha, Karen, and April, just to name a few.

"It's not about her right now. It's about me. I ain't ready for Mrs. Right, but I am getting ready to handle Mrs. Right Now.

An Unexpected Visitor

- Eric -

That fool wouldn't know love if it smacked him on his ass. As a matter of fact, judging by the moans and groans, he may have just smacked love in the ass.

"Knock knock knock!"

I wonder who that is, I didn't invite anyone, and I know Corey isn't expecting anyone. I walked over to the door, tiptoeing so not be heard. Looked through the peep hole, but the stranger was over to the side. They must wanna keep they ass out there!

"Who is it?" I asked through the door, using my deepest voice possible. I know Jehovah Witnesses don't work the night shift in Atlanta, and I didn't order any pizza.

"It's me, Nia," said a sweet but unexpected voice on the other side of the door.

I didn't invite her here; we sure can't start out like that. The only woman that can pop in on me is my momma. I wonder if she is sleep, cause I want to tell her that I called Phelicia."

"Hello?" said the voice again.

I opened the door, and there she was with some hip-hugger blue jeans, and a cut off shirt that showed her sexy mid drift.

Tasty.

"Hi Eric, I know I wasn't invited, so please don't get mad at me, but I really wanted to see you."

"Well, as long as this is the last time you pop up, I won't trip. What's goin' on?"

"I umm."

"Come on now, don't get all shy on a brotha now."

Wait a minute, it's passed 11:00! I've heard of a booty call, but I think I've been a victim of a booty drive-bye!

"I just wanted to be held again tonight, I really enjoyed that the night before."

Held? What the hell do I look like, a babysitter? Yeah, that's me alright, Mr. Asexual himself..., looks like a man, but *just be my friend*. Hell, I thought I left that image back in Indiana.

"I don't know about this, Nia."

"I won't try anything Eric, I promise."

I won't try anything? Did she just say I won't try anything? What is wrong with this picture? This fine woman trying to convince me a man, a grown ass man, that she won't try anything just to get in my bed. She's treating me like I'm that cool gay friend that many women love to be around. I actually want her to try something. I think. I don't want to be the way Gilligan was to Ginger. She could walk in front of him bucky naked and she knew he wouldn't try a thing. They were on that island for over five years, and he didn't see no parts of the body. She's standing here looking like an extra in a rapp video, and... naw forget that, I need to put my foot down. No more Gilligan! I grabbed her by her small waist, and planted a kiss on her like I had just gotten out of the penitentiary (not that I know anything about that). Luckily, she kissed me back; it would have been pretty embarrassing if she hadn't. This was a serious kiss too. I know it was because when I opened my eyes to look at her, her eyes were closed, she was concentrating on enjoying me. Shit, why am I kissing her thinking about Phelicia. I wonder if she is kissing anybody right now. I wonder what she would do if she knew I was.... Bad idea, the shorts are too loose for me to be standing at attention like this, I just know she can feel it. Just then I heard Cory's door open, but Nia didn't budge, she was still enjoying me.

"Nia!?"

She abroptly stopped, recognizing the voice that recognized her. She let go of my embrace.

"Sheila, girl what's really going on, I didn't know you knew Eric and Corey."

"Small world, small world, girl I would talk to you, but I am kind of in the middle of something right now. I'll call you at work tomorrow, that is if you're not to tired."

"No you didn't, I ain't the one streaking down the hall in my man's robe." Replied Nia as they both shared a laugh and one of those I'm trying to exhale looks when they are talking in code. Nia went into the bathroom, and came out with a towel, and returned to the room where Corey was. She had this devilish grin on her face. My boy is putting in work.

"This is to funny," said Nia.

Funny, I just planted the mother of all kisses on her, and now she is thinking of humor. Not cool. She grabbed my hand and led me to my room.

"Do you ever clean up?"

"I wasn't expecting company."

"You need a made, I can see that already. Did your mother clean up your room for you in Indiana?"

I started to tell her that if she didn't like it, she could go back home, I get tired of people coming into my space and complaining. I didn't force her to come over, and I ain't forcing her to stay. I wanted to say that, but before I could get the first word out, she took off her pants and, well, you know....

She climbed in bed with her pink-laced panties, and tee shirt while I sat there thinking about Phelicia. She had a pair of underwear like that. I wonder what she is doing now?

"What are you thinking about, Eric?"

"You." I lied.

"Well don't think about me, join me."

"Do you expect me to be able to hold you all night, while you are wearing next to nothing? It was different the other night, you had on sweats, but now?"

"You don't think you can control yourself?"

She is playing games; she is being a tease.

"And I would want to because..."

"Because you respect me.?"

"I respect you enough to tell you put your pants back on. I refuse to be teased all night long, I mean look at you, what you expect me to do."

"You mean to tell me, you can't lay next to me all night with out jumping my bones."

You know what, she already told me that she loves my body, two can play that game. I took off my shirt, got under the covers, and then I took off my shorts and my underwear, showed them to her and rolled over on my side to go to sleep. She sat there with her mouth wide open in disbelief.

"Eric, what are you doing?"

I played dumb.

"Huh, you talking to me?"

"Who else would I be talking to, you don't have any clothes on, what are you doing?"

"Let's talk about it, you popped up uninvited, and you are questioning the way I sleep. Corey gets congested when the air is up, so I sleep like this, so I won't get too hot, now be quiet, so I can get some sleep. Do you still want me to hold you?"

She lay there very quiet. She no longer had control of the situation, I did. I could no longer be looked at as the penisless friend, because everything I had was out in the open. She had two choices, embrace my manliness, or get up and leave. Just then, she started to squirm under the sheets. What is she doing? She then showed me something and tossed it to the side. Her shirt, she showed me something else, tossed those too. Her panties. Calling my bluff. I swallowed hard.

"Are you going to hold me or not Eric?"

"Uh, yeah, yeah, I'll hold you, come on."

I was on my back, and she put her head on my shoulder, slid her leg up my thigh, and lay there. I had my arm around her, and there we lay. As I lay there, I felt her soft firm body pressed against mine and I liked it. Her legs were as long as mine, almost. I liked it. She snuggled closer to me, and nuzzled her head between my shoulder and neck. I liked it a lot. She then began to kiss my neck, then my chest then my neck, then my ear and then she whispered.

"I want you."

"Take me" I cornily said back.

She began to take. I liked it.

"Do you have any condoms?"

I looked in the drawer of my nightstand, and got the condoms. She took them out of my hand, and continued to take me. I liked it.

Later on that evening...

WOW! That was great. She was great. I was great. It was great, but I'm feeling guilty. I don't know what she wants from me, and I didn't bother asking. I was so busy trying to be the man, that I wasn't man enough to see where this thing is going. I don't know where I want this to go. I know where my heart is, and it ain't here. As I lie here looking at the rotation of the ceiling fan, with sweat running down the small of my back, I can't help but wonder if I am turning in to Corey. I normally get things out in the open before I sleep with a woman, but tonight, all I wanted open were her legs. She obliged. Corey would hit it and forget it. Just like that. I just told Phelicia that I loved her less than six hours ago, and here I am making love to someone else. That's not cool. That's not me. My mother raised me better than that.

She always told me to treat women like you would want a man to treat my sisters. I wonder what Nia is thinking right now? She looks so innocent. So sweet. She definitely has potential.

I don't think she is a very good listener, but most guys I know don't really express themselves, so maybe she has never had a guy to want her to listen, maybe we could work on that.

I don't even know if she can cook. I did fry the fish the last time we had dinner. I was raised on some good food. Soul Food. Moms could throw down in the kitchen, even when we were on welfare. She even got that Government Cheese to melt. I never thought I would like macaroni and Government cheese, but momma made it work.

She also slept with me after only knowing me for five days, what does that say about her character? But then again, I slept with her after five days too, so what does that say about my character? Maybe all she wanted was an orgasm, and that's it? I don't know what she wants. I do know what I want though, to see Phelicia. Then again, if I want her that badly, why I am laying in my birthday suite with another woman. I wonder if Corey goes through this whenever he sleeps with different women. I'm thirsty. I think I need some cold juice.

Breaking Down the Wall of Resistance

Corey

Wow, that was good. I was good. She was great. I can get used to this. She really enjoys being with me, and I really enjoy her as well. Uh oh, I think Eric is rubbing off on me, cause I keep thinking about her being my woman. My girl. I can't go out like that. It is too many women out there for me to be hung up on one. I mean, usually when I sleep with women, all I can think about is the next one that's going to make my bedsprings, sing. Look at me now....I'M CUDDLING! Normally, I can't wait for them to leave, but this time I don't want her to leave. I can think of a million reasons to make her my one and only, but my reasons for not are few and shallow. I have plenty of women who would love to be right here, but I don't know if I want that anymore. Having one woman is something that I haven't experience since college, and it was all that. But when it ended, I wanted to got to the loudest speaker and scream 'FUCK THE WORLD!'

I honestly think I can put up with her on a regular basis. No guessing games. No games period. She has everything that I need a woman to have, but being with her would be so consuming. I know what she would require from me, but since I am feeling her, I wouldn't mind her having certain expectations. She even likes sports. So what she likes the wrong teams, the Lakers, and the Raiders, she is a fan. I am a Pacer fan, especially since they have a brother coaching them. I am glad Isaiah took the job. That is so funny, The two most popular teams in Indiana, the Pacers and the Hoosiers, both have black coaches. I bet the rednecks in rural Indiana are having a fit, about now. I mean Indiana is the capitol of basketball, even though New Yorkers may dream differently.

Look at her. The look in her face says that she can not think of any other place in the world that she would rather be than with me. She gives me that look all of the time. I like that look. I like her. I think I could fall in....naaaahhh.

"Baby, will you get me some water, I'm thirsty?" she said as she caressed my chest, and kissed my cheek.

"Sure."

Corey & Eric

Eric poured himself a tall glass of apple juice and closed the refrigerator door, as a sleepy eyed Corey walked into the kitchen. Corey was startled when he realized that he was not alone.

"Man, you know good and well that you are too dark to be walking around in the dark like that!" Corey whispered sternly.

"Don't hate on the complexion, you wish you were my color." Eric returned.

"Say partner, I heard you had ya girl Nia in there, did you beat it up?"

"Huh?"

"Did you hit it?"

"Come again?"

"Oh, I'm sorry Pointdexter, did you have sexual intercourse with her?"

Eric looked around the room, he wanted to say yeah, but he had just talked to his friend about Phelicia, and felt like a hypocrite.

"Oh, you can't hear now" an irritated Corey said.

"Yeah man, I did it," he finally admitted before walking past Corey, and plopping on the couch in the living room. His thoughts were on Phelicia, and the fact that he cheated. Or at least he thought he cheated, they were not a couple, so how could it be considered cheating?

"You just got some ass, and you looking like you lost your best friend, what's wrong with this picture?" Asked Corey.

"I don't know man, one minute I'm expressing my love to Phelicia, the next I'm doing the do with Nia." Said Eric in an extreme melancholy voice. He looked up at Corey, waiting for some sarcastic remark about being single, sticking and moving, or his philosophy about women and sex, but he said nothing. He actually looked sympathetic. He sat down on the love seat across from Eric, and didn't say a word. He was dealing with his own issues at the time.

"You alright man?" asked Eric.

"Yeah, I will be."

They both sat in silence. Looking around the room, at the ceiling, avoiding each other's eyes. They knew each other very well, and knew that once they made eye contact, they couldn't lie to each other. A pact that they made in the sixth grade always be honest....with each other. Sitting there, they thought they had very different philosophies about women, but at this moment in time, they were almost as one. They sat there in confusion. Their eyes met, and Corey broke the silence.

" I know that Sheila wants to be my woman, and one side of me wants it too."

"Sooooo, what's the problem?"

"The problem is, I don't know if I am ready for a girlfriend."

They both sat there lost in their thoughts. They both had beautiful, intelligent good black women less than twenty feet away, yet they had no idea what they wanted from them.

"If you were ready, would it be her? Would she be the one?" Asked Eric.

Hesitation, he thought about what he wanted, and

what she had to offer.

Corey finally responded, "yeah, yeah no doubt about it."

"What's stopping you then?"

"I am too young, and not in the mind set of having one woman. Why do I even need to address having one woman? This is Atlanta, Mecca; black women are more plentiful than the peaches here. I love peaches."

"It's not about that man; it's about finding that one woman who can compliment you. That connects with you on a totally different level. A woman that you don't mind letting into your personal space. A woman that you want in your personal space, a woman that with out, your personal space seems empty. Nothing else matters when you are with her, everything around you is manageable when you are with her. I know sex is great, but when you are with that special woman, the sex is better, because you are connected on a higher level... that's what I want."

Midway through Eric's spiel, Corey began to realize that Sheila could be that woman, but he would never admit it, at least not now. He totally didn't respond to what Eric said, on the outside, and thought of a way to keep Eric from getting any further into his head. He asked about Nia.

"What's up with you and Nia?"

"I really don't know. She came over here wanting me to hold her all night, and I was like, hold you, you do realize that I am a man don't you, I do have a workable penis. I ain't getting caught in the friendship zone. She had the audacity to get in my bed in panties and tee-shirt wanting to be held."

Corey reared back on the love seat to try to contain his laughter. Eric, puzzled as ever, wondered what he was laughing at.

"What's so funny?"

"She played you. She wanted to get served so she came over here and got served. End of story."

"And how do you know that?"

"Sheila told me. They hung out the other day, and she told her how horny she was cause she ain't had none in over three months when she broke up with Tank. Any woman that strips down to her bikinis and gets in to your bed wants to be held...after the sex."

"So your saying she knew she wanted some all along?"

"That's exactly what I'm saying. Women want it just as much as men do; they are just a little smoother with theirs as all. That's funny. You probably thought you did something special to convince her to have sex with you, man that's classic. I'm going to bed dog, thanks for the laugh, and if I were you, I'd hit it again, and feel guilty tomorrow some time." Said Corey as he walked down the hall with a cold bottle of water to his bedroom.

He paused briefly outside of the door to think about what Eric said. Was he entering a room that housed a woman that he could connect with on that abstract level that his boy spoke of? He entered the room, confused. Sat down on the edge of the bed awaking Sheila.

"Hey, I thought you got lost."

"You were knocked out, you probably didn't even realize that I was gone."

"I did too, the bed got cold when you left." She said as she grabbed the bottle out of his hand and took a sip. He watched her the whole time, imagining that she were his girlfriend. His heart sped up, and he got a little nervous. He stood up.

"Baby what's wrong, why did you get up?" asked Sheila.

"Oh, I needed to stretch." As he went into a routine of a fake yawn and stretch, his heat still raced. Sheila lay there watching, and when he realized that he could fake it any longer, he climbed into bed with her. She snuggled up against him, and looked him in the eye. Corey returned the glare, and she smiled. She has a beautiful smile. She closed her eyes, put her head on his chest, and closed her eyes. She began to take deep long rhythmic breaths. He looked at her for what seemed like an eternity, and his heart slowed down. He smiled at the sleeping beauty, and felt at peace. Could she be the one? Or would she be one of many. She could be the one. Maybe.

Meanwhile, Eric sat on the couch wondering if he had really been played. He sauntered lazily back to his bedroom only to see that the covers had been kicked off of Nia. He stood in the doorway to witness how the moonlight cascaded over the bronze Nubian sister in his bed. She looked like a work of a art, chiseled by a world-renowned sculptor, with his bed as the canvas. Oh how he admired the black woman. A love that started with his mother, and extended to every other woman that he knew, and even those that he didn't. Even those that he didn't like, he loved, appreciated, admired. He walked to her side of the bed, and picked the covers up off of the floor, and placed them at the foot of the bed, and then he lay next to her. Hey turned to his side and propped his head up on his hand while he admired her slim, curvy figure. He began to caress her slowly. She purred like a kitten and opened her beautiful brown eyes. He began to kiss her all over. She laid back and enjoyed it. She engulfed him. She allowed him to take her to the peak of pleasure while her mind let go of all of the stress that had been mounting up in her life, and in one orgasmic moan; she was on a cloud of ecstasy. His mind was on Phelicia, pretending that he was making love to her.

The Morning After

- Eric -

I must have been sleeping hard, Nia is gone and I am just realizing it. I wonder what time she left? She didn't even bother to wake me, that's cold. You don't leave like that without waking somebody up. I feel like a hoe. Just joking. What's that, a note?

"Had a great time, talk to you later?"

Had a great time, that's the kind of stuff that you say after you get off of a ride at Six Flags or something. I bet that's probably all I was to her, a ride. She is not the one. The phone is ringing, it better be her, I know she didn't have to work, cause she doesn't work weekends.

"Hello?"

"Good Morning, Mr. Dukes."

"Phelicia, is that you?"

"Yeah, are you still sleeping Eric, it's almost 8:30."

"I actually just got up a minute ago. You sound awfully perky this morning."

"You know, I'm an early bird. I just got back from jogging a few miles."

Jogging, good, big girls don't jog a few miles, so I know she's still fine.

"Good for you, I need to hurry up and join the gym."

"You didn't get pudgy on me did you Eric, in college you were a firm 195 pounds."

"Well, I did put on some weight, but I ain't pudgy though, I weigh around 210."

"Well, after college, I put on a few pounds myself, 30 to be exact, but I got myself back together, now, I am back to 135."

Thank God.

"That's good to hear, how was your evening?"

"Relaxing, I got home from my aerobics class, finished reading my book, and chilled. I thought about you, reminiscing about old times, looking at the pictures from college. What did you do? Anything interesting?"

I can't tell her what I really did, and I don't want to lie. I actually have no choice but to manufacture the truth.

"I watched the *"Best Man,"* listened to some music, got in bed."

Well, I didn't lie, I did get in bed, I just wasn't alone.

"Sounds relaxing, guess what?"

"What?"

"I have a long weekend coming up, and a Delta buddy pass. If it's cool with you, I can come up there from Thursday night, until Sunday night. What do you think?"

"What do I think? I think you need to be on the first thing smoking! I wish you could come now, I can't wait to see you."

"I can't wait to see you either, but we need to set some ground rules before I come out there."

Ground rules, I wonder what she is talking about?"

"I'm listening"

"Well, I don't want us to sleep together, so I don't mind staying in hotel. If we sleep together, that will give us a false sense of what's really going on. Is that cool with you?"

"I will do whatever I have to do to...um, yeah that's fine."

"Do what you have to do to what Eric?"

"Make this situation comfortable. Make it work."

"Are you sure?"

"As deodorant"

" Still corny I see, well, I need to make some arrangements, I will give you a call early in the week, O.K.?

"O.K,"

"Bye Eric, I…"

"I what?"

"Love you."

"Love you too." Click.

I flopped back on the bed elated that I would finally see my true love, only to ruffle the cover and sheets. The ruffling of the sheets conjured up the aroma from last night's escapade. It smelled like perfume and sex. Sex, not love. What does love smell like? Hopefully I will find out next week. I know she said that she wanted us not to sleep together, but you can not control a fire with gasoline. Together we were gasolines. We always made love like it would be our last time. I'm glad that our last time was not our last time, and I hope our next time feels like the first time.

Anyway, I need to get this smell out of my bed, because it is making me sick. I began to strip the bed, and out fell the condoms from last night. Well, at least I was protected.

Boy's Night Out

Corey

That Georgia sun is awfully bright, my eyes are closed, and I can still tell that it's bright. It's not even July yet. I had a great time last night. I wonder if last night will be our last night. I know we can't go on like this without something changing. I opened my eyes. Sheila is staring right at me.

"How long have you been staring at me?"

"Not long, you look real innocent when you are sleeping."

"I am innocent."

"Last night you were proven guilty, and judging by the tent you are making under the sheets, you must wanna go to trial again. Or do you just have to pee?"

"Both."

"Well, pee first, and we will set up another court date in a few minutes.

She laughed after she said this, obviously amused at the exchange that we just had. I threw something on and went to the bathroom. I hate having to use the restroom when the soldier is at attention. You see, the toilet is down south, and the soldier is facing north. Problem. The worst thing, other than being kicked there by baby shoes, is trying to bend a boner so I can hit the target. Ouch, damn, missed the target, hit the backboard.

Nothing that a little Pine-sol and a sponge can't cure. Women can just sit down and chill, but not us. Speaking of women, I know Sheila wants to spend the day with me, but I don't know if that is a good idea, especially since I am not ready to be on lock down. I mean I am feeling her, but I need to sort some things out first. I washed my hands, wiped the seat, and went back into the room. She is still laying down looking as sexy as ever.

"Say Corey, what are you doing today?"

Here it goes, I know she wants to do a couple things. Can't go out like that though.

"I told Corey I would take him to Run n' Shoot to play some ball today. Why what are you doing?"

"I have to show a house around noon, then I am meeting a friend for lunch."

"What!? You mean to tell me that you got a date?"

"Not really a date, just lunch with a friend."

"A friend who happens to be a guy?"

"Yeah."

"Looks like a date, sounds like a date, you got a date."

"Wait a minute, we aren't getting jealous over a simple lunch date are we."

Starts out as lunch, ends up as breakfast in bed. How is she going do me one night, and have a date with some other nigga the next, that's foul?

"Naw, jealous about what, if that's what you want to do, you go right ahead"

See, that's why I am a player, these women don't want to act right.

"What are you doing, I thought you were coming back to bed."

"Nah, I got things to do, plus I don't want to make you late for your little date with your boyfriend."

The word 'little' always demeans the integrity of the situation.

"Boyfriend?"

"Yeah you heard me, boyfriend."

"I don't have a boyfriend. The man I want is enjoying his bachlorhood, so what's a girl to do? When you want to step up to the plate, you let me know, until then, if a gentlemen wants to have lunch with me, I have every right to except."

"Whatever."

"Whatever? What, Corey, are you my man?"

Ooops, I am back into a wall now. I gave her the brush-off look with the swatting flies hand to match.

"Well, lets put it like this, when you want to be my man you let me know, but don't expect me to wait around too long. I know right now you and I are having a little consensual fun, but eventually it will time for me to get out of this phase of having fun and get serious. I would like to get serious with you, so the ball is in your court. And don't bother acting like you got somewhere to go, because I am leaving anyway, I am going to the Waffle House for a pecan waffle and some southern hospitality."

And just like that, she picked up her things, and scooted off to the bathroom. I walked out and into the kitchen, only to see Eric on the couch watching Sports Center.

"Trouble on the home front, kid?" he asked.

"I'll tell you about it in a minute" as I pointed to the restroom.

"Oh, I hear you. Do you think the Spurs can beat the Lakers in a seven game series because...."

I don't know who in the hell she think she is? I really don't think she knows. Well, she's about to find out. I don't care if she has a date or not, I can find one, as a matter of fact, I will find one. Two can play that game.

"Dog, where you at, you ain't heard nothin I said."

"Huh?"

"Forget it, Corey. You zonin."

The toilet flushed, the water ran, the door opened, enter Sheila.

"Eric, what time you all playin' ball today?"

"Playin ball, I didn't know we were"

Sheila sucked her teeth and looked at me with a pity me type grin, then shook her head. I avoided her eyes, she turned toward Eric.

"Nia still sleep?"

"Nia left early when I was sleep, I don't know where she is?"

"Classic Nia" said Sheila.

"What do you mean by that?"

"I can't put my girl out there like that, but since I like you I will say this, keep your eyes open, and be careful. You seem like you have a heart. She is a good girl and all, but make sure you ask plenty of questions. You have a heart."

That's the second time she said that. Hint taken. Now get gone. You messin up my vibe.

She leaned down and gave me a surpassingly full kiss. I didn't want it, but I love her lips so accept them. She winked and said, "I'll call you later."

I said a nonchalant O.K. and she left.

"What was that all about" asked Corey.

"She gotta date today, let's go play some ball."

"Hold up man, you not upset that she got a date are you?"

"Yo kid, let's go play some ball, you with it or not?"

"You are actually upset that she has a date."

Hell yeah, I'm upset.

"Nope, not one bit, for every one date she can get, I can get three."

"The player got played, that's classic! I bet you probably thought she would be all on your jock for some quality time today, didn't you."

"Later for you, duck. Are you playin' ball or what?"

"Yeah, I'm playin ball, but don't try to get off the subject, you get a kick out of it when you think I'm the one with the female problems, but when the shoe is on the other foot, you wanna get all sensitive I see. That's cool though, I'll leave you alone, but don't bring it to me later about mine."

"It ain't that deep, she's got a date, life goes on."

He was right, and he knew it. I wouldn't dare let him know that he was right though. I talk too much trash.

"Guess what?"

"What?"

"Phelicia is coming next Thursday."

"Seriously?"

"Yep."

"You don't waste no time, do you, dog?"

"A minute wasted is gone forever."

"What in the hell did you just say?"

"Nothin Einstein... nothin at all."

"You don't think that this is kind of soon, I mean, you did just get with Nia last night, I think you should enjoy yourself a little first."

"Corey, will you make up your mind. You and my mom are the ones that encouraged me in the first place, now you wanna throw salt in my game."

I got enough shit on my mind right now; I don't have time to debate with a guy who thinks he is never wrong.

"You're right man, do your thing. You go head and get your gear on so we can go play."

He went back to the room. I sat there angry. I don't have a right to be, but I am. Sheila isn't thinking about me, she's with some other cat.

He was ready in no time flat.

"I'm ready, but we need to stop and pick up something to eat, I am starving."

"That's cool."

We stopped at Chick Fila, for a biscuit, and that world famous lemonade before getting on the I-285.

"Yo man, put some music on, or something."

I didn't even realize that it wasn't on. I wonder what Sheila is doing now?

"What kind of music you wanna hear, jazz, hip-hop,

R&B or what."

"Dang, it feels good to have choices in what to hear, at home it is nothing like this. Put it on Hot 107.9, I'm in the mood for some hip-hop. That's what I'm talking about, Ludicrous, cause I'm gone be throwing some boes today myself."

"Huh?"

"Man forget it, that girl has your nose wide open, you can't say nothing about me, you need to turn in your players card, I think it expired."

"Later for you, I ain't thinking about her? You must have forgotten my name? I'm the man."

I better get some gas.

"I need some gas man, you want some Gatorade?"

"Yeah, that's cool."

I pulled up to a pump.

"Eric, look at that."

"Look at what?"

"That sistah pumpin gas in Maxima up there. That's why you can't get hung up on none of these women, because they are too replaceable. Watch this, I am going to get my players card renewed."

I stepped out of the car. The pressure was on, because I told Eric what my intentions were, so I could not return empty handed. I had to earn back my player's card.

I strolled to the car using my 'it will be a pleasure for you to talk to me' walk.

"Hello" I said to the petite sistah in the Spelman shirt.

"Hi" she replied as she continued to pump gas, not even looking my direction. I noticed she had Ohio plates on her car.

"Tell me something, how do the summers in Atlanta, compare to the ones in Ohio."

She smiled, pretty smile. Small gap in her front teeth, but that gave her face character. She is definitely easy on the eyes.

"I think the heat here is moist, the heat up there is dry."

"Yeah, I agree."

"You agree? What do you know about Ohio heat."

"Well, I am from Indianapolis, and I have family in Dayton, so I spent many summers there." I replied.

"Dayton? I am from Dayton."

Bingo. I still got it, never lost it, need to loan the mammas boy some of it.

"Is that right, I used to go to the Boys Club off of Randolph all the time."

"I grew up off of Dennison Street. I spent a lot of time at the Boys Club."

"Small world, huh?" I said. I knew I had her. Time to close the deal.

"I'm sorry, my name is Corey."

"Nice to meet you, Corey, I'm Kacy."

"How long you been in Atlanta, Kacy?"

I looked back at the car and gave Eric a 'how you like me now' glance.

"I went to school here, graduated two years ago, and decided to make this my home, how about you?"

"I moved here two years ago as well."

"Well, I am done pumping gas, it was nice meeting you Corey."

"Yeah, it was nice meeting you too. May I call you sometimes?"

"Sure, that would be nice, let me give you my number."

"I'll call you later."

"O.K."

We exchanged smiles, and she drove off. I pumped the gas, and got in the car. I noticed Eric looking at me in obvious admiration as well as with a slight touch of awe. It ain't easy being *the man*, but someone has to do it. I finally looked at Eric, smoothed out my goatee, and coolly said.

"Sheila who?"

Things are Happening Fast

-Eric -

I think there are definitely going to be pros and cons about living in Atlanta, for example, why are there so many damn Peachtree Streets in the city. How uncreative can one be? Why are there so many one ways in downtown Atlanta? What if I don't want to go that way? Why are there so many traffic jams, all day every-day? Why is it that there can be accident on the other side of the median, yet people who are going the opposite way feel inclined to stop to look at it? Why is everyone referred to as shorty...even tall people. On the other hand the weather is as beautiful as the women. Jobs seem to be plentiful. There is a radio station for everybody. There always seems to be a concert, a play, or somebody famous in town The Braves are good, the Falcons are unpredictable, and the Hawks suck. I mean, I'm glad my homeboy Allen Henderson is doing his thing on a consistent basis, but other than that, I am not impressed. One good thing about it though, once your at the bottom, the only place to go is up, that is unless you have a shovel. But since I am here, I will root for the home team. There is also a club for every occasion, I mean there are over seven clubs jumping on every weekend, starting on Thursday. Speaking of clubs, I wonder where Corey is taking me tonight.

"This is it, dawg." Said Corey.

"This is what?"

"This is *Run n' Shoot,* a ball players pulpit."

"With this high crime rate in Atlanta and all of this glass, they need to call it Run n' Get Shot"

I always had a fear of a lot of glass. I have drivebyafobia (is that a word?) It all started when I watched that movie *'Colors'* back in the day

"Don't stress it, dawg. It's cool, just bring you're A-game with you, cause it's on."

"I got mine, you better get yours. Yo man, where we going tonight?"

By this time we are walking to into the gym, and there is his boy Roger, the one who D-jayed the party.

"We're going to the spot."

The spot, which spot

"Yo Rog, what's up, baby. You better lace em up tighter than that, cause I'm breaking ankles."

They exchanged pleasantries (trash talk) while they embraced, the way brother's do.

"Eric, what's shaken, baby?" Said an enthusiastic Roger. I like him, he seems genuine. You can tell by his eyes. Real sincere.

"Let's go put our names down so we can run together."

"That's cool." I pretended to know what they were talking about, but I was clueless. My motto has always been, fake it till you make it. I was good at faking it.

We stretched out until our names where called. We were all on the same team with two other guys; one was an overweight weekend warrior who was 45 pounds, and 10 years past his prime. The other guy looked the part; he was at least 6'6 and weighed around 245, built like a wall. He was defiantly a baller.

Our first couple of shots were bricks, but the Larry Johnson look-a-like rebounded both times, and put it back in. One time dunking the ball and a couple opponents went flying. Come to find out this guy flunked out of Georgia State and never went back. He was on full scholarship, and was almost assured a spot on someone's NBA roster if he could just complete a season. He flunked out before basketball season ever started. He now works the graveyard shift at the Super Wal-Mart. I would say he was a wasted talent, but dude comes in real handy when it comes to getting those king-sized sheets on the top shelf. Anyway, back to the game, the game was relatively close, at first, but once we learned each other's game, we ran off eight straight points. Roger was an excellent jump shooter, Corey was good at driving to the bucket, and I was good in the post. The old dude had an old school game. Came to find out he played for Jackson State in the early 80's and he was an extremely good point guard. He was slow, but used defensive angles to his advantage, didn't make any mistakes, and had an adequate jump shot. We won four straight games until we were run off of the court by a bunch teenagers from Mays high school. They only won because we were extreamly tired, at least that is what I keep telling myself. We shook hands with the other guys on the team and headed it to the car.

"Yo Rog, we'll meet you at the spot around 9:30, from there we will hit Vegas Nights." Said Corey.

"Alright Doc, I'm there. I would bring Toney, but he trippen about Sheila, and I ain't down for no drama."

"Drama, I thought he had a girl? Not that I care, it ain't that serious."

"He does, but you taking Sheila hurt his pride, he'll be O.K. But when he gets drunk, he starts talking crazy, so later for him."

"Aiight man, whatever."

We got in the car and headed toward the highway. I kind of like living with Corey; he is like a brother I never had. We get along well eventhough we are as different as night and day. The way I slept with Nia though, I don't know how different we are.

"Say dog, when I get home I'm going to take a quick nap before we hit the spot."

"What is the spot?"

"The ballet."

"The ballet? We are going to a ballet?"

"Chill out, and stop asking questions, you will enjoy it.

Please believe it.

Ahhh, that shower felt good. I don't know what was more soothing, the shower or the Miles Davis C.D. Tough call. I guess I will take a quick nap too, I need to have my energy up for later, and I'll probably end up driving back if Corey has a drink or two. He just recently started drinking, and even though he doesn't drink heavily, he gets sleepy after a small sip. *Yawn. Zzzzzzzzz...*

"How was class today?" I said to Phelicia as I picked her up from her 4:00 class in my 1983 black Monte Carlo.

"The same ole same ole"

She seems upset about something. She had an edge to her voice. She gets upset an awful lot about simple stuff lately, and most times I can't see it coming. Not only does she get upset, but she holds it for a long time, won't talk to me, and I can't stand it.

"What's wrong with you?"

"You must think I'm stupid don't you?"

Here we go again.

"What?"

"I saw the way Lillie looks at you, what's really going on?"

"Nothing is going on, what are you talking about?"

"Why is she in your group?"

"Dr. Johnson assigned those groups, I had nothing to do with it."

"Why you all smiling in her face like that, and why is she flirting with you?"

"I smile all the time, and she does not flirt with me"

"Well you need to stop smiling in her face, you smile at everyone, and you are a fool if you don't see her flirting with you"

"Lillie and I have been cool since freshman year, and believe me, there is nothing going on. I am with who I want to be with.".

"Look, I've been cheated on before, and I ain't goin through that again"

"Have I cheated on you?"

"*I don't put nothing past men, you will do what ever you want to do.*"

"*What, you don't trust me or something, if we don't have trust, we don't have anything.*"

"*Take me home Eric, I don't have time for this*"

"*Time for what? What did I do*"

"*I found her number at your apartment Eric, explain that one?*"

"*We are in a group together; we have to call each other to meet. On that same paper you saw David's, Romona's, Jazzmine's, and Robert's number.*"

"*Yeah, I saw Romona all in your face too.* "

"*You are talking crazy, Romona White from Mississippi? She's been dating Rodney for the longest, they might as well be married.*"

"*Take me home, now!*"

"*What is wrong with you? I told you that wasn't anything going on. I am with you all day everyday. When could I possibly cheat?*"

"*I don't have time for this, take me home!*"

I took her home, and she didn't talk to me for two days. She came back latter and apologized for overreacting, and I accepted it. Incidents like this happen all the time. All the time about any little thing. She likes the way that I treat her, says I am a rare breed, but treats me like I'm disposable. I am really tired of her treating me any ole kind of way when I have not done anything. Sometimes I wonder if it is worth it. There is no doubt in my mind that she loves me, but I don't like the way she shows it. I want her to be my future at times, but other times I just want to be as far away from her as possible. This is my life I am talking about; I can stand turmoil on the home front. Blackmen catch to much hell in the outside world, to put up with that negative energy once at home. It's only two months until graduation, if we don't get any better, I can't see us going any further. I love her, but I love myself more.

"Yo Eric, pick up the phone." Yelled a sleepy voiced Corey.

"Hello" I said.

"Hey Eric, did I wake you?"

"Yes, you did." I said in a matter of fact tone. You didn't have the decency to wake me when you should have, so you get no props for waking me now.

"Oh, I'm sorry, anyway, what are you doing tonight?"

This is Nia, and I don't think I am even going to let her know that she bothered me.

"Tonight, I'm hanging with the fellas."

"Oh, I see, boys night out huh?"

"You got it." I sounded disturbed, I didn't want to sound like that, but I did. I also just tipped my hand that I was somewhat pissed.

"Listen, I want to explain about leaving like I did."

I cut her off mid sentence, "No explanation needed Nia, I'm just glad that it wasn't me who left you like that. I would have been every breed of dog that you could think of, but I guess it's cool when women do it huh? Well don't sweat it, I now understand the ground rules, so it's cool."

"No Eric, those aren't the rules..."

I cut her off again, "Wait a minute, you set the tone, so now you gotta deal with it"

"Eric let me explain."

"No need for explanations, I mean, men have been making booty calls for as long I can remember, so it's only right for a sistah to make one every now and then, so it's cool."

"Eric"

"Nia, listen" I said as I tried to sound as cold as I could " keep your cell phone on and maybe you can meet me at whatever club we go to, and we can talk then, but I am going back to sleep for now, I am tired."

Silence

"O.K., but don't forget to call me, we really need to talk."

Later that evening...

Corey and I drove north on I-285 and exited Bankhead Highway. I had heard a lot of things about Bankhead, and it wasn't all good. He made a right off of the highway, then another quick right. I saw a liquor store on the right, and a place called the Blue Flame on the left. I read the sign, and saw the words adult entertainment on the sign as well. I heard all sorts of tales about Magic City and Gentleman's Club, but I have never heard of the Blue Flame. This is why he called it the ballet, because they are dancing. Duh!

"I don't think you are ready for this dog," said a grinning Corey. "This definitely ain't Indiana."

I know Corey, and when he has this look on his face, it's time for me to be afraid. Very afraid. We walked up to the door and this huge security guard patted me down, damn near violated me, and took mine and Corey's admission. We walked inside, and on stage was this woman that made me stop in my tracks. Literally. He was right; I wasn't ready for this. She was magazine gorgeous. *Jet* beauty gorgeous. Tall, muscular legs, nice butt, and breast that said ëas perfect as we are, I don't mind you staring'. I know that music was on, but I couldn't hear it. It was if she was dancing in slow motion, and everything around her was a blur. Oh, my goodness, she was damn near perfect. I was frozen in her beauty. I was in the presence of greatness. I can't understand for the life of me, from looking at what I was witnessing, why brothas loved white women. Not all brothas, but the ones who do, need to spend some time right where I am right now. I felt like I was a deer with car coming at me full blast with the bright lights on. Frozen. I heard laughter faintly in my right ear, it sounded like Corey, but all of my five senses were focused on this woman on stage. I was in love.

"Close your mouth, and lets go grab a seat, dog. I knew

you weren't ready for this!"

"What?... huh?" I know he said something. He then grabbed my arm while leading me to a seat on the side.

"Corey, do you actually you see that sistah on stage, she is unbelievable."

"Slow ya role, dog. You ain't seen nothin yet, look around."

"I mean, I can't believe this, you can actually come witness this any time... any day! This is crazy. I would spend all of my money in here. I can't come here often, I would go broke. You see her on stage? She can have all of my money..." I went rambling for the next few minutes when Corey finally turned to me and said, "Eric, will you relax before you have a stroke?"

And low and behold, there were over fifteen women walking around in practically nothing, who were just as beautiful as she. They came in all shapes, sizes and colors. Any thing that your heart, and penis, desired was walking around. I thought I'd died and gone to Hugh Heffners house on Black Bunny day.

"Is it always like this?" I asked Corey. I know I sounded like a kid who just arrived in Disney Land, amazed at seeing all of his story book heroes up close and in person.

"It actually will get better, it's only eight o'clock, and the Saturday night shift is when the top guns work. Checked that out"

He pointed to a small petit innocent girl, walking next to a tall voluptuous sistah with a duffel bag who went in the dressing room.

"You gotta excuse me dog, this is absolutely unbelievable" I said to Corey as I dapped him up. And before I could finish giving him a pound, a tall dark and built, brick house of a sistah approached the seat next to me, put a towel on the chair and sat right next to me. I looked at Corey with a "now what" look on my face.

He smiled and whispered "relax, she's only a woman."

Only a woman, it's not everyday that a fine but ass

naked beautiful woman sits next to you in a red g-string and a bra on. I mean I have seen stuff like this on TV, but this is real life. I mean, you can't appreciate the size of Shaquille O'Neal, until you stand next to him. I stood next to him and I felt like a black Stuart Little.

"How you doin?" she asked.

"I'm good, and you?"

"I'm fine, my name is Chocolate, what's yours?"

Chocolate? I always did have a weakness for chocolate.

"I'm Eric." I said as I extended my hand to shake hers.

"Wow you have soft hands. You seem out of place, this your first time?"

"Yeah, it is."

"Would you like a table dance, Eric."

"Tell me how this works first."

"Well, I take off my clothes and dance for you for five dollars a song."

"Sounds good to me."

"I'll wait until the next song. Is that O.K. with you?"

"That's cool."

Note to self, I have a hard time saying 'no' to women with hardly any clothes on.

"Yo, dog. Pace yourself, we got an hour to kill in here." Said Corey.

An hour my ass, I ain't ever leaving, you can forward my mail right here.

"Eric, did you here me?"

"Yeah dude, I heard you, I'm trying to concentrate."

Just then, the DJ Put on some Florida booty shake music. I think it was Trick Daddy. And with that, Chocolate stood up, all 5 feet 8 inches of finess, and took of what little she had on, and went to work. I didn't know where to look; each part of her body was involved in an event that I didn't want to miss. It was like sitting in the very front row of a 3D-movie theater. You can only see bits of the screen at once; I wanted the full view. I couldn't believe it. Except for her shoes (which were extremely high heels) she was just as naked as the day she was born. She moved with the syncopated rhythm of some exotic African dance ritual, isolating different parts of her body to the beat for my viewing pleasure. I felt my eyes drying out, cause I was scared to blink for the fear that I would miss something. Don't get me wrong, I've seen naked women before, but always naked with preservations about some aspect of their appearance. This woman was naked and confident! Most of the women I saw naked were trying to cover up something. This women wasn't covering up a thing. And just when I thought I saw it all, she turned around and showed me one (of many) reasons that I just love black women. The structure of her posterior anatomy (her butt) was practically majestic. It illuminated the room, I felt like I was in the presence of greatness. And to top it off, she made it clap. Yes, clap! She made her booty clap. I sat there with my mouth wide open, giving her my own private standing ovation. How in the hell did she do that? My mind immediately went toward how she could possibly use her superb physical skills in the bedroom. The song ended. She put on her g-string, what a lucky piece of cloth. I put a five in her garter belt, and she asked me if I wanted another one.

"I need to recuperate from that one first."

She laughed. "Did you enjoy it?"

"You have no idea."

"So Eric, how long you been in Atlanta?"

She remembered my name. She is a good listener.

"I've been her for almost two weeks."

"Really, you like it so far?"

"You just made it a whole lot better. I'm sorry, that probably sounded like a line."

"No it didn't, I can tell when someone is sincere. I can read your body language."

She seems like she's kind of smart. I wonder if this is all she does. I want to have an intelligent conversation with her, but her breast keep waving at me. I find myself wanting a glass of chocolate milk (that was a joke).

"What do you do in your spare time?" I asked her.

"Spare time? What is that? When I am not in here, I am studying or in class."

"Class! You mean you are in school?"

"Don't sound so surprised, I am a junior at Clark Atlanta, majoring in political science. This job helps me pay tuition and rent."

"The next booty on duty is my girl, Chocolate!" yelled the DJ over Ray J's new joint.

"Well Eric, that's me, don't move, I will be back when my set is up" she said as she kissed me on the cheek, and scurried to the stage with all eyes on various parts of her anatomy.

I looked at Corey while he was getting a dance from some petite high yellow sistah with large breast and an ample butt. She was really getting into it with him. Her dance was a lot more suggestive, she even grinded on his lap for five seconds at a time when the oversized bouncer wasn't looking. Corey seemed to enjoy that part the most. When the dance was over, he slipped her a ten instead of a five. I gathered that the extracurricular lap activities were an extra five. I guess you get what you pay for.

"You alright, kid?" asked Corey.

"Yeah man, just trippen off of these beautiful women in here. That girl that danced for me is a student at Clark."

"Don't believe that shit, man. These hoes will tell you anything to get in your pocket. It's all about the money with them, and don't let anybody tell you anything different."

"I don't know, dog. She seemed pretty sincere. I see you back to callen em hoes again, huh?"

"I callem like I see them."

I shook my head with a disgusted look on my face at

Corey, this look always agitates him, he replied.

"Damn momma's boy! You *do* realize that some people will tell you a lie to get what they want sometimes, don't you. Have you always been that naive? Don't let these hoes get in your head like that! You are here to see some ass. Period. Don't get caught into any deep philosophical conversations with them, because all of their conversations lead back to money, and how they can get it from you. First of all, they are naked. So what head are you thinking with? Secondly, their job is to do all the things your woman won't do. Or, at least, make you think that they will do all of the things that your woman won't do. And once your money is gone... so are they. Don't get it twisted. So when they tell you that they are in school, they are. They are trying to school you out of your money!"

"I hear you." I said that not because I agreed with him, but I didn't want to hear any more of his sermon. I know you can't lump all people into the same category. Everyone has different circumstances. She may be in school, who am I to judge? All I know is, she seemed nice, and if she wants to dance, I *will* watch. And if she wants to talk, I *will* listen and if she wants to do anything else... I am down for that too.

Chocolate was finished, and she headed toward the dressing room. Corey had been joined by Roger, but I didn't see him come in. The disc jockey gave him a shout out, and a couple of girls ran to Roger like they knew him. Corey was getting another dance from a girl who had that innocent, girl next door look about her, and she was working up a sweat. He told me to pace myself, yet he is on his third table dance, and second beer.

Chocolate came back out and ignored five brothers who wanted her attention, and she sat by me. I felt so special. I began to look at her with admiration, I don't know why, but I was glad she came back. She handed me a piece of paper with her number on it, but the name Chocolate wasn't on it. It had what was apparently her birth name, Stephanie. I smiled at her.

"You have such nice teeth, did you wear braces as a kid?"

"No, I didn't, but thank you for the compliment. I would start paying you compliments, but we would be here all night."

"You are so sweet," she said as she pulled he chair closer to mine.

Just then, Corey tapped me on my shoulder and whispered, "Could you take her home to mom?"

I shot him an evil look; he didn't have to say that. That ruined the whole mood. He was persecuting this girl because of her job. That was wrong.

"Why you say some ignorant shit like that, man? I am only talking to the girl!"

"I know how you are, and I don't want you to loose sight of reality, besides, you know what they say."

"No, Corey! What is it they say?" I said sarcastically.

"You can't turn a hoe into a housewife."

" Later for you, man. You handle your business, and I'll handle mine."

"Don't try to reason with me, you the one who had two beers. I don't need no alcoholic knowledge, right now!"

"Nigga, ain't nobody drunk. Stop getting all sensitive and shit. I'm just havin some fun, it's the weekend baby!" He said as he gave me a pat on the back and smiled.

I smiled back; maybe I was loosing site of reality. What did I really want from this sistah? I didn't know her, or anything about her, other than that she was drop dead gorgeous, and half-naked.

"Ooh, I love this song, can I dance for you again Corey?"

The song was Musique SoulChild's Love. I liked it too.

"Be my guest."

She slowly stood up, provocatively undressed and began to dance. This time I looked her in her eyes, and they were captivating, yet sad. She had sad eyes; I wonder why she was so sad. The eyes are supposed to be the mirror of the soul. I wonder if her soul is struggling against what her present reality is? I guess she is sad because she has such a good mind and heart, but all we see is her body. Maybe she feels degraded. I wonder what she is thinking, she is smiling on the outside, but I know it's fake. I then let my eyes venture to other parts of her, and my thoughts went directly to sex. I imagined what it would be like to be in bed with her. Is she as confident one on one as she is in here? Can she duplicate those same movements horizontally? She mouthed the words of the song, and I could tell that she wanted to be loved. How could she find true love working in here? Maybe that is why she looks so sad. If I did give her a call, would I be too afraid to introduce her to my mother? If this same woman were a librarian, would I hesitate to call her? Is she a bad person, or a hoe, cause she works in here? The song ended. She dressed and sat down.

"My feet are killing me."

"I guess so, I don't see how you can dance on those stilts."

"A girl's gotta do what a girl's gotta do." She replied.

Yeah, but do you have to do this?

"Thanks for the number... you caught me off guard with that," I said, in a genuine tone.

"I normally don't give my number out like that, but you seemed different."

Is that a line? I wonder if she is just saying that to get more money.

"Yo dog, it's time to bounce." Said Corey.

Bounce, I don't want to leave! I will stay here until it closes down, I don't want to leave! I felt like throwing a tantrum like my little rock head cousin, Cedric does when he doesn't get his way. But I didn't.

"Stephanie, you mind if I call you Stephanie?" I asked.

"I don't mind, I'd rather you call me that than Chocolate."

"O.K., Stephanie, we are getting ready to go, but I will give you a call sometimes."

"O.K., call me tomorrow after church, I guess around 3:00."

"Sure, I'll do that."

She stood up with me and gave me a really nice hug. Really nice. She pressed her perfect half-nude body against mine, and I tried to savor the moment. This hug lasted an awfully long time. So long, she looked at me in a surprised, yet satisfied, 'please do that again soon' look.

"Let's go, man. I don't want to be in line." Said Roger

We walked out of the door, and headed to our cars. With all the money this place makes, you'd think they do something about this parking lot.

"Where are we headed now, Corey?" I asked.

"I don't know. Yo Rog, we going to Club ESSO, Vegas Nights, or Liquid?"

"I got us on the list at ESSO, so lets hit them up."

"The list?" I said, "if we are on the list, why do have to leave here, I was feeling it."

"That's why we left, rookie." replied Corey. "You were feeling it a little too much. I didn't want you spend all of your little savings in there."

Am I Corrupting My Boy?

Corey

I really need to watch my boy. I mean, I knew that he was a strip club virgin and all, but he worried me. I've never seen him behave like that. His eyes, when he looked at those women, were that of a blind man that was just blessed with the gift of sight after 25 years of total darkness. That's what his momma gets for sheltering him like that. He got a real taste of freedom now, and has no experiences to draw from. He needs to understand that all that glitters ain't gold, every attractive woman that gives him the time of day, doesn't deserve the energy that he puts toward getting to know them. Then again, he treats everyone with comfort. I know one thing though; I will take it upon myself to expose him to as many women as possible. Speaking of women, I wonder how Sheila's little date went. Not that I care, I am just curious as all.

"You ever been to this club?" asked Eric.

"Yeah, I've been here a few times."

"How is it?"

"It's actually jumping. Hot 107.9 broadcasts live from there every Saturday night," I replied, as I turned the radios dial to that station. And as usual, the music was hyped. The Host of the party, I think his name is Surcy, kept talking about how the ladies always out number the men. They get in free before ten, so I guess so. I am not complaining though, the more women, the better. It has been my finding that at most clubs, the party is at it's peak from 10:30 until around 12:30, after that it seems as if the men began to outnumber the men, and the women who are still there after 1:00 am are so tired of the pestering brothers, that they are irritated, and refuse to give the average brother the time of day. Not that I am the average brother.

We parked in the makeshift parking lot, and got out. The line was full of ladies trying to get in free. I bet these same women who are getting in free, are the main ones begging for a free drink later. Buy your own damn drink. Better yet, buy me one!

"I think I am going to like Atlanta," said Eric as he scanned the lines of scantly dressed, sassy looking attractive black women.

"Don't get to used to it, dog. You trying to settle down with Phelicia, remember?"

"Oh, so I can't like Atlanta with her here?"

"Yeah, but you can't get the full effect like I can, so don't push up too much, you know how jealous she is."

"She ain't that bad."

"Yeah, and hell ain't that hot." I replied.

"You probably know from experience, don't you." He shot back.

"The only experiences that I have are with your sister!" I laughed.

"Oh, I see you got jokes, huh?"

We shared a lighthearted laugh as we entered the club. Since the ladies had their own free line, the guys got in quickly. The business savvy club manager let the ladies in a few at a time, this kept a nice line of honey's on the outside, which will attract any club-seeking brotha. This also cuts down on the amount of ladies who entered free. The cop at the door patted us down, while the dreadlock wearing cutie took our money. The inside of the club wasn't very packed, so me Eric and Roger took a seat in the lobby area as we watched the women come in. They checked us out, and we checked them out. We exchanged smiles and eye contact with the exuberant crowd of ladies who got in free. I didn't want anything else to drink, I had two beers already, and I didn't like that comment that Eric made about my alcoholic logic. Just because my dad drank a lot, doesn't mean that I will. Besides, I just started experimenting, and it doesn't do anything for me. It won't be a habit.

Roger broke the silence. "Eric, you like the Blue Flame, huh, son?"

"No doubt, man. I am still trippen on how fine they are."

"Don't trip son, the A.T.L. is like that. Once you get over the initial shock, you'll settle down."

"I hear you."

"What was that girl talking bout, I think her name was Chocolate?" asked Roger.

"Not much, man. You know, about school and stuff like that."

"She gave you her number, you gone call her or what?"

"I don't know, man, I might."

What ever. He will probably call first thing tomorrow morning, he ain't foolin me one bit.

Roger and Eric kept the conversation flowing, I tried to join in, but my thoughts kept heading back to Sheila. I played that Boys II Men C.D. and all that stands out in my mind is the Chorus, "Don't let real love pass you by." I wonder if she thinks that she is my real love? I do keep thinking about her. I wonder what it would be like to be in a committed relationship?

"Hey you, you following me?" said a seductive female voice.

I turned around and recognized the petite beauty to be the one and only Kacy, from the gas station earlier.

"Hey Kacy, what's goin on?" I said as I stood up and gave her a hug.

"Nothing much, you clean up really nice" she replied as her eyes went from my Kenneth Cole Shoes, to my cream colored v-neck tee shirt. It wasn't one of those extra tight, 'look at my bulging muscles'- type shirts, but because of the material, you could tell that I was working with a little sumthin sumthin. She had two girlfriends with her; both wore shirts that revealed tight flat stomachs, one with a stomach ring, untamed curly hair and a cute round face. The other had on hip hugger pants, a shirt with sequence letters that read "Respect" and short curly natural. I sized them up and then introduced my boys.

"Stephanie, these are my boys. This is Eric, and that is Roger" they both stood up like gentlemen and shook Kacy's hand.

She followed suite and introduced her girls, "These are my Soror's, this is Lisa, and this is Regina." We all shook hands. Roger, being the true mack that he is, stepped to the one with the untamed curly hair. He was on the rebound from his crazy girl Dawn, and needed to get back in the game. Eric's shy ass stood their looking stupid, until I gave him a look that said, 'what are you waiting for'! He offered her a seat, and we all began conversations on our own.

"Kacy, which sorrority are you in?" I asked.

"Guess?"

"Oh, hell naw, the last time I did that, I pissed someone off and never heard from them again." I replied. She had a light complexion, and was real prissy, so my first thought was AKA, but her friends fit the stereo type of the Deltas, but you can't really go by that anymore.

"No, I want you to guess, I think you will guess right. You better guess right."

"Well", I looked at her girl's key chain and the answer

was clear. "As fine as you are, you've got to be a Delta."

"I like you, lets go dance!" she said as she grabbed my hand and took me to the floor. The club filled up quick, and the floor was packed. I like the way she dances. We were grooving to R.Kelly's *Fiesta* when I realized that she was a good dancer. She had a seductive, cool thing going on. Hips were practically hypnotic, and she came closer and closer. I can tell she was feeling me because she put her arms on my shoulders and looked me square in the eye. Nice smile. I wanted to get into the dance with her, but every female in the club with a certain haircut, I though was Sheila. Especially that girl dancing with some short brother on the edge of the floor. Wait a minute, that is Sheila! She is dancing awfully close to that midget; well two can play that game. I put my hands on Kacy's petite waste, and pulled her even closer, she obliged. I looked up at Sheila again, and she was pushing the guy off of her, I think his hands were a little too active. That's my girl handle your business, she walked off of the floor. The midget followed.

"Stephanie, I'm going to stop now, we will definitely dance and talk some more latter, I'm going to the rest-room."

"O.K., don't keep me waiting to long."

Waiting, no no no, I don't want her to wait for me; I am trying to loose her. I walked off the floor and went into the rest room. I hate going to clubs where there is pressure to give Hustle Man a dollar for some shit I can do myself. If he'd stop taking all the paper towels out of the dispenser; I wouldn't have to pay his broke ass. Get a real job. But since I've got to pay you, I am getting my money's worth. I used lotion, cologne, a breath mint, two sticks of gum and a tic-tac.

By the time I left the restroom, Kacy was no where in sight, but Sheila was. Some guy was playing her real close, but I didn't care, I wanted to talk. She leaned against the bar, as the clown in the shirt that was so tight you could see his pulse continued to irritate her ear. She looked like she didn't want to hear a word that he had to say. She looked like she was thinking about me (wishful thinking). I strolled up to the bar right next to her and ordered two bottles of water, all the time not acknowledging her presence. I noticed her noticing me out of the corner of my eye. She smiled this wicked grin, and I didn't fully turn my head her way, still ignoring her. When the bartender gave me my two bottles of water, I gave him a meager tip, and turned around and handed her the water. The tight shirt wearing brothah shot me a mean glare, and she gave him a kiss, told him it was nice to meet him, grabbed my arm and walked off with me.

"Thanks for saving me, I owe you one." She said as we walked arm and arm to the Reggae room downstairs. Arm in arm, all of these women seeing me escort Sheila, and I don't care. Oops, there is Stephanie, she doesn't see me yet, so I unlocked my arm and scratched my head as I walked by.

"Hey sexy" mouthed Kacy as we walked by.

I winked and kept going.

"You are so smooth it's a shame." Laughed Sheila.

"You saw that?" I asked.

"She wanted me to see that, but it's cool, I know where I stand." She said

"And where might that be?"

"I stand on the side, for right now. When I need a change, I'll stand somewhere else."

She is so nonchalant it's a shame. Maybe that's a harsh word, she is so *mature*, yeah that's it, *mature* is a better word to use. I like that. I think?

"Sheila, where do you want to stand?"

"I don't know anymore, I just take things day by day with my eyes open. I make my own choices, and deal with my own consequences (pause)... This is getting to deep for a club, lets dance to some reggae mon!"

We went to floor while DJ Doc blasted the seductive sounds of the islands. I love it. I love to see women dance to it. Sheila obviously loved it too because once we made it to the floor, she seemed to be in a trance. Her shoulders down to her pelvis performed a sensuous fluid like motion as she closed her eyes. I was definitely turned on, as I moved as close as I could and matched her movements. It took me a couple of beats, but when I finally caught up with her, it was something short of erotic. The dance floor was dark and sweaty. The air was laced with incense, and marijuana. Someone was in the middle of the floor dancing and smoking a turd sized joint as if it were legal. We danced for what seemed to be an hour, and my clothing was soaked. I can't remember what kind of cologne that I had on, because it had been washed away and replaced with musk and marijuana. Sheila and I walked to the bar to get another round of bottled water, and found a spot on the wall. I initially stood next to her, until, out of nowhere, I grabbed her and gave her a hug. After we hugged each other, we just stood their, front to front, oblivious to everything around us. She smiled at me, I smiled back, but I couldn't help but wonder what she was thinking.

"What's on your mind?" I asked her.

"I hear it melting again."

"Huh?"

"The ice on your heart, it's melting again." She practically whispered this in my ear. I could feel her breathe on my lobes.

"Maybe."

"I'm going to the ladies room, will you be here when I return?"

"Yep."

She walked to the restroom. She was adorable. Her once neat hairstyle has taken on a life of it's on with the perspiration and her shirt clinged to he body. I wanted to cling to her body.

"Is it my turn yet?" asked Kacy, out of nowhere, she kind of startled me.

Damn.

"Give me a minute, I am burning up."

"I see, you are sweating something terrible, you having a good time?"

"Yeah, I wish they had better ventilation down here though, this has to be a fire hazard."

She laughed, I wish she would leave though, Sheila will be back any minute now.

"I am going to get a drink, I will be right back."

Take your time, Kacy, and Sheila hurry up. There she is, making her way through the crowd, and once she got to me, she assumed the position that she was in before she left. Front to front.

"Help me find Eric, I am ready to get out of here."

"Yeah, me too, lets go to IHOP I haven't eaten since lunch."

"Oh, you mean on your lunch date?"

"Baby, jealousy isn't very becoming."

"Whatever. Let's go before I change my mind and make you pay."

"Whatever."

I Can Hardly Wait...

-Eric -

This club is off the chain, except for the five stuck up females that were too stuck up to be social. All I wanted to do was dance, not father their child. This club is called E.S.S.O, and that's what I got turned down by, Every Stuck-up Sistah Out there. I mean, I even understand not wanting to dance, but must they be so rude about it? I hate when a woman stands close to the dance floor, bobbing her head to the music, practically dancing where they stand, but when you ask them, they say 'no.' There should be a section in the club where people stand when they don't want to dance, so we won't even waste our time. It is a lot of pressure on men to initiate the socializing in a club, especially when you have a lot of stuck up women infiltrating the room. I wish the DJ would say, 'All of you who do not want to dance, please have a seat in the back of the club, as far away from the floor as you can sit, all of you who came to have fun and party, stand in this section.' That would be great.

"Eric, you ready to roll?" asked Corey from behind me.

"Hey Sheila, yeah, I'm ready. I don't close the club down like I used to back in the day. Did you tell Roger that we were leaving?"

"Yeah, I saw him. He was hugged up with that girl that he met earlier. Did you get a chance to hollah at her friend?"

"I did, I did. We danced, chit-chatted a little. I'll probably call her."

"Probably!" said Sheila, "Did you tell her that you would call her?"

"Uh huh."

"Well, I know I am all up in your business, but if you say that you are going to call, then you should call. Women hate it when men say that they will call and don't."

"O.K., you're right, I'll call."

"Such a sweet heart."

"I know. Ain't he the cutest?" joked Corey.

"Shut up, punk."

"Say E., you wanna roll to IHOP with us?"

"Nahhh, I'm tired, dude. Give me your keys, I can find my way home."

"What? You must be crazy! If you get lost, who do you think is going to answer to your mother?"

"Stop trippen, the highway is up the street and around the corner. I ain't got time to be watching you two love birds slobber all over each other."

Corey gave me a funny look, I guess the love bird statement was overkill. No use in him getting mad though, it is what it is. He tossed me the keys, better yet; he threw me the keys. I'm glad I have quick hands though, cause if I didn't, he would have had my head.

I was in the mood for some mellow music, so I could think. I went up and down the dial with no avail; everyone was still in party mode. I can't be mad though; it was only 2:00 in the a.m. I finally decided to turn the radio off and listen to the volume of my silence. My ears were still ringing from dancing too close the speaker anyway. Just think, in five days Phelicia will be here. Phelicia. The mere mention of her name brings back memories of the best four years of my life. Is that why I am still enamored with her. Enamored. I haven't used that word since I studyied Shakespeare with Phelicia in college. At one time I could not even bring myself to think of her without thinking about our future. Now, I don't even know if we have a future. What will I say when I see her? She had the clearest skin I've ever seen. She only had one dimple, and it seemed like it showed, no matter what her facial expression showed. She is left-handed, which made ideal for us to hold hands while we ate. Phelicia represented my fairy tale. Why didn't I try to work it out, what if we have grown apart? If this doesn't work I have no one to blame but myself.

A couple of days later...

"Eric, what are you thinking about, you have not said two words since we've been out here. I thought you excepted my apology for leaving like I did Saturday."

I know I should not have agreed to let Nia take me to dinner. My focus is on tomorrow. Phelicia is coming. On top of that, Nia and I have talked on the phone extensively this week, and she has made it crystal clear that she wants to get out of the dating game, and do a one on one thing. With me. Not happening. Her explanation for leaving me like I was a two dollar hoe was that she and her girlfriends always met early on Saturday to walk on the track and that she didn't want to wake me.

"Nia, I accepted your apology, I just had a long day and I am tired. I took 15 children to Six Flags today, they wore me out." I tried to explain to her.

"You are probably thinking about that Chick that's coming this weekend."

"Chick, her name is Phelicia."

"Whatever. You worrying about some one who lives eight hours away and you have me right here. Am I not good enough for you or something?"

"That was totally out of line, and uncalled for."

"You all kill me, I don't understand men one bit. You got a good, educated woman right in your face, and you are thinking about some girl from college that you have not seen in over three years. You think the grass is greener in Louisiana?"

"You know what? I ain't got time for th-"

"You ain't got time for what? You had time for me when you were sleeping with me. Just like a nigga!"

I reached in my pocket and took out two twenties and a five, placed them on a table for the bill and got up. I can not stand anyone trying to loud talk me. Trying to put a brotha on Front Street. I know I didn't drive, but I refused to deal with this foolishness. And to make it even worse, I wasn't finished with my food. It was my first time at the CheeseCake Factory. I was enjoying my food. My good overpriced food.

"I'm out, I told you, if I wanted drama, I could rent me some at BlockBuster!" I said this in an intense whisper, and walked out. I didn't know where in the hell I was going I knew there would be a Marta Station somewhere. I needed to catch the southbound train to the Five Points Station, from there, I would take the West Bound Train to the Hamilton E. Homes station. From there, catch a cab. As I began to walk, I heard the click clack of a woman with long strides and expensive shoes. I knew who it was before I even turned around. By now I was in front of the ESPN Zone. She grabbed my arm; I didn't stop, so she put her arm in mine like I was escorting her. I wanted to snatch away but I didn't want to be loud talked in one of the busiest sections in Buckhead.

"Eric, I'm sorry."

"Yeah, I agree."

"I deserved that." She took a few long quick strides, and I found her in front of me. She stopped me in my tracks. I stopped, I felt sorry for her, don't know why, but I did. Although she was an unstable nut case, she was very pretty. Tall, brown, with nice full pouting lips. Kissable lips. Did I mention that she had a big butt and a nice smile? Poison. Now that I think about it, maybe she isn't crazy, maybe she just isn't used to guys not sweating her.

"May I have a hug?" she asked.

Before I had a chance to say 'no,' she had given me one, she then grabbed my hands and looked me square in the eye. Damn those high heel shoes!

"Listen, I will be the first to admit that I was a little jealous. I mean, when I slept with you that was special to me. I didn't think I would like you like I do, but I do. I think you are special, and I don't want you get away. I kind of knew you were special when I saw you at the party. Most guys would have taken full advantage of having all of the attention from the women at the party, but not you. You seemed uncomfortable with it, real humble. You didn't have to be, but you were. You are nice looking, educated, and warm. Any woman would love to have you, and most men would sleep with every one of them, but not you. I really like you. What other man would let me lay in his bed and not force me to have sex? I know you put it on me the second time, but by then I wanted you anyway."

"Nia, I like you too. I think we definitely would have to do some serious talking before we thought of the next level, but overall, I think you are a good woman. Having said that, Phelicia represents a part of my life that I need to take a serious look at. A serious look. If I didn't, I would be cheating myself. I need to stay true to myself. I enjoyed sleeping with you, but I probably should have not. My pride got in the way, I mean, you were treating me like I didn't have a... Nia, you were treating me like I wasn't a man."

"Mr. Dukes, you are all man. Well since I can't do anything about this person coming down, will you do me a favor?"

"Yeah, what's the favor?"

"Promise that if she doesn't work out, you'll let me be a part of your life? I mean, I don't know how long I am willing to wait, but give me a call."

"I can do that."

She gave me a warm hug, and she grabbed my face and

184

forced a passionate kiss on me. A long one. I could have pulled back, but I guess I didn't want to. She then looked at me and said, "Take that with you." She grabbed my hand, led me to her car. The conversation on the way home was non-existent. We both listened to *The Quiet Storm* on V-103. Joyce Latell has one of the sweetest, most soothing voices that I've ever heard. She must have read my mind cause she put on Anita Baker. The song *"You Bring Me Joy"* made me think of what I really wanted. Corey said that I would have a difficult time enjoying Atlanta with Phelicia living here, but I beg to differ. I think I would gain even more of an appreciation for it with her here. Atlanta is more than a place to party, it's a cultural hub. It is filled with a lot of quaint, off-the-beaten-path restaurants with a very low-key romantic atmosphere. That is at least what I have heard. I want to try new places with her.

"Thanks for the company, Nia." I gave her a peck on the cheek before leaving her car. She gave me a weak painful smile, and drove off. I wonder if I hadn't had sex with her, if she'd be acting like this? I watched as she turned the corner, wondering if she and I could actually make a connection if given a chance. I mean, I don't think she can cook, she doesn't seem to be the best listener and she is not down to earth enough. She doesn't seem very attentive, and I think she is too much of the glamorous type. She hardly has any of the qualities that Phelicia has.

I walked up the stairs to our bachelor pad, and I opened the door. There Corey sat on the couch with two sodas on the table in front of him. I didn't see Sheila's car out front, so I know she isn't here. He looked at me and said "what's up." He looked like he was ashamed of something. Just then, his bathroom door opened, and out comes Terri.

"Hey Eric, long time no see."

"What's up, Terri, how's Dawn doing?"

"Why don't you call her and find out, you know she was kind of liking you."

"No, I didn't know that."

"You got some messages on the machine, dog. I didn't erase them."

"Aiight, I'll check them out." I walked in my room, not before giving Corey a curious glance. It was almost a somewhat judgmental glare. A 'what happened to Sheila?' glare. But I shouldn't have. I'm the one who has a women coming to spend time with me, yet I just got threw swapping spit with Nia? I can't judge him.

Feelings of Guilt
- Corey -

"Corey, why are you so quiet, you haven't said much since I've been here. You O.K.?"

"Yeah, I'm cool, just trying to get into this movie. I like Denzel's style"

"Yeah, I like more than his style!"

"Yeah, you and every other woman in America."

We shared a lighthearted laugh. She was right, I was distant. She wanted to give me some, she wasn't obvious about it, but I know the signs of future pleasure when I see them. You know the ones, laughing at all my corny jokes, touching me every chance she gets, making sure that she is as close as possible. I just thought of something, Sheila hasn't called me since lunchtime, and she wanted to hook up tomorrow. Tomorrow, not today. Terri wanted to come see me today. I wanted to see her as well; at least I thought I did. When she came in wearing Capri Pants, and a tight fitting cut-off sleeveless

T-shirt, I didn't feel a thing. Not even an attraction. She has been on my lap, and I thought about Sheila, she has fed me grapes, and I thought about Sheila, she has kissed me on my neck, and I thought about Sheila. Everything that she did, I thought about Sheila. Now she is rubbing my groin, and I am thinking about sex. Sex with Sheila. Making love to Sheila. I think she knows how I like it, and I know how to make her back arch as well. Terri stood up at the end of the movie, and grabbed my hand. As she led me to my room, I watched her walk that sexy walk, hoping to get aroused. And although she has a nice back porch, I don't know if I want to swing on it. I followed anyway. She lay on the bed and pulled me to her. She then rolled me over and straddled me. She kissed me on my neck and then sat up. While looking at me, she removed he shirt. No bra. She has been here for two hours, and I am just now realizing that she doesn't have a bra, I am loosing my touch. She placed what was under her shirt into my mouth, and I did my best impression of a newborn. I was getting into it physically, and that was it. My soldier was ready for battle in the valley of the flesh, but my mind toyed with something that was totally foreign to me. Stopping. Me, stop now? My mind isn't in it. My heart is with another so maybe I should stop. I am proud of myself. Keep in mind that I still have one c-cup in my mouth and the duplicate in my hand yet I am contemplating stopping. Just then something even more foreign than my initial thought happened. It all started when she took the twins out of my mouth, took my shirt of and began kissing me. She started at my neck, then to my chest, then to my navel, then to my soldier. She kissed the soldier, and he was at ease! This is MAJOR!! Normally the mere breath from a sistah sends him to the firmness of granite and NOW he is at ease? She looked up at me as she felt him loosing even more life and said "What's wrong, don't you want me?"

What in the hell is happing to me? That damn momma's boy is rubbing off on me. I am supposed to be receiving/enjoying some serious oral stimulation right now, but instead, my conscience is taking over. I looked at her with a blank stare. She couldn't take it. She got up, snatched her shirt put it on and shook her head at me.

"Corey I'm leaving, and please don't bother calling me!" She stormed out of the door while talking to herself about me, (calling me every no good so and so in the Richard Pryor handbook) and left the apartment with a loud wall-shaking slam of the door. Shirtless, I walked to the door locked it, sat on the couch and turned the radio to the quiet storm. I buried my head in my hands. I wanted, make that, needed to talk to someone. I couldn't talk to Sheila about what had happened, so I decided to talk to Eric. His conscience is what I think got me hear anyway. He owed it to me. Instead of knocking on his door, I turned the music loud, very loud. He will be out here in five, four, three, two, one.

"What's wrong with you, dog?' he asked as he scratched his butt, rubbed his eyes, and walked down the hall to where I was sitting. Note to self; don't touch that right hand.

"Nothin man, just winding down."

"Man, how long have I known you? Almost sixteen years right? I know that when you wanna talk, you beat around the bush instead of saying ëI need to talk'."

"O.K. I need to talk."

"I can see that. It's cool though, with Phelicia coming, I wasn't seeing any parts of the Sand Man."

"These women, these women, these women."

"I take it your having women problems?"

Smart ass.

"It's Sheila, man."

"Sheila, wasn't that Terri that just left here?"

"Yeah, but because of my feelings for Sheila, I couldn't even get a..."

I can not bring myself to admit that I couldn't get a stiffy.

"Couldn't get a what?"

"I couldn't...how can I say this."

"Just say it man...wait a minute. You mean you couldn't rise to the occasion?"

"Yeah man, but this better stay in this room" I yelled as I stood up in front of him, feeling less than a man.

"Yeah, like I get together with the fellas and talk about your dick. It happens, man. Having sex can be just as mental, spiritual, as much a physical thing."

"Nigga please, don't bring that 'ole sensitive, R&B shit to me..."

He cut me off.

"Well, you explain it, then. You had a girl in here with a body like she should be in a rap video, and all you could do was go limp. Your mind was not there. Your mind is with Sheila. You got a Jones, and you don't even know it. Well, I bet you know right now, don't you, softy." As he laughed.

"Oh, you think that this shit is funny, don't you?" as I through a pillow at his head.

He ducked and popped me in my forehead with a folded sock. I then rushed him, and it was on. Just like old times; two friends wrestling and tussling all over the furniture. Just like old times, except this time his mother is not running in the room with her house shoe, swinging like Ali and cursing like a mad sailor. We are both on the brink of stepping to two women that we have fallen for, on the brink of doing something that men are supposed to do, and we are acting like 3rd graders. I guess we are getting it all out of our systems. The childishness, that is. I think in our minds, our subconscience, we were resisting the fact that we were growing up. And if we had to, it would be on our terms.

As soon as I got him in my world famous sleeper headlock, we heard sirens and a loud knock at the door.

"Open up, Police!!"

We both froze, hoping that if we were very quiet, maybe they would go away.

"We heard you in there, you either let us in, or we are breaking the door down." Said a voice that was trying hard to be deep, but just wasn't quiet there yet.

I stood up, and ran to the door. I opened the door, and there was a husky black lady cop standing next to a tall lanky, brothah cop.

"Is there a problem officers?" I asked.

"Yeah there is, we had a call about disturbing the peace, possibly a domestic violence case." Said the female as she walked into the apartment cautiously, only to see Eric standing near the couch in his boxers. Her face immediately sank into her robust chest. The male waited for her to continue, when he saw Eric as well, and felt the awkward silence. He smirked and shook his head, almost as if he had taken pity on us.

"You two having a lover's spat?" he asked.

Aww, hell naw! This dude thinks we're gay!

"Lovers? Man, no disrespect officer, but hell to the naw!!!" I said.

I looked at me. Shorts unzipped no shirt, and a hickey on my neck. Corey with boxers and a wife beater, out of breath. This does not look good at all.

"You tell me what it is then?" said the frustrated lady cop.

"We were just messing around, having a little fun, that's all?" said Eric.

"You couldn't think of any other way of wording that, man? *You* made it sound even worse!" I exclaimed to Eric

"Dang, you're right. Officer, we are not lovers; we are just two homeboys rough housing. That's it, we are sorry if we were disturbing the peace. It won't happen again."

"Let me talk to you for a second" said the lady cop, as she led me to the balcony. The man did the same with Eric as he took him to the kitchen. It just so happen that they separated us to see if our stories were the same, if they are not the same, the aggressor is the one who is put out of the house for that evening.

We went to the balcony and the attractive, husky woman said, "with all of the nice looking women in Atlanta, how could you be screwing around with a man?"

She looked angry. She had the anger of every black woman who could not find a decent black man pumping

through her veins. Pumping at a rate that was so power-
ful that her temple looked as if it could explode at any
minute.

"Look officer, I know this looks strange, but it ain't
what it looks like. I am all man, 100%; I love women,
black women. A man can't do anything for me but fix my
car. That dude in there, shit, we grew up together, been
knowing him since elementary school."

This caused her to show a hint of a smile, her stance
softened and she looked away, almost in embarrassment
definitely relieved.

"I'm sorry for snapping at you like this, but I see this,
well not this, but I see homosexuality between brothers
all the time. I ain't judging nobody, but hell, we can't find
a man, because most of the brothers that I see are wanna
be gangsters, lazy, gay, or with a white women."

"I hear you, but you can rest assure that that ain't us. I
am not a gangster, I don't like white women, and I got a
job"

"Our work here is done Officer Swain." Said her lanky
partner. I guess Eric convinced him that he was straight
also.

"You two keep it down, alright?" said Officer Swain.
"We will."

They left. Eric and I stood there looking at each other.
"This episode will not leave these walls."
"No doubt man, this is too embarrassing."
Silence.
"So, what time does Phelicia's plane land tomorrow?"
"Seven thirty."
"You ready?"

He flopped down on the couch and leaned back as far
as he could go. He looked up at the ceiling, and watched
the fan. This dude has a deep fixation with ceiling fans,
whenever he is in deep thought he stares at them.

" I'm a tell you like this. I want this to work, but if it
doesn't..."

He got silent again and looked again toward the fans. I should get that damn thing removed.

"What man? If it doesn't work, what can you do, what will you do?"

"I don't know, dawg... I mean, in my mind, she is on this extremely high pedestal. I put her up there because I didn't think I would ever see her again. Not seeing her again meant she was safely tucked away in my heart, a perfect woman. When we hook up again she has got to be perfect. If not, it would destroy something."

"That's some dangerous territory, man. I read a book one-day where this man met his baseball idol, and he was an asshole. From that day forward, he never watched baseball again."

A Date with Destiny

-Eric -

I want my face to be the very first face that she sees when she gets off of that plane. No, no, no, let me take that back, I think I will stand off to the side and get a good look at her, before she can see me. Yeah that's what I'll do, stand to the side. Why is it that when you are waiting for someone to get off of an airplane that they are the last ones to get off? There she is.

Be still, my heart. My heart is beating with the speed of a humming bird flapping its wings. My palms are sweating, and my mouth is getting dry. She doesn't know her way around Atlanta, I could leave right now, and she would never find me. Should I approach her? I see her looking around for me, but what is she really looking for? I am the one, who called her, what am I looking for? Why didn't I leave well enough alone? She could be the best thing that ever happened to me...or the worst. I remember the days that she would put me through hell, giving me the silent treatment for hours, days even ... because of a simple, explainable, misunderstanding, or because of her own insecurities. She would treat me in a way that she knew bothered me, only to come back and apologize later. I wanted her to see my heart and to realize that above all, I would not purposely hurt her, nor would I do anything that would jeopardize our relationship. I wanted us to be us too badly. How can you accept the apology of a person who continues to do the same hurtful things over and over again? She knew that she was hurting me by giving me the silent treatment, then lashing out like she did. I mean, how sincere were her apologies? Why do I think things are going to change, things couldn't have changed that drastically in three years. I should have left well enough alone. I know I can meet that special person in Atlanta eventually, look how quickly I found Nia. Maybe Nia is the one that I should be with; we had a great time the last time she was here. Why didn't Corey like Phelicia? Maybe I should have set down and had a man to man with him, to see what was really going on, that's what I should do, call Corey.

Come on, get a grip, man. Just because she is here, doesn't mean that we have to get together for the long haul. She is still a resident of Louisiana, and if it doesn't work out, she can get her ass back on that plane, and the hell out of my life.

Look at her, just look at her. Gorgeous, simply gorgeous. Hair pulled back in that classic ponytail. Her hair is so wavy, it looks like a steel life picture of the Mississippi dipped in black. That beautiful mane resting so gently on her soft brown shoulders. She would sit at my mismatched kitchen chairs, pouring over an over-priced anatomy book, and I would come behind her and place my hands on her shoulders. I used to love to massage her shoulders after a long day of boring lectures. Her shoulders would always be so tense, and tight. It was as if all of the stress knew I would be paying attention to her shoulders. I would even venture to say that all of her stress would simply leave her temples, and her heart, and form large masses where I could get to them; smooth them out with baby oil using deep circular movements with the tips of my fingers and the palms of my hands. Her eyes, her deep dark brown eyes..., eyes that always looked like that could break out into a smile or a cry at any giving moment. She has high cheekbones and skin as

smooth as a baby's butt. Medium brown, with red undertones. She could say she has Indian in her blood, and you
would actually believe her. She's picked up a little weight,
but in the right places though. She looks more womanly
now. Nice child rearing hips. I walked up behind her,
close enough to smell her hair. Her hair always smells of
fresh fruit. Peaches usually.

"You looking for someone?" I asked as I tapped her
shoulder.

She turned around and flashed me her wide, slender
smile, and hugged me. Really hugged me. I felt the body
pressed up against mine that I have been missing for so
long. She felt like the long lost piece in the puzzle that
was me. My empty spot was filled. We were both intense
in our hug. At one point I even picked her up and twirled
her around.

"This seems like a dream," I said.

"I know."

I felt a tear filter through my polo shirt. I felt her heart
race. I felt a wave of emotion burn through my body, but
I didn't cry. There we were, hugging in the middle of
Atlanta's airport; hugging like I just returned from
Vietnam. I was happy, elated even. A little scared, but
mostly happy. This is what I have been waiting for. I
hope this dream doesn't turn into a nightmare, or as
Langston Hughes called it, a dreamed deferred. We
stepped back and looked at each other, while speaking
unspoken words of love. I didn't know what to say, so I
picked up her bag, grabbed her hand, and walked toward
the escalator. We didn't say anything else for what seems
like an eternity. We would look at each other, smile, and
then keep going. This routine went on until we got to
my car. I popped the trunk, and led her to the passenger
side. I opened her door.

"Still the gentleman.. I see."

"Yeah, mom taught me well."

She smiled at me. I liked that. Do women really realize how much men appreciate loving eyes, and a warm smile? I don't think so, but the ones who do are special to be around. I can't stand to see a woman frowning up all the time (I bet the ones who frown would probably blame some no good brother for putting that frown there). That look that she gave me made me so happy. It made me realize why I stayed with her when time got tough, and why I cried so deeply when we broke up. I remember wanting to break up with her sooner, but not being able to because I knew I would get that smile and those eyes again. Those eyes and that smile began to come further and further apart. I simply could not take it when I didn't see it. I think that look of unhappiness hurt more than anything else.

She touched my hand before I put the key into the ignition. I felt an emotional charge in her touch. Her palms were sweating, her palms used to sweat when she was under pressure. We wanted to speak, but words would not have done this moment justice, only belittled it. I don't know if the Creator has blessed us with words that could describe the magnitude of a moment such as this. Yeah, the word *love* is in our vocabulary, but the word love has gone commercial. That word *love* seems to be used with reckless abandonment. I heard someone say that they love their car, they love a certain song, they love a movie, they love fried chicken. I couldn't use that same word to describe what we were feeling now. What I think I am feeling right now isn't that easy to describe. What word do you give to the feeling of warmth, fear, hope, anxiety, happiness, elation and vulnerability? My air conditioner is on high, yet I have beads of sweat on my nose, what is that about? Is the word that describes that in the dictionary? I know it's not a hot flash- like the ones that I hear momma talking about, cause when those things hit her, watch out! I can't think of any words to describe my feelings, so I guess until I write the folks at Webster's Dictionary with my verbal discovery, I will settle for *love*.

I feel like I am at a crossroads right now. The traffic is coming head on. I see lights at the end of the tunnel, but I don't know what the lights are attached to, and it seems like the lights are coming for me. It could be a tricycle, a motorcycle, an Expedition or a train. Will that lighted ëthing'stop and pick me up, pass me by or run me over? How fast is it coming? Am I in harms way? Why are my feet cemented in the ground; I can't move. Phelicia is that light.

I drove; I drove in total silence. We listened to the soft music, and gazed at the Atlanta Skyline.

"Which hotel did you reserve?"

"I am staying at the Holiday Inn downtown"

"That's not far from here, I think."

"Oh lord, you 'bout to have us lost."

"Don't sweat it, I got a full tank of gas."

"If you say so."

"Are you tired?"

"Not really."

"So what's on the agenda?"

Agenda? Dang, I forgot all about making an agenda, I have been so caught up in a hurricane of emotions, that I didn't even plan anything.

"I don't know, I guess we can do that Jill Scott thing."

"I heard her CD so that can mean a whole lot of things."

"I mean take a long walk. What kind of guy do you think I am? I hope you don't think you're getting any, do you?"

She laughed. I almost forgot how that sounded. I enjoyed hearing her laugh. She had a laugh that was so deep and feminine at the same time.

"You are so silly."

We pulled up into the parking lot, and she checked in. I carried her luggage to the second floor room and sat on the bed. It was one bed, a king sized bed. She came and sat on my lap.

"Thanks for inviting me, Eric"

"Thanks for coming."

Silence, long silence and eye gazing. She was looking for something in my eyes, but what? I looked away.

"Why did you look away?"

"No reason."

"You still look the same, you looked like you picked up a little weight, but you still have a baby face."

"You look like you have blossomed a little yourself."

"You talking about my butt, aren't you?"

"No, but now that you mention it..."

Nervous laughter. We were both waiting on a kiss, yet scared to initiate it. She had on lip-gloss, so her lips where that natural shade of shinny brown.

"We better get out of here, Eric. I know that look."

"What look?"

"That is the look you gave me the night we first went all the way, that look and that sneaky crooked grin."

I kissed her. I couldn't resist any more. She pulled back quickly, then she gently grabbed my face and met me head on. We kissed and kissed, and kissed, and kissed. When we finally came up for air...we kissed again. I didn't want to stop, if she didn't put a halt to this, I won't stop. I just had a two piece from KFC, and I used the restroom when I first got to the airport, so I don't have any reason to stop. I opened my eyes, and hers were closed. She looked like she was in deep concentration. I kept my eyes open because keeping them closed felt too much like a dream. I don't mind dreams, dreams are good, but I needed this to be real. Her body was on top of mine. All of her erotic parts where matched with mine, nothing separating them but a couple layers of denim, my cotton fruit of the looms, and whatever secrets she may have on.

"Eric..." she stops kissing me long enough to whisper sexily in my ear.

"Yes?" I whispered back while nibbling in her lobe.

"Stop, you know what that does to me...and stop smiling like that."

I chuckled; I stop with the ear action, and went for the neck.

"Ooh, you need to quit."

"You don't sound very convincing." I had her going this seemed so familiar, like there was no elapsed time since the last time we where together.

She sat up and adjusted her blouse. She walked over to the window. Meanwhile, I am laying on the bed ready to explode.

"What's wrong, Phelicia?"

"This is too fast, I mean honestly, I had a feeling we would probably kiss and touch each other, but not this soon. We need to talk and... this is just too fast."

She went on and on for the next infinity. I don't know what it is about guys, but when we realize that sex is not the next step, our concentration diminishes considerably.

"What do you think?"

"Huh?"

"Eric you didn't hear a thing I said. Did you bring me down her just to sleep with me, because if that is so, I can leave right now, I am on an open ticket, and I can leave when ever!"

I jumped off of the bed and trotted to where she was, I gave her a hug and a kiss on the cheek.

"Relax...Phelicia. Relax. I brought you down here because I can't stop thinking about you. I wanted to see you... to see if we still had it?"

"It?"

"Yes, *it*."

"Do you want '*it*'?"

"Yes, I want '*it*'. Do you want '*it*'?"

"I want '*it*', as long as '*it*' isn't pain, and a broken heart."

"I never intended for anyone to get hurt, I would never

do that."

"And I believe you, but since we know what happened last time, what are we going to do this time to prevent what happened last time?"

"I don't know, but I do know that everything is different. We are not 20 years old anymore, we are not in college, and we are a lot wiser."

"But when it is all said and done, you are still Eric, and I am still Phelicia."

She said that and turned around to gaze at the hustle and bustle of downtown Atlanta. This is hard. We can't travel very far with all of this unpacked luggage. Every little step we take, something is falling out. Instead of a shirt falling out, it's pain. Instead of pants falling out, it's insecurity. Either we pack up these bags, or we don't travel. Together. I sat back on the bed; this is weighing me down. My shoulders are slumping, my head is in my hands, and I am at a loss. What in the hell have I done? This is supposed to be perfect. I know if I had let her heal properly, we would be married or engaged by now. She has all of the qualities that I look for in a woman. This is the woman for me, yet there is a wall in my way. I need to break down this wall and get to her heart, if this is what I really want, but how do I do that?

You know how you can feel someone staring at you without even raising your head? I felt it. I looked up, and she was within inches of me, squatting down in front of me so we were face to face. She had dreamy, uncertain look on her face. She raised up and put her hands on my shoulders, while gently pushing me to my back. I was now lying on the bed; she snuggled up against me, put her head on my chest, and sighed.

"Eric."

"Yes?"

"All of my girlfriends told me not to come down here."

"So, why did you?"

"Because I remember how much in love I was with you, I remember that you were a good man, and I couldn't stay away. They thought I would get hurt again."

"You must have made me out to be a monster in their eyes."

"No, they just saw how depressed I was when I first started working at the hospital. I was the new girl, and they helped me get out of my funk. I didn't tell them anything bad about you, but they knew that only a man could cause a woman the kind of pain that I was feeling."

"I hate how that sounds, I caused you that pain. Is that fair to me? I was hurt as well. You know how women are, they probably think I cheated, or pulled an Ike Turner on you. I mean, we were hurt, and I don't think placing the blame is going to make it any better."

"Well, the bottom line is that we were together, and then we weren't. Now we are going to see if it is worth trying again."

"So, what do you think, Phelicia? Do you think this is worth trying again?"

"When I think about what we could be in the positive since, I think, yes. When I think about the worse that could happen, I think, no."

"Are you an optimist, or a pessimist?"

"I'm a realist."

Corey

"You are being such the gentleman today, Corey. What have I done to deserve the royal treatment?" asked Sheila.

"I'm always a gentleman."

"Yeah, you are, but something is different today. I can't put my finger on it, but you seem... more here than usual..., more attentive. I like it."

I smiled at her, she smiled at me. Her smile had more of a glow this time than usual. I guess she is feeding off of the energy that I am giving her. She is wearing an orange summer dress, an autumn type burnt orange. She looked good. I stroked her hand and smiled at her while she consumed her grilled chicken and pasta.

"O.K, who are you, and what have you done with Corey?"

"Why are you trippen, this is me."

"This may be you, but something is very strange?"

"Can't a brotha enjoy his woman with out getting the third degree?"

I just called her my woman. I haven't called anybody my woman since my days at Ball State.

"Your woman? I didn't get that memo." She giggled, not sure how to take my comment.

"Yeah, my woman, you told me when I was ready to let you know, well, I am ready."

"Boy, get out of here, you are not ready, you are just jealous because I had a lunch date, lets keep it real."

"I am for real. I know that you are a good woman, and I am tired of playing games."

"Oh, so you think I'm supposed to jump into your arms cause you think you are ready?"

"Uh, yeah, that would be nice. I thought you would be excited, or happy, or something?"

"I would love to be excited, really I would, but lets be honest. You're a player, and I don't have time to be wondering about who you are with when you are not with me. I mean, before it was no big deal as long as we were protected and casual. If you are going to be my man, we need to get somethings in the open."

"Like what?"

"I don't share when it comes to my man."

"You won't have to share. What else?"

"Well, that's a start, other that being an ex-player, you are a great person. As long as you turned in your players card, we will deal with everything else when it comes up."

"I'm with that."

She reached over and gave me a hug. I hugged her

back. My armpits aren't sweating, my heart isn't racing, I must be happy. Yeah, that's it, I am happy!

"Let's hurry up and get out of here so I can go home and celebrate by making love to my man."

MAKE LOVE??? Uh-oh, my armpits are starting to sweat.

"Check please!" said Sheila.

My last meal as a free man.

We held hands all the way up to my apartment. Am I a dead man walking, or am I walking into what could be something special? One thing that I am sure of is that Sheila looked happy. Her guard was down, she didn't have that tough exterior. As we entered the house, we began to kiss. This kiss seemed to be more passionate than any other kiss that we have ever shared. Her hands where everywhere. I am not complaining at all. I like a woman who's not afraid to take matters into her own hands, if you know what I mean. Sheila has always been a champ in bed, but this time promises to better than the others based on what I am seeing thus far. We haven't come up for air in a while. Not complaining though. She jumped when she heard Eric's keys jiggling in the door. We both stopped. Eric walks in with a younger version of his mother, Phelicia.

"Hey Corey!" she yelled as she ran and gave me a genuine hug. Eric looked surprised at her genuine display of affection toward me. It didn't seem fake, and for what it's worth, I was glad to see her as well. I want whatever will make my man happy, and that's real.

"Hey Phelicia, how you doin? You lookin good, girl." I returned as I stepped back to see what nature has blessed her with.

"Thank you, so do you, a little less hair, but it looks good on you."

"Thanks Phelicia. Hey, this is my girlfriend, Sheila, this

is Eric's 'um, friend, Phelicia." I wasn't sure how to introduce her. As I continued my introduction, I could feel
Eric looking at me funny from when I called Sheila my
girl. I gave him a wink, and he broke out in this big 'ole
kool-aide grin.

"Girlfriend, huh? When did this happen?" asked Eric.

"He came to his senses today." Said a smiling Sheila.

"About time."

"Let it go, dog. Let it go!" I said.

"So Phelicia, I have heard a lot about you" said Sheila.

Again Eric shot me a funny look, with raised eyebrows
this time. I guess he was wondering what Sheila new.
This dude can have a full conversation just using his eyebrows and facial expressions.

"I hope they were good things" returned Phelicia.

"They were."

"Eric, what are you getting into tonight?"

He gave me this devilish grin that let me know what he
would like to get into, and Phelicia caught him. Gave
him a playful punch.

"I see you still nasty." said Phelicia.

This time it was Sheila giving me a weird look, I bet she
is wondering what she meant by calling me nasty. I gave
Eric a high five, and he reluctantly returned my hand ges-
ture.

"You trippen, dawg. I don't know... I was just showing
Phelicia where we live."

"Showing her, you mean she's not staying?"

He sort of dropped his head, and shook it no.

"Not this go round... We are taking it one day at a
time."

"Good for you, girl. If it's yours to have, it will be
yours." Replied Sheila.

"Who are you supposed to be Oprah or somebody?" I
wondered.

"No, but you can't blame them for taking it slow, that
is the smart thing to do. When is the last time that you

two have seen each other?"

"It's been about three and a half years ago."

"Awww, this is *so* sweet!" said Sheila.

"Don't be getting all mushy on me."

"Yo Corey, what are you all doing tonight?"

"I don't know, kid. I'm sure we'll find something to do."

"Yeah, you better leave it at that." Said Sheila as she shot me a slight elbow.

"Well, I can take a hint. I'm going to take Phelicia back to the hotel, I'll be back later."

"That's cool, I won't wait up for you."

"It was nice meeting you, Phelicia, I'm sure I will see you again before you head back. How long are you staying?"

"I will be hear until Sunday."

"We should all go out tomorrow, I know this nice jazz spot up on Roswell."

"CafE 290, yeah, I heard of that spot" I interjected.

"Sounds good to me" replied Phelicia, while Eric nodded his head in agreement. She put her arm around his waste. They looked so natural, so innocent, so happy. Maybe they do belong together. Eric and Phelicia said their good-byes, and headed toward the door.

"They make a cute couple. They almost look like they could be related." Said Sheila.

If only you knew how on point you are.

"Yeah, she may look good, but if she's anything like she was in college, they won't last long. She seems different now, more mature."

"Well, didn't you say that she wasn't ready at the time? She was on the rebound, they were doomed from day one."

"Well, I hope you're right, I know how bad he wants this."

She moved closer, kissed me on my neck and whispered seductively, "how bad do you want *this*?"

"About as bad as Patrick Ewing wants a championship

ring"

"Huh?"

What a wasted metaphor.

"I want you bad."

"Well it's yours now, and I won't hold back anymore."

Hold back? Did she say, hold back? Anticipation of love making is often more stimulating than the act itself. Almost.

We went into the bedroom, and she put it on me. She really showed me how a woman is supposed to make love to her man, and what made it even better is that she looked me in the eye the whole time. She wanted the lights on. That did it for me. When you look a woman in the eye at her point of ecstasy, you can really see the essence of satisfaction all on her face, all through her mind body and soul. She made love to me so intensely that she had me saying her name. First, middle, last, and nick. She's got skills.

"Wow"

"You like that, huh?" she asked.

"Wow!"

She cuddled up next to me, placing her head on my chest, sweat glistening on both of our bodies. The room smelled of extreme, physical, erotic activity mixed with my Wings cologne.

"Thank you."

"Why are you thanking me" I asked.

"Thank you for making me your woman."

"Thank you, for agreeing to be my woman."

Ring, Ring..

If I ignore it, maybe it will go away.

"Isn't that your phone Corey?"

"Yeah, I'll get it."

Damn, I forgot to turn my ringer off, I must be slipping. The cordless phone was on the kitchen table, I half trotted in there, hopping they would hang up, and grabbed it on the third ring, I didn't recognize the cell phone number from the caller I.D.

"Hello?"

"Hey, boo, this is Yolanda, what you up to?"

Yolanda, the energetic, perky, college senior. She was notorious for making booty calls after turning in a long assignment. Not complaining. She sounded like she was in a car.

"Nothin much, I was in bed"

"Really, you mind if I come up and join you, I got a sorror who stays in the same complex with you, I am over here right now."

Just as I was about to answer her, I felt some eyes burning the back of my baldhead; I could feel my new girlfriend eyeing me. She came all the way in the room, practically naked (she had on the button up shirt that I had on earlier) and sat at the table and looked at me curiously. She had one eyebrow raised like the Rock, and I was afraid if I didn't do the right thing, I would catch a smack down.

"Corey, you there?"

"Yeah, yeah, I'm hear, I was just sitting hear looking at my girl, she just walked in to keep me company."

Sheila smiled at me, I acknowledged her presence while on the phone. I think I passed the test.

"Oh, you gotta girlfriend now, my bad. Listen we are still cool, don't loose my number, you never no what may happen in the future. Bye."

Damn, that was easy. I loved that about Yolanda, she didn't want to be tied down, didn't trip, took it all in stride. Besides, she's got some Ivy League cat waiting on her in Boston. This dude is in Harvard Law School; they'll probably be married within a year of her graduating. I hung up the phone.

"That was pretty smooth Mr. C, I liked the way you handled yourself."

"I told you, no more games. I don't know what's going to happen next with you and I, but as long as we are together, I'm gone be true."

"I also understand that some women don't care if you are involved or not."

"True, they don't have to understand, because I do. That's the bottom line, my understanding, and appreciation of what I have." I winked at her, she smiled at me. She liked what I said. She took me back to my room, and showed me how much she liked what I said. She put it on me again. I was barely able to rise to the occasion this time, but the soldier of love did not let me down. I'll sleep good tonight. I hope she doesn't want to talk.

Someone to Talk to

-Eric -

"You are awfully quiet, what's on your mind?"

"I don't want to say."

"Why?"

"Because."

"Because is not an answer."

"Before I came here, I made a promise to myself that we would not sleep together, now I want you, and I feel myself getting vulnerable...Eric, I don't want to sleep with you, it wouldn't be right."

"Listen, if you feel that strongly about it, I'll stay in the car. I refuse to force myself on you again. I did that before, and look at what happened."

"Thanks, I'm glad you are being strong, because I don't know if I can resist you, I would be all over you the moment you set foot in that room."

"You keep talking like that, and I don't know how strong I can be, so chill out."

"Sorry, I didn't mean to make it hard for you."

She's trying to test my strength. If she keeps on, she is going to see how strong I'm not.

"Are you trying to be funny?"

"No, I didn't mean for it to come out like that."

"Whatever, man."

"Man? I am all woman."

We smiled as we rode down I-20 and as I pulled up to

the hotel, she noticed how pretty the water fountain is at Centennial Olympic Park.

"Let's walk over there, it's beautiful."

We got out of the car and walked hand in hand to the park. It's just across the street. We found a bench to sit on and gaze at the water, the stars, and all of the high rise buildings in Atlanta. She sat in my lap. I held her close. I smelled her hair, her skin, her breath. I let her feel my moist breath on her neck. I noticed that she was getting excited (her blouse was thin).

"You ever dream about us, Eric?"

Only when I'm sleep.

"Occasionally."

"Really, what about?"

"I have dreams about the way we met, how much fun we used to have, the love we used to make, things like that."

"I have dreams too"

"You feel like sharing?"

This is perfect, sitting, sharing, and gazing at the stars, my only true love sitting in my lap. I have that feeling that nothing can go wrong this evening, this is too right!

"I dream about what could have been. I dream about what we could have become if you hadn't broken your promise."

Ouch!

"That's the way you look at it? I broke a promise and that's why we're not together? What about the other stuff that went on, what about how you treated me."

This conversation could get ugly. She jumped out of my lap and put her hands on her hips. Her eyes looked like she didn't like what she was looking at. She was looking at me. There were tears on the other side of her eyes, ready to burst out at any minute. How long has she been holding this in, and where did it come from. I should have let it go, not said anything. I have a hard time keeping my mouth shut when I know I am not wrong. I am very easy going, but extremely stubborn.

"Treated you? I told you that I wasn't ready to be in another relationship, I had just broken up with J.T. You're the one who forced me! Gave me an ultimatum, I didn't want to loose you. What was I supposed to do?"

"You didn't have to lash out at me every chance you got. You could have been nice to me! You didn't have think I was sleeping with every girl who smiled at me. Romona and I were good friends, and you blew it all out of proportion, I haven't spoken to her since, and I can't say that I blame her."

"Why you bringing up, Romona? She ain't got nothing to do with this!"

I lowered my voice, softened my stance, and put my hands on her shoulders. I tried to hug her; I didn't want this to get anymore out of control than it already was.

"Why are you raising your voice at me? All I ever wanted to do was love you, Phelicia. You know that. I was always true and sincere about everything I said and did."

She snatched out of my embrace and pointed her finger in my face. Her finger looked like a gun, aiming at my dreams, my heart. Ready, aim, fire.

"You don't know what love is, if you loved me you would have been patient!" she practically hissed at me.

Boom!

"Yeah, well if you loved me, you would have trusted me!"

"You should have given me a reason to trust you. You know what? You probably slept with Romona!"

"What? I didn't sleep with anybody but you."

"I knew I should have listened to listened to Keisha, she told me not to bother coming here!"

"Keisha? She didn't want you to come because she wanted you to be miserable like her, she ain't had a man in ages. She probably wants you for herself, anyway."

"I don't have to put up with this crap, I'm going back to my hotel!"

She stormed out of the park and across the street. I watched her. I wanted to follow her but I couldn't move. My heart stopped beating. I was paralyzed. I felt heavy. I know she was safe because one of those security guys on bikes heard her raise her voice, and escorted her to the hotel. Before he did that, he looked at me and shook his head in disgust. I hated that look.

What in the hell happened? We went from sugar to shit in no seconds flat. The more things change, the more they stay the same. I wish life had a rewind, or an undue button. If it did I would definitely go back over this horrendous episode, maybe change some things. I would definitely avoid this damn park. I hate this park. There should be more statues of brothers here anyway. Our events are what make the Olympics exciting. People don't get excited over archery, and fencing, they like the track & field, and basketball, things like that.

This was supposed to be perfect. Supposed to be like old times. Maybe that is the problem, it was too much like old times. In my effort to see the positive in every situation, I ignored the negative, and it bit me in the ass. Why did I think things would be different? They say that time heals all wounds, but they also say that all things don't apply to all people. Can you heal a broken heart with a band-aid? Now what? Do I give up on her, or try it again? I've come too far to give up like this, I am at the point of know return. I took out my cell phone and dialed her number.

"May I have room 221 please?"

"Just a second, sir."

"Hello?"

"Hey Phelicia, it's me."

"What do you want?" She sounded like she had been crying. I felt like crying.

"I want to talk."

"Not tonight, Eric. I have a headache, call me in the morning. Click!"

Just like that, she hung up.

I drove home in complete silence. I wanted to turn to *The Quiet Storm*, but for some reason, I couldn't. I guess it's because, every time I do, they are playing a song that is so appropriate. That's eerie. What the hell, may as well. I clicked on the radio, and a commercial was on about how to increase your sexual stamina. Luckily, that's not one of my problems.

My fingers where crossed, hoping that the radio Gods would spare me, play something light hearted, something that I could bob my head to, but not put to much thought into. No luck. The next song was an Earth Wind and Fire classic, "*Reasons*." While listening to that song, I could not help but ponder the reasons that I kept dreaming and wanting Phelicia. Am I afraid that I will never find a love like that again? Am I afraid that I won't find a woman like my...

Was Corey right, did she remind me of my mother? I do know that she is one of the only women that my mother liked. My mother always told me that I would marry that girl. I hate letting my mom down. My mother has never been wrong when it came to me, so why would she be wrong now? She did resemble my mother..., just a little. She does act somewhat like my mom, that is until she flips the script, with that funky attitude. How important to me is it that my mother likes the woman that I bring home? Afterall, I am the one who has to be with her, not mom. I've dated plenty of women that have nothing in common with my mom...I just can't think of their names right now.

I don't like feeling like this. Helpless. The more I reflect on the situation, the more I realize that that ugly conversation could have, and should have been avoided. She didn't have to go there. Why do women love drama so much? I don't like drama, try to avoid it, but it follows me whenever I am around women. I know I am not just putting out that type of vibe. It seems that every good thing I try to do, comes back to haunt me. To bite me smack dab on my ass. I need to talk to someone. Let me call Stephanie. Stephanie is the dancer I met at the strip club (please keep up with me).

"Hello"
"Hi, my I speak with Stephanie please?"
"Yeah, this is she, who am I speaking with?"
"This is Eric"
"Eric, Eric who?"
"I met you at the club last Saturday."
"Oh, O.K., I remember you, I gave up on you, I didn't think you were going to call."
"Yeah, I know. Sorry it took so long. So, what are you up to?"
"Nothing much, just studying, I got mid-term exams this week."
"Is that right? Good luck."
"You don't need luck when you study."
"You got it like that, huh?"
"You know it."
"You know what, your phone number sounds a lot like mine, what side of town do you stay on?"
"I stay in Cobb County, in this sub division called Secret Gardens."
" Secret Garden, that's where I stay!"
"Boy, stop lying."
"I'm telling the truth, I stay in Secret Garden, those Spanish style apartments off of Campbell Ave. and 285."
"This is funny, it's a small world."
"Sure is."
"Why don't you come see me, are you at home?"
"I'm five minutes away?"
"Good, I stay in apartment 4451, we can go get some ice-cream, bye bye."
I can't believe this! I didn't actually think I would ever see this... this..., I don't even know how to explain her.

She seems so cool, and down to earth. I don't think I need to be going over there though, Phelicia is in town. Hell, forget Phelicia. She just went off on me for nothing, I ain't thinking bout her. Yes I am. What if she cools off tomorrow and wants to act right? Yeah, she may act right, but for how long? It has always been a cycle being with her. For every good time, there was also a bad time just around the corner without fail. Do I want to live like that? On the other hand, no one could make me as happy as she made me.

Knock Knock Knock.

"Who is it?"

"It's me, Eric."

She opened the door and gave me a hug. I always wondered how this body would feel pressed up against mine, it isn't the effect that I was looking for, but it's a start.

"Hey cutie, how you doing?" she asked.

She had on baby blue sweats, and a loose fitting Nike t-shirt. Her hair was in a short Anita Baker type cut, no make up, but still fine. She looked shorter today, I guess without those six inch heels, that was bound to happen. I bet she's got some jacked up toes. She looked like the girl next door. She lived on the opposite end of the complex than I did. It's a small world after all.

"I'm doing fine, good to see you again."

"Yeah, good to see you too."

"You look different than you do at the club."

"Oh, you mean with my clothes on."

"No, I didn't mean that, you just look more relaxed."

"I should be, this is my element, and I don't have to worry about no fake, wanna be ballers grabbing at me all night."

"Yeah, that makes sense."

Stephanie and I talked for the next two hours about everything from psychology, to traveling. She was very intriguing. I really enjoyed talking to her. Sex didn't come up not one time, even when she said that she was hot, and took off her sweats and changed into some short shorts (she didn't change in front of me, but I have a hell of an imagination). I was honest with her about Phelicia being here, and I even gave her a true history about us, and you know what she did? She listened! Not once did she pass judgement or give me advice, she just listened. We laughed, talked, drank grape kool-aid, and watched talk shows (same topic, different day!).

"I have to ask this. How does it feel to take your clothes of in front of thousands of men everyday?"

"I got bills, tuition, dreams, and no one to take care of me but me."

"Yeah, I understand that, but how does it feel to be a stripper?"

She got quiet while she searched for words.

"It's what I do, not who I am. I am a strong black woman who refuses to live off the system, or some wanna be, high rolling pimp. This stripping thing that I do is short term. I have enough money in the bank, and in investments to only have to strip for six more months. After that, I won't have to do it any more. My tuition will be paid, my Hundai will be paid off, and my rent will be paid up for a whole year. After that, I will get a job in the mall, and enjoy my senior year. You know, Eric, I see these women come in there living from day to day, with no future; smoking there money up, turning tricks, living from man to man, it's depressing. Every time I go in there, I feel like it puts additional years onto my life. To be honest with you, I hate the club. When I leave the club, I scrub myself off in the shower, then I take a ten minute hot bath. I feel filthy when I leave."

"I see. You have a good head on your shoulders. I see why you can't meet guys in the club, the club doesn't betray who you really are."

"Would you be ashamed to date me?"

"I'll be honest with you, I wouldn't be ashamed, it's just that I wouldn't like the fact that all of my boys could see my girl naked when ever they wanted to. I mean, I see why you do it, and I understand why you do it, it's a means to an end, but I don't know. You know?"

She looked at the floor and didn't say a word for a long time. She shook her head and chuckled.

"I am playing the cards that I was dealt Eric, that's all I'm doing...playing my cards. I am a good person, a good, god-fearing woman. My father left me and my mom when I was eight. We moved to the South side of Chicago because that was the only place we could afford. She lost her job, got on welfare, got addicted to crack, died of an overdoes my senior year, and left me all alone. My aunt wouldn't take me because her husband wanted to sleep with me. He got drunk and told her so one day, and she has hated me since. I stayed where ever I could, on friends couches, in parks, homeless shelters; where ever, after graduation. I knew I wanted a better life, so I applied to a few colleges. As soon as I graduated, I begged, borrowed and stole all the money I could. With that money, I bought a one way ticket to Atlanta, started dancing, started school, and here I am. Yeah, I could have done things differently, but I did it my way, and I can live with it."

"That's cool, I really admire you. You are taking full control of your life, not being a victim. That's cool, I like that."

"The only thing I hate, is when a guy tries to talk to me at the club, it's because I dance. When I meet a guy out-side of the club, they don't want to date me because I dance. I'm damned if I do, and damned if I don't. When I asked you if you'd date me, I wasn't expecting you to say yes, the timing is all wrong. You're not ready for a girl like me."

"What is that supposed to mean?"

"You are too caught up with what society tells you about women who dance. You are probably even worried about what your momma would say. I understand though, I ain't mad at you. One day, every man that had an unfair reason for dating me, will be sorry. Please believe it."

"It's not like that, I mean..."

"Stop Eric, you don't have to explain, if you were a male stripper, I would have reservations about dating you as well. I don't like the cards I was dealt, but you better believe that I am going to play the hell out of them. So let's just talk, and be friends, is that cool?"

"Yeah, that's cool. I really admire you. I would like to be your friend."

"Good, I have one stipulation though. Since we are friends, you can't see me naked anymore, when you wanna see some booty, you gotta go to Magic City, or the Gentleman's Club, or somewhere else. Is that a deal?"

"But you look sooooo good naked, that's not fair. If you were really my friend, you wouldn't deprive me of something so beautiful."

She threw a pillow at my head.

"You better promise before I come over there and headlock you. Living in Chicago taught a sistah how to fight."

I started to challenge her to fight, but fighting would lead to touching, and I was too horny to get into a wrestling match with a stripper... I mean an intelligent black woman who just happens to be a stripper.

"I promise, but can I see your booty one more time, just for nostalgia sake?"

She mooned me. I can't believe it, but she mooned me, pulled her pants down and showed me all of her glory. I was shocked, but I enjoyed it. It was quick... beautiful but quick. She then cracked up.

"Take that with you, I hope you got a great memory, cause it's the last time you see this, unless you marry me... I'm joking Eric."

I laughed, but I would love to marry a woman who is as independent, smart, and strong as Stephanie. Not only is she strong, smart, and independent, she is beautiful. She reminds me a lot of my... never mind. Stephanie and I talked for what seemed like forever, we talked about everything. When I finally looked at the clock, it was three o'clock in the morning. I reluctantly said good bye, and left for home, feeling lonely as ever. I'm glad I'm not a drinking man, cause I needed one...bad. I laid in my bed, I didn't even take a shower, just stripped down to my boxers, and laid there, watching the ceiling fan. It went around and around and around. Life does that, goes round and round. A cycle. Nothing new under the sun. My life has a strange cycle to it, and it normally ends like this, in loneliness. No matter what happens during other periods of my life, I end up right here, laying on my bed wondering how I got here. I know what I'm doing wrong, life is playing me, instead of me playing life. I live by everyone else's rules but my own. I don't make my rules, I react to what everyone has on their own agenda. I would rather keep the peace and be miserable, than to put my foot down and risk getting someone upset at me. Instead of putting my foot down in college and not accepting the way Phelicia was treating me, I just accepted it. Instead of getting to know Stephanie, I'd rather follow the rules of society, and not date her because she is a dancer. What do I want to do? This is my life. What do I want from it? I do love Phelicia, and I am not going to give up that easily, she said what she said, and got some pent up frustration off of her chest, now she may be ready to move on. I know one thing though, I must do more acting and less reacting. I need to look at self, and see what I want. She needs to understand that I am not just going to be a punching bag for all of her emotional outbursts. We need to work things out better than what we have done in the past.

"Oops"

- Corey -

She is beautiful when she sleeps. She looks so peaceful, I bet she's dreaming about me.

"Baby, what time is it?" asked a half-awake Sheila.

"It's 7:00, what time do you show that house today?"

"10:30, but I need to get home, get dressed, and stop by the office. What time do you go in today?"

"I need to be there by 9:00."

"You wanna meet me for lunch today?"

"Yeah, lets go to Justin's."

"That's cool, Corey, you wanna take a shower with me?"

What does she think I am going to say, no?

"That's an offer that I can't refuse."

Sheila and I took a shower together and it was nice. Even though we didn't do anything, my back was squeaky clean. That's one good thing about having a woman, your back is always clean, and lotioned up. When I was single, my back was always itching, but not anymore. I guess that's why married men never seem to scratch their backs.

"Corey, do you have a pair of sweats I can put on?"

"Yeah, look in the closet."

She went into the closet to get the sweats, and before I could turn around good, she was back in my face with a blue dress that wasn't hers.

"What is this?"

Damn, I know what it is, I just don't know who's it is.

"That's a dress."

"I know it's a dress, but whose dress is it? The last woman who stayed the night, and didn't want to wear it home. It looks like someone has tried to mark her territory."

I don't like the face that she was using to stare at me, almost as if this is what she expected from me. She wasn't surprised one bit. Her lack of surprise actually surprised me.

"I don't know what to say. I don't know how long that dress has been in there, but I do know that I haven't been with anyone since you and I start kicking it, and that's real."

"You know what, since we just became official last night, I am going to let this slide, but you need to do some house cleaning. Make sure this is the last piece of anything that I find."

"You know what, you're right, but I don't know if I like the tone in your voice."

"Well, put yourself in my shoes, I don't like going through my mans' closet and finding some hoe's dress. That doesn't sit to well with me."

"Well, it won't happen again. But I really need you to know that that dress was there way before you and I even thought about getting together."

The silent stare down was on. She was right as hell, but I wouldn't let her know it. I don't allow any woman to talk to me like she is my superior. Ain't gone happen. If I let her start out verbal punking me like this, it won't end. Momma didn't raise no punks. Please believe it!

"Corey, have you ever had an Aids test?"

"No, have you?"

"Yes, I had one last month. I wanted to get some life insurance, and I needed to take a test. If we are going to be together, I would like for you to take a test."

An Aids test? I don't know if I want to take one of those, I can't even begin to count how many women I've been with. I mean, I used protection most of the time, at least 95% of the time, but what about the 5% that I didn't use it on in the past six years. I've been doing well though; I've worn a helmet every time for the last four years.

"Corey, you listening to me? You look scared?"

"Me, scared? Hell naw, I ain't scared, I was just thinking."

"About what, how many women you've been with?"

"Come on, girl, I ain't thinking about that."

"How many have you been with then?"

"I don't know, it ain't like I sat down and counted them."

"You can't count them, can you? It's been that many? You lost count haven't you?"

Hell yeah!

"Hell naw, Sheila, what kind of a guy do you think I am?"

"Ok, well, whose dress *is* this then?"

"Um."

"Just what I thought. Baby, you need to get a test, I will not sleep with you again until you get a test, and if it comes back negative..."

"What you mean if? I ain't got nothing."

"Like I said, if it comes back negative, we will make love like you've never made before."

"Wait a minute, you mean I can't get anymore until I take a test! That ain't cool."

"Better safe then sorry. I won't cut you off all together. We can still bump and grind, and when that doesn't work, we can get the Vaseline. Besides, this abstinence will test to see how much you care for me, we can get to know each other."

"This is torture, how long does it take to get the results back?"

"You can have them back in a week. The sooner you go, the quicker the results will come back."

"The things men do for women."

"Baby, you ain't doing this for me, this is for your health. You don't want stuff to start falling off of you, do you?"

"That ain't funny, don't be talking about stuff falling off of a brotha like that."

"Well, listen baby, I've got to go, I will see you at Justin's at 12:30 sharp."

She kissed me and left. An Aids test. I sure wish I could study for this one. How many women have I been with? If I have something, I don't want to know, but if I don't have anything, I want to know. I just thought about it, I slept with Angela on the first night I met her, the condom came off, and I haven't seen her since. I didn't know Angela at all; all I knew is that she had a big butt. I received oral sex from a stripper at Chauncy's bachelor part last year, and I don't even know her name? Can you get aids from oral sex? Shit! It is definitely time to turn in my player's card, I don't want it. I love sex, but it aint worth dying for. If I am clean, I am sticking with Sheila, she's fine, strong, and pleasant to be around and she can work it in the bedroom. What more can a man ask for? Thinking about this will drive me crazy; I need to get my mind off of this.

I wonder what happen with Eric and Phelicia last night, I bet he got some. He probably ain't even home yet. There is no way she could come all of the way to Atlanta, stay in a hotel, and he not stay with her. The best sex is had in a hotel. He better not have his black ass in that bedroom, let me go back here and make sure.

"Man, what the hell you doing here? What's wrong with you, why are you not with Phelicia?"

"Get out of here, you see me trying to sleep, don't you?"

"Sleep hell, I want details. You been dreaming about this girl, thinking about her non-stop, keeping her picture in your raggedy ass wallet, and now you trying to sleep. What's really going on?"

He sat up on his bed and scratched his butt. Why is he always scratching his butt? He needs a bath.

"We had an argument, and I came home, end of story."

"An argument... all ready? Damn, that has to be a record! What happen?"

"She said we would be together by now if I had broken my promise, I said some more stuff, she said some stuff, she stormed to her room. She vented on me, plain and simple, vented on me. I could have accepted what she said, and we would be fine right now, but I can't do that anymore. I'm tired of taking peoples shit, just to keep the peace! Peace and unhappiness is what I end up with. Unhappiness and no peace of mind. I'm sick of that shit man, this nice guy boy next door shit! That shit is played out! If she and I are going to be together, I ain't taking her shit, man."

Whoa. He doesn't really curse, and he has said shit at least three times in the last three sentences.

"Chill out before you catch a stroke! It's about time you got some balls, and stop dodging arguments and conflict for the sake of peace. Now send her ass back on that plane, and enjoy Blacklanta!"

"Send her back on that plane? It ain't that easy, man. She said what she said, and got it off of her chest. Today is whole nother day. She had a chance to sleep; maybe she's come to her senses. She might be ready to deal in the present, and leave the past in the past."

"Whatever dude, that's your love life, I can't comment on yours until I get mine right."

"I'm surprised to see you trying. I knew Sheila was a good girl, but I didn't know that you knew it."

"I knew it, I just had to make sure."

"I feel you, so how did it go last night?"

"Check this out dude, everything was on point last night, I mean it was off the charts, my toes are still curled from last night, but this morning... Sheila went in my closet searching for some sweats to put on cause she didn't want to put on her clothes from last night, and found another broad's dress. And to make it even worse, I didn't know whose it was!"

"You serious? Did she bug out?"

"Nope, and that's the bad thing about it too. She made it seem like she expected that kind of shit from me. It's like she has low expectations of me, or something."

"How do you feel about that?"

"I don't like it. That ain't the worse though, she is making me get an AIDS test! Can you believe that?"

"You have been with a lot of women, dog. You can't blame her. That AIDS stuff ain't no joke, man."

"Have you been checked out?"

"Yeah, I got checked out before I moved here. I knew I was fine, but the wait had me loosing my mind. Now that it's over, I am relieved."

"I'm scared, man. What if I have it?"

"What if you don't? The life you save may be your own. Being a player isn't the same anymore is it?"

"I know man, I'll get tested today. If she didn't say anything, I probably wouldn't, but now that we've discussed it, I need to know."

"You don't have anything man, you'll be O.K."

"How do you know?"

"I just know, dog. I just know"

Hearing him say that made me feel much better. You can't be too sure.

"Eric"

"Sup?"

"Let me ask you a question."

"What?"

"How many women have you been with, I mean have you ever actually counted them?"

"To be honest with you, I don't really know, that's not something that I actually think about. I am sure I haven't had as many as most, but I have had enough to know what I like, and don't like. I hate to admit it, but

I got burned one time by not protecting myself in college. That was my wake up call, that was the worse feeling in the world, man. Why do you ask that?"

"Just curious, I've been with quite a few in my day, and I used a condom on practically all, but the ones that I didn't..."

"Yeah, you never know, man. When I finally found out that I was negative, I dropped to my knees, and thanked the creator, and promised never to do it again without protection."

We both just sat there in silence. I am not making any excuses for being with all of those women, because I didn't hurt any feelings. And if I were single, I don't know if I would turn any down, but you can rest assure that I will wear a condom all the time, hell, I will even wear one during masturbation if I have to...not that I masturbate or anything like that.

"Guess what?" Asked Eric.

"What?"

"Remember that dancer that gave me her number last week?"

"Yeah, what about her?"

"I went to her apartment last night"

"When, after you left Phelicia?"

"Yeah."

"Phelicia pissed you off. I know you hit it, didn't you? That's my boy!"

"Naw man, we didn't do anything, we just talked all night."

"Was she feeling you?"

"Yeah man, I mean, we were both digging each other."

"Let me get this straight, you were digging her, she was digging you, she is a stripper, and you didn't hit it?"

"No man! I wasn't trying to hit it, I needed someone to talk to."

"When you need someone to talk to, you don't go to a stripper. You go to a stripper when you want to hit it, you know, make that booty call."

"It ain't all about hitting it, with me. I needed someone to talk too, I found her number in my pocket, I called her, we talked, end of story."

"Did you, at any time during the conversation imagine her naked?"

"Well, yeah, but I mean, it ain't like that."

"You know what? You starting to piss me off. You had this fine ass stripper who you were feeling, who was feeling you as well, and you did nothing but talk? I don't want to talk about that anymore. What about Phelicia?"

"Phelicia is still Phelicia, nothings changed, I just needed someone to talk to. Me an ole girl is just going to be friends."

"How are you going to be friends with her, knowing you want to hit it? You all will be friends until she feels sorry for you and gives you some. You don't want to be that girls friend, man. Be real with me."

"Yeah, I know she's fine, but I like talking to her, she's cool."

"Whatever. Look, you can pull that cool stuff with some other knucklehead. You let her throw it on you... I *bet* you catch it."

"You think what you want to think. As long as Phelicia is in the picture, ain't no room for nobody else."

"Sounds like she wants out of the picture."

"Well, I'm getting ready to find out."

"Do your thing kid, I'm getting ready for work, this adult shit is getting on my nerves."

"Aiight then."

Maybe things will be different

- Eric -

"Hello, Phelicia?"

"Hi, Eric."

"Were you sleep?"

"Nope, I didn't sleep much last night, I had a lot on my mind."

"Yeah, I bet... I think we both did."

Long silence. I am getting a strange vibe. This conversation is almost awkward. I broke the silence.

"Would you like to see me today?"

"What kind of question is that?"

"After last night, it seems like a good one."

"Don't raise your voice at me."

"I didn't raise my voice at you."

"You did too."

"Look, I didn't call to argue with you."

"Well, why did you call me then?"

"I called you because I want to see you."

Silence.

"I want to see you too"

"What time should I be there?"

"How soon can you get here."

"Less than hour."

"See you then sweetie." Click.

Sweetie? I can't believe she called me sweetie, one minute she's fussing, and the next minute she is calling me sweetie. WOMEN??????? That sweetie comment just threw me all the way off, how can I have my guard, and my BS detector up, when she is saying sweet things like that? Maybe she has dealt with it, and is trying to move on with our, I mean her life now. Should I be saying our?

An hour later...
I don't even know what to say when I first see her. Do I give her a hug, or do I shake her hand?
Knock, knock, knock.
"Who is it?"
"It's Eric."
She opened the door, and she had a towel on. She knew exactly what she was doing, she had an hour to put some clothes on, and she didn't. Women!!
"Well, give me a hug," she said, flashing a beautiful, yet uncomfortable smile.
I gave her a hug, all the while wondering what she had on under that towel. Thinking how well I used to know the contents of what was on under that towel. Wanting to take that towel off of her and get reacquainted with her body. She pressed her towel wrapped body against mine, and while she was hugging me, I noticed that if I just rocked her from side to side that the towel just might come undone, especially if I put my hands on her back just like this. I know I should not be doing this, but I can't help it! O.K. now we are rocking, and the towel is loosening up more and more, and...bingo! The towel unwrapped. Her whole backside is exposed, and what a beautiful sight it is, nice round and firm. I need to write her mother a thank you note for producing such a heavenly body. I know she feels that draft, but she is not phased by it at all. Is this her idea, because it seems like this is part of her plan, but why? We had a not so good day yesterday. She is still hugging me! I am so glad that black women are blessed with such a nice posterior. Should I touch it? I want to touch it. It would be a crying shame if I didn't at least touch it. That does it, I must touch it with at least one hand. Wow! It is firmer than I thought. She is still not phased by my octopus

impression. I wonder if she would mind if I put both hands on it, it is definitely enough room on her butt for both hands. The way I see it, it's only fair for me to put one hand on each cheek. WOW, this feels good! O.K., now she's sucking on my neck, and I like it. I know where this is heading. She backed away from me, and the towel dropped to our feet. My goodness, working out is working for her, because everything is nice and firm. That's what those Destiny Child girls where talking about when they said *booty-lishus*.

"That's not fare, Eric. Me standing here in my birthday suit, and you standing there fully clothed" she seductively whispered in my ear.

"So what you are saying is, either I take off some clothes, or you are putting yours back on?"

"Exactly."

I began to take off my clothes, and I noticed how intently she was looking at me. That's cool, it feels good to be wanted, and this made me go even slower. She obviously got tired of my amateur peep show, and began to help me. She seemed excited. This excited me, literally, as she practically tore my clothes off of me. As I stood there in my birthday suit, standing at full attention, she seems to be taken by what she saw. I did suck my stomach in a wee bit, but other than that, she was staring at all that God gave me.

"I see you've grown in more ways than one." She commented.

"So what are you saying, that I used to be little?"

"No, you were never little, I was always satisfied with you."

As she said this she pulled me closer, and began to kiss me, I followed suit. The foreplay lasted so long, I now understood what R. Kelly meant by twelve play. I was relieved that I had some condoms, yet pissed that they where in the car.

"Do you have any condoms, Eric?"

She must have been reading my mind.

"Yeah, but they are in my car."

"That's O.K. I'm prepared, I knew this would happen eventually."

"I'm glad you are prepared."

She took out the condom, put it on, then put it on me. It felt like old times, until I looked at her. She looked like she was enjoying the sex, but not enjoying me, if that makes any kind of sense. She and I had made love many times before, but this time I felt like I was being, excuse my language, butt fucked. It seems weird that I, a full-blooded man, would mind such erotic stick tuitiveness, but I do. She never did me like this. The more I looked at her riding me, the more it seemed like she was in an erotic race for an orgasm. Like she had this planned the whole time? It seemed like she was having sex for the last time. I watched her as she arched her back, never making eye contact with me, she reached her peak. She let out a high pitched moan, then her body went limp. I think I saw her eyes get real glossy. She rolled over off of me, took a deep breath, got up, and went into the bathroom. Not once did she look at me. She ran water for a long time. This didn't feel right to me at all. I felt dirty, almost used. How could she do this? Why did she do this? This is the second time that I have felt used after sex in the last week and a half, what is wrong with this picture. The door opened after what seemed like an eternity, and she came out in her clothes. By this time, I am really angry, almost hot. I don't have to put up with this shit! I don't even want to look at her. Why am I in such a hurry to settle down anyway, I am only 25, I am still in my prime, and I have nothing but time on my side. I just read that book, "Who Moved My Cheese" and I now realize that if she is not the one, I need to move on, and stop analyzing every damn segment of a relationship that has been over for three years. If she does not have cheese (love) for me, I need to find it else where, period, end of story.

"Eric, we need to talk."

"You damn right we need to talk, don't you ever pull no shit like you just pulled. I deserve better than that, and I will not let you fuck me like I'm some faceless penis that you met in the club!"

I raised my voice, I don't do that often, but it felt good to speak my mind.

"It wasn't like that."

"The hell it wasn't, I was there, I know what it was like!"

"Please don't raise you voice at me."

"Considering what you just did, I can speak how in the hell I damn well please!"

"I'm sorry, Eric."

Tears began to seep out of her eyes.

"Tell me why you did it? Is that all I'm worth to you right now?"

"No, you will always be special to me, but after last night, I know that I still hold a lot of anger toward you that will not go away. I will always love you, but I think our time is passed. I wanted to feel you inside me one last time before I said good bye...for good."

"So this is good-bye?"

"Yeah...it is."

"So you are not even willing to give us another chance?"

"I want to, I want too very badly, but I am not there yet. The more I see you, the more I think of how you just left me. You promised me that we would be together. I can't be with you without thinking of how hurt I was when you left me. I don't trust you with my heart anymore, I thought I was over it, but I'm not... I'm sorry."

I felt my heart stop. My eyes began to swell. I cried. I haven't cried like this since my little cousin GeJuan was killed in California last year. He was innocent, trying to do the right thing, and was gunned down just like that. One minute he is a nurse with a promising career, in a position to make my Aunt Carolann, and everyone else happy, and his life was taken from him, just like that. This situation does not compare to that, but this is how I was sobbing at his funeral. I feel like, again, something is being taken from me, and I have no control over it. I thought that book about the cheese, would help me right now, but it's not. Maybe if I reflect on it later it can help me, but not now. Now all I feel is pain. She tried to hug me, but I didn't want her to touch me. I didn't want her to see me cry, but I couldn't move to go to the restroom, I was paralyzed.

"Baby, please don't cry. This is for the best. I will always love you."

How in the hell can she quote a Whitney Houston song at a time like this? I heard her, but I couldn't respond. I had in mind what I wanted to say, but it would not come out. I just put my face in my hands, as gravity pulled the tears from my eyes, and dragged them through my fingers, down my arms, and on to my thighs. Phelicia stood up, grabbed her packed suitcases, that I didn't even realize were packed... kissed me on the forehead, and left. Just like that, she was out of my life for what seemed like would be forever. I wanted to run after her, and convince her that we should be together, but I did that in college. I felt my insides start to bubble, and I rushed to the bathroom. My stomach can't stomach emotional intense situations like this. I had to go sit on the toilet, and I barely made it. I handled my business, then I flushed. It all went... just my like my relationship with Phelicia, down the toilet. How about that for a metaphor? I just rid myself of some shit that was no longer useful in my life. I thought to myself, maybe this is a blessing in disguise. This disguise was an extremely good one, cause I couldn't see the blessings for the pain. I stopped crying. Not because I wanted to, but I think I have exhausted my tear ducts. How long have I been holding this in? I didn't cry after graduation when I left

Grambling. I guess I was so relieved that an under achieving highschool student could actually graduate from college. Speaking of college, now that we aren't together, I wonder if my years spent with her were a waste of time. The time spent with her could have been developing long lasting relationships with like-minded brothers and sisters. No regrets, I absolutely loved and learned from everything that we went through together. I am a better person because of what we went through. I can probably appreciate love much better, now that I have experienced such pain. Pain. Why does pain have to hurt so much? Here I sit, alone, without the woman that I thought I would be with till death due us part. God, why me? Why did you allow me to get in touch with her again if you knew how it would end? Am I being punished for some former sin, or will this lesson go in my Holy layaway?

I now have a headache. Checkout time is not for another few hours; I need to lie down for a while. The sheets smell of Phelicia. I wrapped myself into the cheap memory of our act and the scent left in the linen on the bed, so I could inhale what she left me with. I guess it's time to move on with my so-called life.

"House Keeping... Anyone in here?" yelled a Spanish woman from the other side of the door. I jumped up, and opened the door.

"Knock yourself out, but I wouldn't open that bath room door for another hour."

I rode home in total silence. I could not bear to turn the radio on for fear that I might hear an Anita Baker song. I couldn't handle that right now. I need to be alone with my silence. I need peace. My heart is barely beating right now with the thoughts that Phelicia and I are not going to be together. I kept saying that to myself over and over, and each time I said it, it hurt worse. My mother is going to be crushed. She knew that Phelicia would be here this weekend, and she's probably waiting to get an update about when the wedding date is. I hate to disappoint her. I think she will be very disappointed that I could not seem to make this happen. To close the deal, so to speak. Phelicia is the only girl that my mother ever wanted for a daughter-in-law. The pain that I feel when I think of upsetting my mother is equally as painful as loosing Phelicia. I want my mother to always be proud of me, but now that I don't have Phelicia, how can she be proud? I won't call her; I'll wait for her to call me. I need to lie down. Today is Saturday, and I am off until Monday, so maybe I won't have to get out of bed until then. Hopefully Corey will spend the weekend at Sheila's house, and won't bother me.

I see that someone has left a message on my voice mail.

'You have two new messages. To listen to them, press two, followed by the pound sign.'

"Hey Eric, this is Phelicia. You were the perfect gentleman this weekend, as usual. And when I finally let go of all of this baggage, I think you and I will be great together, but I realize that I am not ready. I know a man like you will not be around forever, so I don't expect you to wait for me to come to my senses. I love you, and I am sorry that we are not together, but then again, who knows what tomorrow may hold. I won't call you, but know that you are in my thoughts."

Second Message

"Hey Baby, this is your mother, call me and tell me about your weekend! I've been excited all day, just knowing that you to are getting back together. Love you. Bye.

Can things get any worse? Spoke too soon, Corey's home.

"What are you doing here?" I asked.

"I live here?"

"You know what I mean."

"Man, I took that Aids test, and I couldn't concentrate at work so I asked my boss if I could have the day off, she said yes, here I am. Why are your eyes so red, you been drinking? Where is your girl?"

"She left. Got back on the plane about an hour ago. Couldn't deal with the fact that I broke up with her the first time after promising her that we would always be together. She's gone, dog."

"Damn, just like that?"

"Just like that."

"She hurt you, huh?"

"Yeah... yeah she did. I never felt like this before."

"I can tell. Listen man, I know Phelicia and I had our differences, but I was hoping for the best for you two."

"I know. But you know what? Maybe this was the best thing for us? Maybe it wasn't in the plan for us to be together."

"Yeah, I guess your right. You gone be O.K?"

"Yeah, I'm cool. Life goes on, you know?"

"Have you told your mom?"

"Not yet, she'll probably take it harder than I did."

"Let me ask you a question. Do you think you'll ever find a woman who measures up to your mother?"

"I don't know if that woman exists."

"Do you still want a woman like your mother?"

"Can you think of a better person for me to find someone like?"

He paused and thought long and hard.

"You know what kid? I ain't mad at you. You have a great strong mother, and if you found someone anything like her, you better hold on to her, because if you don't, I will."

"I'm glad to hear you say that, man. Thanks."

"I meant every word of it, kid."

He stood up, and we embraced. The way brothers do. He walked to his room. He was really worried about the results of his test.

I went to my room to call my mother.

"Hey, Debbie. Is mom there?"

"Yeah, you sound upset. You O.K.?"

"Yeah, I'm cool."

"You're lying, I can tell."

"Put mamma on the phone, ole big head girl."

"Shut up, Black! Mamma, telephone. It's your baby."

I need to sound as upbeat as possible, cause if I don't, she will see right through me.

"I got it. Hello?"

"Hey mom."

"What's wrong."

Dang, I can't hide anything from this woman.

"Nothing ma, just calling to see what you're up to?"

"What *I'm* up to? What are *you* up to, and where is Phelicia?"

"Well, she went home. It's not going to happen. I'm sorry ma."

"Are you O.K.?"

"Yeah, I will be. I didn't mean to disappoint you."

"Disappoint me? Don't you ever let me hear you say that. You have not disappointed me since God has blessed me with you. I don't think you can disappoint me."

"Well, I know how badly you wanted us to be together."

"Baby, I want you to be happy. If she is not the one for you, it's better for you to find out now, than later, after you've had three anniversaries, and two kids."

"Yeah, that's true."

"Eric, you are only twenty-five years old. Take your time. I like Phelicia, but I love you. You are my heart, and any woman that does not realize that is a fool."

"You think?"

"I know.... Do you need me to come down there? You sound awfully upset."

"No mom, that's not necessary, I'll be O.K."

Mom could always detect when I was upset. She always want to be there to hold my hand, comfort me, tell me that everything is gonna be all right.

"You sure? Me and your sister can be down there by midnight if you need me."

"I know mamma, but I'm fine, I promise."

"O.K baby. I love you."

"Love you too."

"Bye."

Click!

That was easy. She didn't take it as hard as I thought she would. I know she's broken up though, I can hear it in her voice. I can tell when she is not happy, just as she can with me.

Just think, I've been through all of this drama, and I've only been here for three weeks. I am emotionally drained. I don't want to do anything this weekend. Times like these, I like to rent movies like *Love Jones*, *The Best Man*, or *The Five Heart Beats*. I don't want to go out, I don't want to talk to any women, and I don't feel like being bothered with the fellas. I just need the solitude of being by myself. I need a hot bath, a jazz CD and solitude. I don't even want to think about my future with women. Don't get me wrong, my future is centered around women, but I am done searching and seeking them out. I've heard people say that you can't look for love, love finds you. When you least expect it, it happens, and at the strangest places. I for one don't except it, so I guess that means I should expect it since I am so unexpecting. I know that that doesn't make sense, but nothing make sense anymore. I do know one thing; my expectations for women have not changed. I still want a strong, well rounded sistah, one who can hold her own in any situation, one who is beautiful and who knows how to love unconditionally. One who excepts me for me, and appreciates what I am bringing to the table, as much as I appreciate her. I would love a woman who can cook, and who knows how to make me feel like I am an important part of her life. Did I just describe my mother? Yes I did. Am I a momma's boy? Yes, and proud of it!